HATEMATES

FOREVER YOU - BOOK 1

MICKEY MILLER

Edited by
SUE GRIMSHAW

Edited by
ELAINE YORK

1

ALEX

I stare out of my window as the farms and the vast green oasis of cornfields hum past me to the beat of the train. With the sun shining bright, it's crazy how corn can look like waves of the ocean. As the scenery continues to fly by, the motion of the train relaxes me, I realize how far I've come. I'm from San Francisco but my mom grew up here in the Midwest. When I was eight, right before she passed away, she gave me some advice I was too young to fully comprehend at that age:

Tall, handsome, and rich: pick two.

My daughter, you've got to compromise in life. And two of three isn't bad. You don't get everything, though. Or else you'll end up like me.

It occurs to me in a flash that my mother wasn't just pulling this advice out of thin air. No, she was literally warning me not to fall for someone like her husband.

AKA *my father.*

It's funny how a truth can be right in front of your nose your entire life before you see it.

"Next stop," the conductor announces. "Galesburg, Illinois. The Greene State University stop."

I grin. I've made it.

Greene State University is often called *The Harvard of the Midwest*, so they say. Just with better athletics.

The stop is announced and I haul the two giant suitcases off the train with some help from a nice older gentleman.

The first thing that strikes me when I step off the train is how flat everything is. I couldn't step out of my house in San Francisco without going either up or down a hill. But here, I can see for miles and miles with no end to the horizon in sight. Even the clouds in the distance look longer and more stretched out. I came here for a visit last fall, but the terrain seems different now and beautifully endless.

I smile, and positive electricity rolls through me down to my core. I chose Greene State for the academics, not the ambience. Most students from my high school wanted to go to Stanford if they were studious, and USC or Arizona State University if they wanted to party. Although I got into Stanford, I chose to come to Greene for its renowned psychology research program, well, that and the healthy scholarship they gave me as long as I keep my GPA above a 3.5. My Aunt Mia put the school on my radar, and the more I researched it the more I liked it.

Right now, my gut is telling me I very much made the right decision. I feel I'm going to have a distinct lack of distraction here at Greene State, unlike my friends attending party schools.

I walk up to one of the taxis parked in front of the station, and the driver gets out and helps me load my suitcases into the trunk. I get in and we leave the train station.

"How is your day going, Sir?" I ask him once we're on the way.

"Oh, it's fine. So, you're attending Greene State University, eh?" the taxi driver says in a gravelly voice that denotes years of smoking, as we ride toward campus.

"Yes. I'm a freshman."

"You're living in the bubble, then."

"What's 'the bubble?'" I ask, using quotations.

"Greene State is clean. Crime free. A utopia. But drive just west of the campus edge and the crime rate spikes. You've gotta watch out for yourself." He glances at me in the rear view mirror as we drive.

"Oh, thanks for that information. Are you saying that the town doesn't really like Greene State? Like, do they think the students live in a bubble not in tune with the world?"

"Oh, we like it alright. Keeps the rest of us alive, what with the youth coming in. There's always a buzz when the students come back. Plus, you got that superstar quarterback now who's coming in this year. He's going to make it exciting to watch the football games again."

"The town comes to watch the games?"

The driver laughs. "Ain't nothing much else to do around here! From what I've heard, this guy has a cannon for an arm. Like a young Tom Brady. Ain't seen anything like it in my whole life. Well, in person, I ain't seen it."

"What's that building?" I ask as we drive past an at least eight-story apartment complex. I'm thinking it's student housing.

"That's the old-folks' home," he says. "I got a great aunt living up there. Doesn't get too many visits from anyone other than me and my kids."

He pulls into a U-shaped parking lot in front of a building, then gets out to get my bags, struggling to get both of them out.

"I mean, damn," he says, wiping his brow. "What have you got in here, gold?"

"Shoes and clothes. A few books."

His eyebrow raises. "Books? I'm surprised the next generation still likes to read those. I thought all they read was Twitter."

"Some do. Personally, I've always been a paperback girl. I prefer the feel of the pages."

The short ride is only five dollars, so I give him double for his tip and wave goodbye.

It's a hot September day, and there's a buzz about the campus. Students mull about, moving in with and without the help of their parents. Concrete paths cut across grass quads in various patterns. I notice fraternity letters on a few houses, and what are probably administrative buildings. I can make out the field goal posts of the football field and track far in the distance on the other side of campus from where I am.

After I check in with student services and get my key, I head back outside, pull up the map of campus on my phone and look for *Dalton Dorm*.

The roommate I thought I would have, dropped out midsummer, and I was switched to Dalton from my original dorm which was on the outskirts of campus in the quads. I use my fingers to zoom in on my phone and try to figure out which way I need to go, but it's confusing.

"You look lost." I hear a young woman's voice, and look up to see a very pretty brunette grinning back at me. She wears tight, stylishly ripped jeans, a tank top that shows her belly button, and a confident smile.

She is gorgeous.

"Do you need some help?" she adds.

"Yes, I'm looking for Dalton Dorm."

She gives me a funny look, then glances down at my suitcases and scoffs.

"Why do you need to go to Dalton?" She makes me feel stupid just from the way she asks the question.

"I'm a freshman," I fire back.

Is it not obvious?

"Oh, uh...alright. And I'm a sophomore." She shrugs and rolls her eyes exaggeratedly, then points. "Well, it's just that big building in the center of campus right there."

Wow. It really is dead smack in the middle of campus.

"Thanks."

"The hottest guys live in Dalton, I swear," she adds with a sly grin. "There's this new quarterback for Greene State who lives there...thinks he's hot shit. And honestly—he is."

"Uh, okay?" I shrug.

Why does everyone feel the need to talk about this guy? I know Galesburg is a small town, but there have to be more topics of conversation available than some silly quarterback? I chose Greene for the academics, not the football.

And on a romantic level, jocks have never been my type, so all this quarterback talk doesn't do much for me.

"Good luck," she adds, in a dismissive tone. "Whatever you are doing in there."

She heads off in another direction, and I furrow my brow, puzzled by her words.

Whatever I'm doing in there? What did she mean by that?

I shake it off and pause for a moment in front of the building. The late afternoon sun beats down on my tan Italian skin and black hair. A breeze picks up and it feels good to cool off a little. Inhaling a deep breath, I smile.

A train horn sounds in the distance. It's been a long road to get here, and today is about celebration, not frustration. I fought hard in high school to get enough scholarships to afford Greene State U, and nothing will derail my focus, especially not a slightly passive-aggressive student. I mean, she *did* give me the directions after all, didn't she?

I head inside of the building and look for the elevator, seeing a few students nervously walking around with their parents. A smile comes over my face, and that anxiety I was feeling one minute ago dissipates.

I highly doubt there are many students here who are as used to being without parents as I am. Mine have been dead for years. In high school Aunt Mia gave me more trust and freedom than most teens have. It was rocky at times, but the end result is me feeling very comfortable with independence. Sometimes I think helicopter parenting can be a curse and cause kids to never grow up.

I take the elevator up, and when the doors open to the third floor of Dalton, I see a family walking toward me, arm in arm with big smiles. It's a tall, middle-aged man in a suit with his arms wrapped around the women on either side of him, who I assume are his wife and daughter. She's very pretty and what, maybe sixteen or seventeen? The wife is attractive, blonde, and carries a sign that says *We'll Miss You, DJ!* in feminine handwriting.

I give them a gentle, polite smile as I pass them in the hallway. They don't wave back, but look at me confusingly.

I know this look. This is the look I get when traditional folk run into me and they've never seen a girl like me.

One tattoo is one too many for some. And I have more than one.

What can I say? Rudy, my ex-boyfriend in high school, was a tattoo artist. After a couple I started to enjoy the pain. For me it was therapeutic. I liked Rudy trying things out on me, and he liked trying them out. Ah, Rudy. I hope he's happy on his year-or-so pilgrimage in South America to 'find himself'.

The point is, it makes sense that a *Leave It to Beaver* family would give me a doubletake.

And my gosh, what an attractive family they are. If you were into older men, that man would be in your wheelhouse. Fortunate wife, I think.

I hope for a moment that I have a hot husband like that someday, and then my mother's prophecy about 'tall, handsome, and rich, pick two' flits through my mind.

Or do I?

"Three twenty-nine..." I say softly out loud, looking at the numbers on the doors to figure out which direction I need to go.

A few different guys pass me in the hall, giving me odd stares.

Judging by all the guys I've been seeing, this is a co-ed dorm. I wonder if there are separate wings or areas? Honestly, I was hoping for the all-female dorm, but co-ed will do. I really wish my roommate and dorm hadn't been switched at the last minute.

When I find the room, the door is partially open.

I set my suitcases down in the hall. As I push the door, something in my gut coils. The vibes are similar to when I got off the train, except more intense. Even before the door is fully open, I get the feeling there's something *off* about this room.

The smell, for starters. I'm a girl, so I'm rooming with a girl. So why does this room smell like a man?

Not that I was expecting this room to smell like lavender candles from day one, but this room really has a piney, masculine scent emanating from it.

Once I open the door fully, I look down and find the answer to my question: Duh, there's a man in here.

The man doesn't even notice me at first—normal for carpeted hall floors which enable you to walk quietly. I watch as he cranks out shirtless pushups. Jesus, that is one chiseled back.

After some time, he finally stands up, breathing hard but he's not as winded as I would be after a ridiculous amount of pushups. He squints at me, mouth-half open. I blink three times again wondering if there's drool dripping out of the corner of my mouth.

"Hi," I manage to say.

"Hi," he says, his sweat-glazed chest rising and falling. "Can I help you with something?"

My insides tumble.

"Oh, sorry," I stumble over what to say. "I'm just looking for room three twenty-nine."

"Okay...well, you found it. Are you my roommate's girlfriend or something? He hasn't arrived yet."

I squint. "Why would I be your roommate's girlfriend? What on Earth are you talking about?"

His radiant blue eyes don't leave mine. Well then, this is an unexpected development. I wasn't expecting to meet Chris Pratt's younger, sexier, ripped secret twin today.

Much less have him as a roommate.

"Three twenty-nine is my room. So...I'm just wondering what you're doing here?" I say, and as soon as the words are out, I hate that they sound unsure, almost like a question.

"You're lost," he says firmly, and his self-assuredness only serves to make me shake. "This is the male dorm. And you're...well, let me back up. I shouldn't assume anything. Are you a woman?"

I'm suddenly tongue-tied. I had a lot of daydreams about

how my meeting with my roommate would go, but this was not one of the ways it happened.

"I don't know, are you a man?" I bite back. The question sounds silly as soon as it's out.

He screws up his face and gives me a funny look. "I'm not sure, actually. Hang on." While keeping his eyes on me, he reaches down and grabs his cock right over the athletic shorts he's wearing and smiles, looks down, and back at me. "Yep. Still a man."

My heart hammers in my chest, and my jaw hangs open.

"This is getting confusing," I say, shaking my head out. "I was assigned to Dalton."

He cocks his head. "No, you weren't. That's impossible. This is an all-male dorm. This is my room. My roommate was supposed to be this guy from France, but he dropped out, so they assigned me a new roommate. I haven't talked to him yet because it was so last second, but his name is Alex. Alex Reyes, I think."

"That's...me...I'm Alex Reyes." I swallow down the lump in my throat.

So much for my plan of a stress-free, undistracted college experience.

He looks me up and down. "You're a girl, though."

I imitate the face he just made.

"I'm not sure, actually," I say sarcastically. "Let me check."

2

ALEX

I'm flustered, to say the least.

Of all the crazy, college-roommate scenarios I imagined, this was not one of them. When I roll my suitcases inside the room, he stares at me like he's eyeing a guilty defendant in a courtroom.

"Your name is Alex." He emphasizes my name slowly, like he's still not sure. "And you're a girl?"

"I don't know, let me check again. Hang on." I touch my breasts and act like I'm really thinking about it, then shoot him dead eyes. "Yep. Still a girl."

Dick.

He winks. "Made you feel your tits."

My blood boils.

I don't think I'm going to make it one hour with this guy.

Let alone a full *year*.

I roll my eyes. "Good one. Really? That's what we're doing now? I thought this was college, not eighth grade."

He smiles. "Look, if we're going to be roommates, you better be able to take a goddamn joke."

I open my mouth, then shut it. Why do I feel my self-assuredness flying out the window in this man's presence?

Aunt Mia taught me that if you're embarrassed, just picture your audience completely naked.

Unfortunately, that little trick is not having the desired effect with him. I can feel my body heating up from the inside as he stares me up and down.

"I don't believe you're really my roommate. Did Luke put you up to this? I'm not falling for another one of the seniors' practical jokes."

I flinch. "I got an email telling me my room was switched because my roommate pulled out at the last second."

"Yeah? Let me see." He puts his hands on top of his head, and with every inhale, I can see all eight of his ab muscles. Is he flexing?

Concentrate, Alex!

I pull up my phone, do a quick search of my emails and hand him my confirmation for room three twenty-nine from the official Greene State email address so he can see with his own eyes.

"Alex Reyes," he reads, scrolling through the email with his index finger. "Well, I'll be damned. Welcome to Dalton dorm, your home for the next year. Guess they thought you were a guy because your name's Alex."

"Great detective work, Sherlock!"

He winks and hands my phone back to me. "Thanks, Watson."

"So, what's your name?" I ask, brushing off his dig.

"I'm DJ."

The DJ from the sign. Now I'm not surprised at how ridiculously attractive he is. The apple does not fall far from the tree. He's got the cleft chin, the height, and the attractiveness you would expect.

"Well, it's a pleasure to meet you, DJ," I say, trying to put my sword away for a moment.

He walks to the door and looks out, then lifts an eyebrow at me. "You're sure no one put you up to this?"

"Put me *up* to this?"

"Some of my friends have been known to pull terrific practical jokes."

"I showed you the email that was from the school address."

"You'd be surprised the elaborate lengths Luke and my friends will go to pull off a prank."

I wish this were a prank.

"I swear on my..." I hesitate. I've never found swearing on my parents' graves to have much impact. I pull back. "I swear. I really do. Who's Luke?"

"Just this hilarious senior on the team with me."

"Which team do you play for?"

"The football team." He says the answer like it was a question that I should have already known the answer to.

I cringe internally but I have to ask the follow-up question to satiate my curiosity.

"What position?"

"Quarterback."

My body stiffens. The conversation with the taxi driver and with the girl outside comes full circle.

Now it makes sense why he's so unflappable. He's *that guy.*

I offer a polite smile. "So where are you from, DJ?"

"Davenport, Iowa. You?"

"Born in New Mexico, moved from there to San Francisco when I was eight."

Our room window is open, and a train horn sounds in the distance.

"Is it just me, or is that noise really loud?" I ask.

"You'll get so used to it after a week or so and you won't even notice it."

"You've been here for a week?"

"For three weeks, actually. Football training camp preseason starts before classes."

He grabs a bottle of water from his desk, backs up to the window and sits on the sill with one thigh and looks out. I walk over to the window to see what he's looking at. It's early September and the weather is pleasant in the late afternoon, if a little on the hot side. We can see students congregating on the wooden patio at wire mesh-patterned tables.

I lean a little, and my shoulder grazes his.

"Oh. Excuse me," I say.

He doesn't say anything, just stares.

"Wow," he remarks. I catch a glimpse of his blue eyes, and they're this impossibly handsome mix of deep blue sky and turquoise ocean. He's so handsome it's infuriating.

"Wow, what?"

Looking me up and down, he brings his eyes back to me and locks on my gaze. "You are absolutely stunning."

The way he says it is so matter of fact, so objective. He tells me I'm stunning in the same tone you'd say 'nice evening out tonight, isn't it?'

And truth be told, I feel this anxious tightness start in my chest and infiltrate my entire body until my toes are even tingling.

Did my nipples just get a little hard?

Say something back, dammit. Play it cool.

"Yeah, thanks," I say with a shrug.

Fuck. I played it *too* cool. Showed I thought too much about my response.

"I like your tattoos." He smiles and touches the one on my right shoulder. "What's this one mean?"

Of course, he zooms in on the freaking phoenix on my upper arm, the first one I ever got, and the most significant tattoo I have. It's the one I got for my mom when she died.

"It's a phoenix," I say, really not wanting to go into the whole back story.

"I know," he says, then looks at me and takes another sip of water. "What's it mean to *you*, though?"

I have to force myself not to stare at his arms. I can't help wanting to wrap my hand around his chiseled forearms. In comparison, Rudy was the Mick Jagger skinny hot type. Not the ripplingly defined muscles type. So seeing a man like DJ up close is new to me.

"I don't really want to talk about that right now."

DJ notices me looking at him and cocks his head a little, then slants his eyes back toward me.

"Thirsty?" he asks.

"Um, excuse me?" I recoil. *Is he coming on to me already?*

"Do you want some water? Alex," he says, lifting the water bottle up to my eye level. "Are you thirsty?"

Well, great. Did I just unconsciously reveal that I think my roommate is a thirst trap within the first fifteen minutes of meeting him?

"Nah," I say, waving him off. "Not thirsty."

He nods and takes a big sip of water, then points through the window down at a guy and girl sitting at one of the picnic tables on the patio outside.

"There is great people watching from this room. You can see everyone out on the patio down there."

"Ooh, I like that. I'm studying psychology."

"Perfect. Well, let's play my favorite game on this windowsill. Look at that couple there."

Just then, the guy at the table he's pointing to stands up and makes a big motion with his arms, followed by an airkick.

I nod. "What about them?"

"From their body language, do you think they like each other?"

The girl doubles back in her chair, laughing. The guy is very tall—and handsome, as far as I can tell from up here on the third floor.

I grin. "Your favorite game is to people watch couples on the patio?"

He winks. "Super creepy, right?"

I laugh. "Well, that couple, obviously they like each other's company."

"Grant and Maya. Both freshmen. I've seen them hanging out there every night."

"How do you know this?"

He shrugs. "Gossip flies around this campus. You'll understand once you're here for a few days. So you think they like each other. Do you think they're hooking up?"

I squint and look closer. She leans in and puts her hand on his shoulder. "It wouldn't surprise me."

DJ grins and looks at me. "Do you think they'll get married?"

I begin to sweat. "You seriously think they might? I mean, they're freshmen in college. And eighteen or nineteen is pretty young to meet the love of your life."

"So, if you meet the love of your life when you're too young, are they not the love of your life?"

I sigh. "I don't believe in the 'one love of your life' concept. It's a bit silly, in my opinion."

"Well, you're the one who said they really enjoy each other's company."

"Sure, but what's that got to do with marriage?"

"So married couples shouldn't enjoy each other's company?"

I take one more look out at the quad, then head over to my desk and sit down. "You're really curious about them. Why are you asking all of these questions?"

DJ shrugs. "My dad met a girl on the first day of his senior year, a freshmen, whom he married. So I'm just curious what you think. You never know, Watson."

"Do your parents enjoy each other's company?" I ask. At a glance in the hallway, they seemed so happy. But I figure I might as well verify.

DJ's eyes glaze over as he continues staring outside. This is awkward, the silence almost deafening.

"I'm not going to unpack my things," I announce when he doesn't respond to my question. "I'll head to student services right now and see if I can get my room switched to the girls' dorm."

Without turning, he gives me a thumbs up. Still sitting on the windowsill, he looks out the window, seeming to be lost, deep in thought.

"What are you thinking about?" I ask.

He shakes his head. "Nothing."

I don't know if it's the golden hour lighting or what, but when he turns his head this time, I can see the oblique line on his left side, and damn him for being in possession of my kryptonite.

He's not my type at all, though, I remind myself.

Which is true.

I got so sick of the jocks hitting on me, like the totally ignorant assholes in high school did—I swore I'd never date another one. And I'm not.

Is DJ objectively (and devastatingly) handsome? Sure.

But he's just the first guy I've met in college. There are plenty of guys here to ogle, of that I'm certain.

If I'm really going to be rooming here—which I'm not sold on yet, I'm going to have a little talk with the university right now—an attraction between the two of us would be a constant distraction. And if we ever crossed a line as roommates, it seems like a situation with huge potential for total disaster.

He finishes the rest of his water, tosses it in the recycle bin, then grabs a shirt.

"Going for a run. Gotta go. You sure you're not thirsty?"

I shoot him a look and open my mouth to talk but don't say anything. Is this thirsty thing a come on?

"It gets hot, and I have some bottled water in the minifridge that you're welcome to if you're thirsty," he adds. "Roomie."

Oh, right, the *water*. I'm imagining things.

Although, I swear he was lacing his tone with innuendo.

"Don't get used to calling me roomie. This is going to be a temporary thing," I say. "I'll get it straightened out as fast as I can."

"Aww, really? What, you don't like me? I thought we had the whole Sherlock Holmes and Dr. Watson thing going on. Coulda been magical."

"I'm more of a Harry Potter girl, to be honest."

He frowns exaggeratedly, then moves his finger down his cheek like a tear. "Wow. My heart just broke. I thought this was true love, Alex." He pauses before he leaves, with his hand on the doorknob, and turns toward me. "Oh, and one more thing. Don't touch any of my shit. That goes without saying."

"Don't touch any of mine," I call out as I watch him leave.

Not my type, I repeat to myself.

I look at myself in DJ's mirror.

Another voice pops up in my head, mocking me.

Yeah, you keep telling yourself that, Alex. That man is every woman's type.

My mom's warning flits through my mind like it did on the train, and I realize something.

Yes, he is *every* woman's type. Good looking. Cocky. Superstar. Damn.

Every one of those reasons are exactly why I'll be staying away from him.

The first thing I need to do is go to student services and let them know about their giant mistake.

3

ALEX

Worthless.

The student services director is absolutely *worthless.*

I work my way back across campus in a huff, the afternoon sun burning into my skin. Fred Makem, though his office is packed with all sorts of people this afternoon, informs me that there has been a record enrollment this year. According to him, I'm 'one of the lucky ones' because I at least have a 'real room for the year.'

Some students, apparently, have to live in a hotel while the university builds new student housing as fast as they can.

All I can say is thank goodness that's not me.

There is a waiting list for female students to get into the girls' dorm. And as a student with a room, I'm not even near the top of that list.

When I get back to the room, DJ is mercifully absent. Something about being in his presence unnerves me, and if this is really going to be my room for the foreseeable, although awkward, future, I need to settle in and unpack my things and set up my new life in an orderly way.

THREE HOURS LATER, the place is starting to feel a little more homey. The room design is divided into two nearly identical halves, with a desk and a bed on each side. DJ's side has a little more space, and he's set up a TV and chair right next to a minifridge that has some of those magnetic scrabble letters on it. My side has a closet, which is already filled with lots of DJ's things, including shoulder pads, gym shoes, sweatpants, and a suit.

I push them to the side and hang up my shirts, capri pants, jeans, and hoodies that I brought with me. Obviously, I'm more about comfort than fashion, but whatever. Envy crops up in me for those girls who get to college and discover they are about the same clothing size as their roommate, which means they instantly double their wardrobe. My best friend in high school was like that with her sister.

I take a video of my room, then send it with a text to Aunt Mia so she gets the idea. I'll just leave out the part about having a male roommate for now. Is it really that big of a deal?

Ugh. Maybe it wouldn't be with some guys. When I went to the bathroom in Dalton on the way back from student services, half of the guys I ran into in the bathroom today were too awkward to look me in the eye or do anything other than grunt. I did see one other girl in there, the girlfriend of someone on the floor, I think. So at least I'm not a total unicorn in here.

I'm still scratching my head about the way DJ told me I was stunning and I couldn't even tell if it was a compliment or not. I have no doubt that the females around campus are fawning over him.

Good looking as he may be, he's just not my type. College is a sea of new men, and I'm certain I'll run into some quirky artist types somewhere here who have a similar magnetic field around them but also aren't so full of themselves.

When I'm done unpacking, I hear a knock on the door and I get up to answer it.

Stress nerves course through me when I see the same girl I saw this morning, the one who gave me passive-aggressive directions to Dalton Dorm.

It's almost eight p.m., but she looks like she's in full makeup and ready for the club. And if I thought she looked gorgeous earlier, well, that was nothing compared to how she looks now.

She looks like a young Megan Fox but with bigger boobs.

I mean I have boobs, too, but I mostly just keep them hidden to avoid stares. And I have a feeling that's a good move since I'm living in a male dorm for the foreseeable future.

She, on the other hand, apparently doesn't feel that way.

"What are you doing here?" she says, screwing up her face at me. She steps inside without asking permission, then looks at me again.

"Excuse me," I bite out. "I didn't say you could come in."

She bites her lower lip. "Well, I'm friends with DJ and this is his dorm."

"Well, DJ isn't here. As you can see."

"Are you friends with DJ, too?"

I furrow my brow, not sure what she means. "DJ didn't

invite me. I live here. I'm not his friend, I just met him. I'm his roommate."

"But this is an all-male dorm."

I sigh, I have a feeling I'm going to be explaining this situation to a lot of people. "There weren't enough dorm rooms available for females. So they put me in here by accident because I have a name that is usually male."

"Whoa," she says, sitting down on DJ's bed. "Oh! You're that girl I gave directions to earlier."

I sit down on my bed and face her. "That's me. I'm Alex."

"I'm Jessica. *Now* it makes sense why you wanted to go to Dalton Dorm. I thought you were mistaken."

"Yes."

"So you're a girl in a guy's dorm. You're rooming with DJ." She fixes her hair and cocks her head, then looks at me like it's the first time she's really seeing me.

I feel self-conscious, even though I'm not trying to impress anyone tonight and I wasn't even planning on going out. I've got on red pajama shorts and a baggy grey t-shirt. Definitely not clubbing attire.

"Wow. This is awkward. I totally thought you were like, trying to steal my boyfriend."

"DJ is your boyfriend?"

She shrugs. "We went to the same high school and were together back then. We broke up for a little while last year, but now we're getting back together."

"Uh, okay. Good to know."

"Do you think he's hot?"

My skin prickles. This feels like some sort of trick question, one where I'm damned no matter which answer I give.

"He's a good-looking guy," I say. "Not my type, though."

She gets up and walks to the window where she looks down at the patio, then turns back toward me. Eerily reminiscent of what DJ did earlier today when he told me I was stunning. "Don't bullshit me. That man is every woman's type."

I shake my head. "Not me. I'm more into the indie rocker, tattooed types. Want to see a picture of my ex-boyfriend?"

Jessica raises her arms out and forms a T, and when she stretches, her tank top comes up, revealing a toned midriff.

She turns around, and any trace of niceness is gone from her face. "That's good to hear. Because, just so you know, DJ is mine."

Her expression deadens, and the eyes she shoots me are like daggers meant to intimidate.

"So he's your property?" I spit back. "That's funny. He didn't seem like the one-woman type, if I'm being honest."

She crosses her arms and frowns. "Are you making fun of me?"

"Just stating facts. He's tall, handsome..."

"And a superstar. He's destined for greatness. And I'll be hitching a ride with him to the top." She steps toward me. "He doesn't like girls like you anyway."

Adrenaline surges through me. I'm finished with this *Mean Girls* B.S.

I go to the door and open it.

"Well, Jessica, DJ's not here, so I think it's time for you to go."

She pauses a few moments.

"Be seeing you around, *Alex.*"

I close the door behind her, then sit down at my desk.

Jesus H. Crimeny. Well, I was right about one thing: DJ is *that guy*. He's the one who turns girls crazy when they can't have him.

I fire up my laptop and connect it to the campus WiFi.

I crack my knuckles.

Time to channel my inner Doctor Watson and do some good-old fashioned online social research. This encounter with Jessica has convinced me I'd better find out as much as I can on the Internet about the man.

I do a search for DJ Dalton on Google, and his picture comes up lickety split, along with a healthy number of stories about him.

I click on a news report from the *Davenport Star*.

Hometown hero heads to Greene State U to join father's elite football program.

Another:

DJ Dalton: Can he climb out from under his father's shadow?

After some more clicking and reading, I find out DJ comes from quite the family. Dalton dorm is even named after his Grandfather, who left a ton of money to the school. DJ's father was destined for greatness until he busted his knee in his very first game in the NFL and never played again. So he became the coach here at Greene State.

Another click leads me to DJ's Instagram page.

My stomach coils as I scroll through.

First of all, he's got a number of followers, like numbers in the mid five-figures. A cursory glance shows that most of them are women.

Great.

Second, it's not surprising that there are ladies after him, given the pics he posts.

A video of him flipping off the diving board into some small lake, then shaking his hair out like a wet dog.

Wait a second, though...

I check the dates for the pictures.

All of them are two years old.

My skin tingles. He was *that* good looking a year ago?

Something about the way DJ carries himself is different, and I can't quite put my finger on it.

That's when I see a picture of him with a very, very attractive young woman wearing a bikini. He's got his arm wrapped around her and they appear to be at the same lake where he took the video of him jumping off the diving board.

My skin prickles when I realize that although she's got blond hair now and black hair in this picture, there's no mistaking that siren-like grin: it's Jessica.

I squint, zooming in on parts of the picture, and something dawns on me.

Why hasn't he posted in over two years?

I giggle, thinking of DJ's Watson reference from earlier. It's interesting the psychological inferences you can make from a person solely based on social media. Sometimes you're totally wrong. But other times, you're not.

I lean back and click out of Instagram.

This is getting borderline weird. I should base my opinion on DJ from the person I have in front of me.

But something catches my eye sitting on his desk—a picture that appears as though it's from that same lake. Or, at least *a* lake. I get up to take a closer look and notice that Jessica is in this one, too.

I bend over and look at the picture close up, careful not to touch it. I don't want DJ to think I'm disturbing his things.

"Find anything interesting?"

DJ's voice booms behind me, and I shoot up straight, my face flushing red.

Damn these rugs and how quiet they make it when people walk on them.

DJ scowls. "You're just going to invite yourself to look over my things?"

"I was...just...seeing how you had your desk set up," I mumble.

Damn. Stupid excuse.

"Really? You need to get your face two inches from my desk to do that? I told you not to touch my things."

I swallow. Might as well come clean.

"I just saw this picture on your desk and I was intrigued. Sorry. I should have asked. Who are those people? High school friends?"

He picks up the picture, looks at it, then puts it back, face down.

"Don't worry about it."

"Why are you acting so weird? If you don't want people to look at it, then why have it up?"

"It's my personal desk. This is my personal space."

I nod, then decide I had better tell him about Jessica. "Your girlfriend stopped by," I say.

"My what?"

"Your girlfriend? Jessica."

He opens his mouth to speak, then closes it. For the first time during our interactions, I feel as though he's tongue-tied.

"She's not my girlfriend," he finally says.

"Oh, okay. She seemed to think differently."

He is quiet for a moment. "Look, Alex, I have practice early tomorrow morning. I'm going to get some sleep. Tomorrow, we'll have a talk about roommate boundaries. For now, you mind if we turn the lights off after I brush my teeth?"

I nod. "Fine."

A few minutes later, he turns the lights off, and I head out into the lobby to unwind for a little while.

As much as I am tired on one hand, I'm also wired.

My mind won't stop analyzing every detail, yet keeps circling back to wondering why did he act so strange just now?

4

DJ

When I wake up early in the morning on Wednesday, I hear an unfamiliar sound that confuses me. It takes me a full few seconds to process what the noise is: breathing. A woman breathing.

I open my eyes, sit up, and look over at Alex under just a light sheet. Same way I slept because it got damn hot last night and the A/C in our building has not been working properly.

I swing my feet onto the floor and stretch my arms as I inhale my first deep breath of the morning.

She breathes gently, and I glance over and notice she has her arm hooked above her head. Alex really is stunning: jet black hair, tanned skin and dark features, voluptuous, and with those perky breasts forming mounds underneath the sheet.

Even when I'm not looking at her, she's magnetic. From her tanned skin that I want to run my hands across to test if it's as soft as it looks, to her beautiful, dark eyes, she's hypnotic. And let's not lie, she's got the feminine features that can turn any man loco. From her curvy ass—almost visible in the red short shorts she wore to bed, to her raven-colored hair, she's gorgeous.

But there's something else about her that's drawing me in and I can't put my finger on it.

I throw on my shirt, a pair of shorts, and look for my gym shoes, but I can't help but steal a few extra glances at her.

Where are my damn shoes? I brought them back from my run yesterday but I will need them if we lift weights today.

Where are they? I swear I set them right in front of my closet when I got back.

I check the time on my phone. I need to find them soon or I'll be late for morning practice. But if I leave without them, I'll be the idiot showing up with no shoes.

I sigh loudly, and my eyes find their way back to Alex, which they seem to keep doing of their own volition.

She flickers her eyes open and catches me staring at her.

Damn. Busted.

A funny expression crosses her face. "Were you just watching me sleep?" she asks in a sleepy voice.

I heat internally. I might as well own it.

"I'm studying your breathing patterns. They are fascinating."

She grins, flips her feet to the side of her bed, and rubs her eyes.

"Learn anything enlightening?"

"You're a loud snorer. I'm sure you've been told that before."

She purses her lips. "I might do some weird things in my sleep, but I don't snore."

Weird things in her sleep? Hmmm...what could those be?

She opens the blinds, letting the sun stream into our room. She stretches like a cat, almost standing on her toes and extending her arms as far up as she can as she walks over to the window to look out.

My heart starts to palpitate. *What is this strange feeling in my body?* I wonder.

I'm a third-generation Green State U student. My grandfather went here, made a fortune in manufacturing, and donated enough money to the school that they named a dorm hall after him. Then my father managed to piss just about the entire family fortune away. So I've got the prestigious reputation of being a Dalton—not to mention the gossip of being a rich, privileged asshole—without any of the actual inherited wealth to take advantage of.

But the Daltons definitely aren't raised to be wusses and we don't fall for women for no reason. Even the hot ones don't faze me. It's just not part of my constitution to be nervous around them. It's one of my many gifts.

Yet here I am, having to concentrate not to stare slack-jawed as I watch Alex stare out the window, run her hands through her hair, and turn her body around.

Ah yes, I know this feeling happening in my heart. It's known as *your new roommate has an amazing ass and you should probably stop staring at it* feeling.

She catches me staring again, a rebellious smirk on her face.

I swallow, sitting down and scanning the room for my shoes.

"So is this how rooming with a guy is going to be every morning?"

"As in, will I be up this early every day? No, once the

school year starts, we won't have too many morning practices."

She saunters toward me, then she stops a foot in front of me. I look up at her.

"No, I don't mean getting up early. I mean...are you going to stare at me like you've never seen a woman before?"

My face twitches. "I wasn't staring. I don't know what you're talking about."

She chortles. "I could *see* you in the reflection of the window."

I try to stifle the fact that my gut is coiling right now.

"What, I can't look out the window of my own damn room?"

Her eyebrows lift. "Sure, *window* is fine. You weren't looking at the window, though."

My eyes attempt to shift to where my key is on my dresser. I need to get out of here.

And, of course, they accidentally land on her breasts.

Her spectacular breasts.

Wait a second...I think her nipples are hard. She definitely didn't wear a bra to bed, did she?

She smiles. "Even Dr. Watson stumbles across a clue every now and then."

Damn. Busted.

I stand up. It's too early for this talk.

"Look, Alex. Yeah, I was spacing out and looking at you, okay? Whatever cat stretch you were doing over there was fascinating to me." My jaw hardens. "I'm not going to dance around shit if you're actually going to be my roommate. When I'm in my room, I'll look at what I want. And this morning, you're the most interesting thing in the room."

"I'm flattered. But let's keep our eyes to ourselves, okay?"

"Please. After the way you eyeballed me yesterday, you're the pot calling the kettle black."

I go back into the closet, rummaging through everything.

"Are you looking for something?"

"Yes. I need to find my damn gym shoes."

"Oh, I put them over here because they were wet. Did you step in a puddle or something yesterday?" She walks over to the air vent near the door and grabs my shoes.

I look at her, astonished. I don't know if I should be mad, since I spent ten minutes looking for these in vain, or grateful that she did me a favor without being asked.

Her brown eyes sparkle as she hands them to me, and the only thing that's confirmed for sure is that I have no idea what to make of this girl.

"Next time you move these, you need to tell me."

"Sorry, I didn't think it would be a big deal. I wasn't about to wake you up last night. But I will next time if you want."

"Write me a note or something."

I throw my shoes on quickly and head out, humming as I hustle out to early morning football practice. I'm feeling fired up already and it's not even—shoot, what time is it?

As I near the locker room, I see Coach Sal—AKA my dad—out there with his clipboard, and he waves me over.

"Dennis, what the fuck?"

"Morning, Coach Sal."

His gaze is steely, which I've gotten used to. Not like my dad ever has a smile on his face. And he's the only person in the world who doesn't call me DJ. I think he does it to create some separation between me as athlete and him as coach, so the other athletes don't think I'm getting any special treatment.

"Everything okay?" I ask, given the perplexed look on his face.

"It's six thirty-one," he says, tapping his digital watch.

My gut drops. I'm precisely one minute late, but my dad—Coach Sal on the field—is an old-school type.

"You know my rules. If you're early, you're on time. If you're on time, you're late. And if you're late, don't bother coming."

"Sorry, Coach."

He shakes his head, tapping his watch. "The fuck happened? You've been so punctual every day of preseason. You out partying last night with the new freshmen arrivals or something?"

"No. I, uh..."

I think about telling him my roommate situation but I quickly squash that idea. Better to just own it. "It's my fault. I'll be out of the locker room in a jif."

He shakes his head. "This better not become a damn pattern."

"It won't."

He nods grimly, clenching his jaw, then leans forward. "Don't take your position for granted for one second, Dalton. Just because you've got an arm like yours doesn't mean shit if you don't put in the work. And you better believe Farnsworth wants the starting spot, and he wants it bad."

I nod. "Yes. I know. I'm going to get ready and be right out."

When he doesn't say anything, I hustle in to get my spikes and pads on.

He's right, though. Something *did* happen since yesterday.

My gorgeous roommate showed up, and she's infiltrated

my thoughts. Yesterday morning I woke up thinking of nothing but football. Today? She was the first thing I saw, and it was fucking distracting.

I need to get her out of there, I decide. It's the only way. I just have to come up with a plan.

5
DJ

An hour and a half later, I see Coach Sal *almost* crack a smile.

Almost, but not quite.

To make up for my tardiness today, I've been extra focused. Playing extra hard. I've just thrown ten impossible long passes in a row to our senior receiver, Luke Rutledge. He's six foot four with a motor for legs, and although Coach Sal has a grudge against Luke for studying abroad last year during football season, there's no denying his incredible talent.

The crazy thing is that football is Luke's secondary sport. Baseball is his primary.

Luke nudges me as we trot back to the huddle. "Word is he smiled back in 2008. No one really knows for sure, though. You throw another one to me in the impossible spot, and he just might crack a full one."

We break the huddle, and I do just that. Luke hauls down another touchdown pass, and there's a notable awe from the team.

"Damn," Luke says, trotting over to me. "It's not cocky if you back it up, am I right?"

I smirk. "Just doing my best."

"You humble bastard," Luke jokes.

After that, the third string quarterback comes in so the defensive coordinator can focus on his schemes for a bit. Coach Sal calls me over to the sideline.

"What you just did, Dennis, was impressive. I've never seen that in twenty years, that accurate, that consistent. Luke makes that catch, it's unstoppable."

Coach Sal doesn't give out many compliments, so this is a big deal. "Thank you, sir."

Farnsworth approaches from behind. He's the senior who started last year for Greene. There's a palpable tension in the air between the three of us.

He sees what's happening. I just tore up the field, proven my worth, and I'm about to take his spot.

"Farns, you think you could throw the ball like that?" Coach says, turning to Farnsworth.

"I could sure try, sir," Farnsworth says, though his voice is laced with doubt.

"Good," Coach Sal says, tossing him the ball. "Because you're starting on Saturday. I need to be sure my starters can be here at the time I give them, not whenever they fucking feel like showing up. Get out there and run some drills with the first-string squad."

I clench my fists at my sides, feeling the tension flow through my body.

"Yes, sir." Farnsworth puts his helmet on and runs out to the field. I stand there saying nothing, trying to calm myself as I take deep breaths.

Because I could not be more pissed right now.

I can't help but think that this is all part of some test my dad is running on me, seeing if I really am as much of a loose cannon as my hometown reputation.

I watch as Farnsworth runs the same play with Luke that I just ran ten times, and overthrows him.

"Run it again," Coach calls out through clenched teeth, refusing to look at me.

Yeah, what's up now, Coach Sal? Not every man can put a ball in a breadbasket-sized area fifty yards away.

I made that play look so easy that you thought your backup quarterback could do it.

Think again.

"Tell me this, Dennis," Coach Sal says, keeping his eyes on the field. "Why is it that the best talent always comes with the most fucking baggage?"

"Coach, it was six thirty-one—"

Farnsworth overthrows Luke again, and Coach turns to me. "Yes. It was. And practice starts at six thirty. Be in the locker room by ten before. On the field five before. It's not hard."

I shrug. Maybe I'm going about this the wrong way. "Well, see, Coach, I've got this new roommate and—"

He grabs my helmet.

"I don't give a *shit* about your roommate. Be a man. Get here on fucking time. Or don't play for me. Simple as that. Now hit the showers because your ass is done for the day. Maybe you need some extra rest so you can make it here on time."

I suck it up and swallow my pride. Trying to make another excuse is futile. "Yes, sir."

Coach hands me back my helmet. "If I hear one more excuse from you, Dennis, you're fucking gone. I took a huge chance bringing you in here and I won't fall on a sword to keep you here."

. . .

"What the fuck happened?" Luke asks back in the locker room. He's getting his ankle retaped, and I'm grabbing my things and heading back to the dorms to shower since I'm in the mood to just get the hell out of the football area. We don't have anything else going on today until we go over film this afternoon.

"Six thirty-one," I mutter. "I arrived here one minute late."

"Why were you late?"

I tell Luke about the mistake the campus made and about putting Alex in the male dorm. And about how I first thought it was Luke playing a trick on me.

"Dude, no, I didn't, but that's an absolutely hilarious idea for the future." He cracks up. "So she's distracting, eh?"

"I don't even want to talk about it, man. She needs to find a new room."

"Campus is packed this year, though. Supposedly the incoming class is seventy-five-percent female."

"How the hell did that happen? Where did all the men go?"

Luke wraps his arm around me. "The trades? Too busy doing drugs in high school? Fuck if I know. I can't chat, I gotta get out there or Coach Sal is gonna smoke my ass. Anyone ever tell you your dad has a huge stick up his you-know-what?"

I laugh. "More than that."

"See ya, man."

Luke starts to walk off, and then spins around. "Oh, and DJ. One more thing. It's important. Don't sleep with your roommate."

"I wasn't thinking about it."

"You fucking liar. You said she's distracting. And I know how eighteen-year-old male brains work."

"I'm almost twenty," I correct.

"And you're a freshman?"

"I studied at community college last year, and played football there, too. And my birthday is early in the school year."

"Oh, pardon me! You're almost twenty! You old man, you! I'm sure you have zero sex drive and have never thought about an attractive female in your life."

"Okay, fine. The thought *may have* crossed my mind." Albeit briefly. How those thick pink lips would feel wrapped around my...

Fuck. It has *definitely* crossed my mind.

"You're thinking about her right now, I can tell."

Luke moves in closer and grabs me by the shoulder. "Just don't do it, man. Be friends. Great friends. But sleep with her? No. No, sir-ee."

"You know this from experience?"

"I might. Just trust me, okay? You'll thank me later."

I laugh. "Yeah, yeah."

As he steps away, he taps a finger to his head and points at me. "I'm fucking serious, Dalton. The prettiest packages come with the most consequences."

Now *that* I agree with. I still need to fill Luke in on the whole Jessica debacle. But it's not something I really enjoy getting into with anyone.

He walks out and I grab my phone from my bag as I head upstairs.

My heart drops when I see I have a message from my sister saying hello and for me to call her when I'm around.

This early?

I call her immediately.

"Hey!" she picks up after one ring.

"Everything okay?"

"Yeah," her voice is shaky.

"Felicity, I know when you lie. What's going on?"

"I'm just feeling a little stressed after yesterday."

"Did something happen yesterday after you guys visited me?"

"Well, Mom and Dad had the biggest blow-out fight you've ever seen. They weren't even hiding it."

I clench my teeth. "Fuck. Dad start it?"

She sighs. "It started out where Mom wanted to change the music, Dad claimed the driver gets to pick the music, then it just got blown out of proportion. It wasn't about the music, you know?"

One thing I've learned from my parents fighting constantly over the past few years is that it's never really about what they are fighting over.

"Did Dad sleep at home in Davenport, or did he stay at his place in Galesburg?"

"Galesburg. As soon as he dropped us off, he kissed me goodbye and took off again."

"Damn. Well, I guess we did have early practice today, so he probably wanted to get back here after the ride back."

"I know, but it's like why even drive back with us if all he's going to do is start a fight?"

"I know. And how are you doing?"

"I just feel kind of blah. I don't want to go to school today."

"Felicity, you've got to go. Junior year is way better than sophomore year of high school. Trust me on this."

"I know," she sighs. "I just want to be done with high school, though. Start college and move away from here. It sucks with you not here, DJ. I miss you. Mom's whole focus is on me."

My gut wrenches as I walk through the quads.

I knew this would happen. Hell, I stayed behind and played football for one year in Davenport at the community college precisely so I could be there for Felicity after her rough freshmen year. But this year, I had to move and join an elite football program, or I'd never be on the right trajectory for getting drafted.

"Felicity."

"Yes?" There's a softness in her voice and I know I'm getting through to her.

"It's a beautiful, sunny day out today. Right?"

"Yes. It is here."

"Go to school, enjoy it. Don't let whatever's going on with Dad stress you out. Junior year is key for getting into college. You're so smart, and you're going to crush it this year. You know my theory."

She chuckles and I can hear her smiling through the phone. "Mom and Dad wasted all of their brains on me."

"That's right. You got the brains, I got the brawn."

"You're smarter than you give yourself credit for. Have you read those books I left you?"

I laugh. "You just gave them to me yesterday."

"So? What are you doing? Seriously."

A smile crosses over my face. I know Felicity just called because she was feeling *off*, and I can already tell she's feeling better.

"You ready for school yet?" I ask.

"No. I need to put my makeup on."

"Okay. Put me on speaker while you do your makeup. I have to tell you a story that's going to crack you up."

I hear her getting ready, and I tell her the story about me

not believing Alex was really my roommate, and she laughs her ass off.

I can hear the smile in her voice now. "This would only happen with you. Just..."

"Just what?" I ask.

"Just be nice to her, DJ."

"I'm always nice."

"You know what I mean. You're nice to me, but not to some people. You can be intimidating, you know."

"I'm nice to the people who earn it."

"Please? She seems like a good girl. She tried to dry out your shoes for you."

"Yeah, yeah. Stop worrying about me and get to class."

By the time I hang up, I'm almost back at my dorm. I feel relaxed, in spite of my disappointment at not starting this weekend.

I shake my head. I arrived at practice at *six fucking thirty-one* and now I won't be starting? I'm ten times better than Farnsworth. Total bullshit.

I unlock the door and peek inside.

Alex looks like she's fallen back asleep.

I can see the bottom of a tattoo running down the side of her thigh.

Intriguing.

As I disrobe and get ready for the shower, I'm overcome with the urge to touch it.

I exhale loudly.

No. None of that, now. Luke said it. My sister was right on the money, too, with her advice. Be nice, and just be friends with your roommate. Sounds simple enough, right?

I feel a surge of electricity flow through my body when she stirs and breathes.

Sure, you might want her for her looks. But you don't even *know her.*

Perhaps, but attraction is how a relationship sparks, another voice says.

I take off my boxers and throw a towel around my waist, then grab my body wash and shampoo.

As I'm about to leave, a boost of adrenaline rushes through me.

There are a pair of pink panties sticking out from under my pillow.

I squint.

No. She wouldn't have. How could Jessica have gotten in here?

And why would she be doing that? It's just a strange gesture. But Alex did say Jessica came by yesterday.

Luke's right. My sister's right. I need to not focus on women, for their benefit as well as my own. I've got enough on my hands with my hometown ex who thinks we're getting back together. Although I've told her numerous times we will never be together after what she did to me. Jessica doesn't seem to get the message, though, and it's annoying as hell. I might have forgiven her, but I'll never forget.

I sigh, looking over at Alex. I came here for football. Not for deliciously voluptuous, tattooed, sweet-sounding, intriguing, mysterious, black-haired temptresses.

But it's so fun to flirt with her. I chuckle at my choice of words yesterday when I noticed she was checking me out.

Thirsty?

She thought I was talking about the water.

Priceless.

Nevertheless, a romance with my roommate that would

ultimately go down in flames is precisely the last thing I need to kick off my first year at Greene State.

I glance up at the poster of Frank Sinatra on my wall.

You think a cold shower will help this situation, Frankie?

Just then, Alex stirs, opens her eyes, and catches me staring at her. Again.

Shit.

"So do you stare at me all the time while I'm sleeping, or is it just a coincidence I keep catching you?"

"Don't move my shoes again, okay?" I grit out.

"I was just trying to be nice."

"Well, don't."

I take a deep breath and recall my sister's advice. Before I leave the room to shower, I spin around.

"I mean...thank you, Alex. That was nice of you."

Nice.

I close the door and head to the shower.

6

ALEX

I'm still waking up, but I can't help but wonder:

How does DJ manage to sound like an ass even when he is saying something like *that was nice of you*.

I tried to wake up early today to read a little and maybe explore the campus, but evidently my body is still on West Coast time. Sunrise walks always seem like a great idea to me in theory, but they never seem to work out in practice.

I sigh, glancing over at the stack of books on my desk. I have this guilty feeling like I should be starting to study already. My Aunt Mia's secret study method is to show up to class having already done the reading that will be assigned on that day. It helped me so much in high school that I plan on doing it in college, too.

I'm thirsty, so I take DJ up on his offer of water in the fridge. After I unscrew the cap and take a sip, I notice a stack of books over on DJ's shelf. I cock my head a little, surprised at some of the titles.

The Feminine Mystique

The Handmaid's Tale
Man's Search for Meaning

WHY WOULD he be reading those? Is he majoring in gender studies or something? Well, aside from the last one.

After that, I head to the common bathroom down the hall. I see a few guys stealing glances at me.

Boys everywhere. Is this truly going to be my life for the next year? I've got to find a way out of this.

When I go to wash my hands, there's a guy staring at me from the sink next to me.

I take a deep breath and remind myself that this is literally the boy's dorm, and there's only boys in here.

This one is short with frizzy hair, and, honestly, he looks like he could still be in high school.

"Good morning," I say.

"Uh, hi," he says, then snaps his view back to the mirror in front of him, a little too unnaturally.

"I'm Alex," I say, offering a kind smile.

He looks at me like I'm an alien, fists clenched at his sides, and his eyes weirdly strained.

"You're a girl," he says.

I nod, then shrug. "Last time I checked, yes!"

He gives me a funny look, then walks out without saying another word.

Well, hello there, awkward.

DJ might be cocky, but at least he knows how to look me in the eye.

At that moment, I freeze when I hear a booming voice start up coming from the shower stall area.

My heart begins to hammer and I cannot believe it.

The unmistakable deep timbre of the voice comes from DJ, and he's singing "My Way" by Frank Sinatra.

My cheeks redden listening to him.

Wow. That's a hell of a voice.

And maybe it's the Italian in me, but even if I don't like the guy, I can't help but appreciate a good shower song.

I blow out an audible breath, wondering how his voice is so manly and deep, when my other dormmate apparently can't look a girl in the eye, or even tell me his name.

Needing some kind of jolt, I run the faucet and splash water on my face, but when I see something out of the corner of my eye that is oh so distracting, I miss my face and get water all over my shirt.

"Dangit," I mutter, then turn my head in the direction of the distraction.

It's DJ...from behind...and I wouldn't even be able to identify him except that his voice is unmistakable and he's still singing.

He's butt-ass naked and has stepped out of the shower.

Holy Jesus, that is just a...rock hard, smackable ass.

It's like he's smiling at me from behind.

Right as he hits the crux of the song, he's toweling off his upper body and spins around. We make eye contact, which sends a rush of blood through me.

His eyes widen, then narrow.

He doesn't stop singing. Apparently, he's got unbreakable concentration when it comes to singing in the shower.

My eyes widen and stay that way, then drift down his abs, lower, lower...

A million guys have checked out my cleavage in my life, including Mr. Short No-Name two seconds ago. This is just payback.

Maybe I can empathize with those guys a little more

now. Because *I can't help my freaking curiosity as I look at this man's package.*

My eyes linger between his legs and they're frozen.

"Uh...I can see your...I can see everything. I can see it all!" I move my hand in front of me like I'm making the motion for Mr. Miyagi's 'wax off', but he doesn't move.

A wave of heat runs through my body as I bring my eyes back up to him.

DJ smirks, holding the towel around his neck.

Of course, the cocky quarterback of the football team, along with being ripped, is also well endowed. This is just unfair.

"Yes, you can see everything. Why don't you take a picture? It'll last longer," he grins, chuckling.

I've already made an ass out of myself at this point, so I decide to call him on his bluff.

I take out my phone and point it at him.

"Maybe I will."

He smirks. "How's the lighting in here? Are you getting my good side?"

I roll my eyes and put my phone down as he turns at an angle and looks at his ass profile.

"I'm not taking a picture of you," I inform him.

"Oh man, that's too bad," he says, then steps toward me and shrugs. "I'm not the type to ever send out dirty pics, but I feel like if that's what you're into, well, then, that's on you."

Something coils inside my stomach. I'm a unique mix of attracted, recoiled, and angry.

"You're disgusting, you know that?" I tell him, putting my hands on my hips.

"If I'm so disgusting, then why were you just staring at my junk two seconds ago like I was a Big Mac and you hadn't eaten in four weeks?"

His beautiful eyes gaze into mine. He's tall—and why is he the only man on Earth who can apparently look me in the eye without actually checking out my cleavage like he is right now? The guy at the sink a minute ago had the opposite problem.

I take a deep breath and decide this is the time for cooler heads to prevail, despite how riled up this man has the ability to make me.

Man. I keep calling him a man.

But he is. There's just something about DJ that makes him different from the rest of the boys in the dorm. He's got just a few chest hairs poking out already. But above all, it's in the eyes. They're sharp, like a hunter's focused gaze.

"You *are* allowed to wrap the towel around your waist, you know."

"I didn't come to college to have my style cramped."

"And I didn't come to college to get thrown in the all-male dorm. Sometimes things just don't work out the way you want."

He smiles at me and walks toward me.

"Well, I wasn't the one who put you in here." He looks down at the water I splashed on my t-shirt. "Sorry for getting you all wet, though. I'll completely take the blame for that."

7

ALEX

I let out a sigh of frustration.

It's not even twenty-four hours into my college experience and I think my blood pressure has already risen to angry Donald Duck levels.

I take a moment to compose myself in the bathroom. I see Mr. No-Name, who is scared of me, duck his head into the bathroom, and I wave.

He freezes, then walks out. Why is he even back here? Did I frighten him so badly he didn't want to be in here at the same time as me?

Am I that scary to some people? Maybe it's the tattoos. Some guys are just intimidated by me, I guess.

I head back into my room, and DJ is mercifully in boxers.

"Hey, I'm not against nudist colonies or anything like that... but this isn't a nudist colony. This is a dorm. So, what do you say we institute a 'wear pants at all times' policy in our room?"

DJ smiles. "Or we could just have no rules, you know, because it's college and we're now adults."

"Or you could just be reasonable," I counter. "And empathize with me just a tad for having to be one girl in a two-hundred-person male dorm."

He takes a deep breath. "I assume you have to change. I'll turn around like a gentleman. How's that?"

"Thank you," I say, though my blood still boils as I change from my pajamas into jeans, a tank top, and a light cardigan. DJ seems to have no problem whatsoever not looking at me as I change in my corner, closest to the window. Instead, he looks out the window. Well, I guess having a man who doesn't gawk at me as a roommate is better than one who can't stop staring.

"Okay. Done. You can turn around. Thanks."

He spins around and I can tell he's been thinking with the way he's looking at me. "I think I am being reasonable when I say I think we should not have any silly rules for this dorm," he says. "'Must wear pants at all times' is a pretty authoritarian gesture. This is my living space, not a third-grade classroom. We're adults, I'll do whatever I feel like. And honestly—because I can see the wheels in your head turning, no, I wasn't thinking about never wearing pants because that's ridiculous. But now that I know it gets under your skin, well," he throws on a Green State Football t-shirt and looks at me again. "I might just start enjoying it more than usual."

I fold my arms and shake my head. "What's the matter with you? Are you *trying* to repel me with your immature behavior?"

"Is it working?" he grins.

I throw my arms out wide, then slap my thighs. I just don't know what to make of his behavior.

"I'm not going to be your roommate for long. I'm going

to head to student services and get this straightened out asap."

"Didn't you already go yesterday?"

"Yes, but I'm going to try again."

"Well, that would be great. Then I could go back to enjoying myself in this dorm."

"What's that mean?"

Just then, my eyes zoom in on something poking out of the bottom of his pillow.

I walk over and lift up his pillow to be sure I'm not hallucinating.

Pink freaking panties. Not mine.

"What are these doing here?"

He shakes his head. "I have a hypothesis about how those got there, but I'm not quite sure."

"I don't even want to know," I follow up. This is such a change from the DJ I met yesterday, the one who seemed cocky but reasonable. Today it's like he's putting me off on purpose. "I'm *so* sorry for cramping your style. You're not a very nice person, you know that?"

He grins. "Thanks."

"That wasn't a compliment."

"Sure, it was. So shall we head down to breakfast? The café closes at nine thirty. It's past nine."

"You're...inviting me to breakfast?"

"Why wouldn't I? You're my roommate. I'm being nice."

Oh, I don't know, because you can't stop messing with me?

"Fine. I'm hungry. Let's eat."

We head down the steps, past the lobby of Dalton, and into the main café of Greene State.

I get coffee, oatmeal with brown sugar, and some fruit.

"I'm going to grab a table with some of my football friends. Come by once you have your food." DJ goes and sits down at a table with about seven big dudes, who all seem to be whooping in laughter about something.

I look around the café, and there are many pairs of two girls sitting around the café. I feel like every other girl here besides me is getting to know their roommate. A brick forms in my stomach.

DJ might like to mess with me, but he extended the invite for me to sit with him and his friends, and I respect the fact that he's not leaving me out. Still, being the lone girl sitting at a table with the football team isn't ideal. My heart flutters, and I have a flashback to the first three months of my freshmen year of high school, the time before I found my crew. I do not want to go through that again.

I close my eyes and say a silent prayer.

Lord, please help me find some good friends in college. How about some really good ones? I'd love that. I'd be a good friend to them, too.

When I open my eyes, there's a girl staring back at me.

"Are you okay?" she asks, seeming concerned.

"Um, yeah," I say, feeling embarrassed. "Totally fine."

"Oh, okay. I noticed you had your eyes closed and you're standing in the middle of the cafeteria. I just wanted to check on you."

She's got a slight build, but her eyes are some of the most intense I've ever seen, a light brown, almost fiery color.

"Thank you," I say. She lingers for a moment, but I don't say anything, feeling nervous all of a sudden. She's extremely pretty, and has a confidence emanating through her that I can't quite explain.

When I don't say anything else, she turns to go but I stop her. "Wait. I, um..."

She turns back.

I clear my throat. "It's just that I got put in the male dorm by mistake. So..."

Her eyes widen. "You're in the *male* dorm?"

I nod.

She continues. "And you don't have anyone to sit with, do you?"

"I don't feel like sitting with the football team where my roommate is. Just not my style."

I shake my head, and my gut clenches with emotion as I brace myself for her response.

In high school, there was a pretty girl who seemed to get off on torturing my little group of misfits. And this pretty blonde is being almost suspiciously nice. And the more I look at her, the more familiar she seems. Do I know her from somewhere?

Her smile broadens. "Why didn't you say so!? April and I are all alone in the corner..."

She takes my hand and points in the direction of a table in the corner and a huge wave of relief rushes through me. "You want to come be antisocial with us?"

I nod, and follow my new friend to the opposite corner from where DJ and the rest of the football jocks are sitting.

I glance over my shoulder and see DJ looking at me as I sit down with my new friends.

It never ceases to amaze me that sometimes your prayers really do get answered.

8

ALEX

"I'm Maya, by the way," the blonde says to me as we reach her table. "And this is my roommate, April."

"Really nice to meet you, Maya," I say.

It clicks where I know her from: DJ's pointing out the window yesterday at a couple on the patio.

"Hi! I'm April." Her friend, a perky, tall, freckled brunette jumps up and hugs me. "Nice to meet you. I'm a hugger. Did you know everyone needs seven hugs a day to get sufficient human contact? It helps your endorphins. It's true."

She wraps her arms around me, and she does have a knack for a solid hug.

"I should have hugged you, too," Maya says, then smiles at April. "So, are you always going to be one-upping me like this?"

April grins as she sits down "Please. Hugs are an infinite resource."

"I'm Alex."

"Ohhh! Are you the Alex who got put in the boys' dorm?" April exclaims.

I pull back in surprise. "How do you already know about that?"

"Some guy in our dorm got a text from some other guy who's in Dalton."

"I'm just mystified at how fast gossip gets around this campus," I say. "I mean, it's not as if it's anything malicious, but still."

"Well, whatever the case, it's nice to meet you, Famous Girl of Dalton dorm," Maya says. "So, tell us about yourself. What are you studying?"

"Well, I'm from San Francisco...mostly. And I'm here because I really like the psychology department. I'm a little bit of a nerd, I've been reading Professor Flores's and Professor Hanks's research since one of my high school teachers introduced me to them."

"That's amazing," April says. "What area of research are you most interested in?"

"How people heal from trauma."

They look at each other, then Maya turns to me with a giant smile.

"I...*love* you," Maya adds, then cocks her head and glances around the room like she's thinking really hard.

"What's the matter?" April asks.

Maya squints at me. "You ever get that feeling like you just had a really important moment in your life? Like there's a little thing that happened to you that will have a butterfly effect on your life forever? I just got that. Why were you standing in the middle of the café with your eyes closed? And the only reason I had gotten up was because I thought I forgot my coffee, but I didn't. Now you're sitting here with us, we're talking, and you have great vibes. That's like divine intervention or something."

April, Maya, and I look at each other, and a chill rushes down my spine.

"Y'all, I feel like we might be friends for a long time," April says.

I nod.

"You never know."

Our special moment gets broken up when another girl walks up to us.

"Well, hello there, gitbid."

"Gitbid?" I jerk my head up and see Jessica's smiling face.

She's got short brown hair, a rack that could give Nordstrom a run for its money, and her smile is not from the eyes.

"Gitbid—Girl In The Boys' Dorm."

"What about the second I?" I point out.

She smiles again, so fake it actually scares me a little.

"Silly details. So...I heard you were flirting in the shower with my boyfriend today?" she says.

"What on Earth are you talking about?"

"I have little spies," she giggles.

My gut clenches.

"I've no interest in DJ, okay? So you can cut it out." I bite back. "What do you think, just because we're sleeping in the same room that I'm hooking up with him?"

She crosses her arms and rolls her eyes.

I take a deep breath and channel my inner Aunt Mia who teaches yoga. "Look, Jessica, I think we've gotten off on the wrong foot. Why don't we call a truce and go back to square one. I really don't want DJ."

I stick out a hand to shake hers, and she draws hers up.

"Sorry. Sticky hands. Really nice to meet all of you, though. Is that...oatmeal with brown sugar and blueberries?"

"Yeah, it's my favorite."

"Interesting combination. I just think sometimes that things aren't meant to go together. Blueberries. Yuck." She laughs loudly, a little awkwardly, and heads off.

Maya inhales loudly.

"It's okay, Maya," April reaches out her hand and grips Maya's forearm. April turns to me. "That's Jessica Pearson. She's not the nicest."

"Clearly."

"That's putting it mildly," Maya says, shooting darts toward her.

"It's DJ's high school girlfriend," Maya says, shaking her head. "She's a year older than us. And, well, so is DJ. He stayed in Davenport last year for personal reasons. Meanwhile, Jessica was enjoying her status as Greene States' resident hot girl. She cheated on DJ, he found out, now she wants him back."

"Holy crap! Why did DJ even decide to go here?"

April chimes in. "DJ accepted the offer to come to Greene State before he knew she was cheating. When he found out, well, it was too late for him to change schools. He had already signed the papers."

"Who was she cheating on him with?"

April frowns. "That's the funny thing. No one knows who the guy was for sure. No rumor ever got confirmed. But DJ called her out on Twitter last year. He's since taken down the tweet."

My Watson alarm bells go off. Maybe this has something to do with the lack of social media posts, at least on his Instagram, almost two years.

"How do you know all this?"

Maya shovels a piece of pineapple into her mouth.

"We've both been on campus for a couple of weeks already for preseason since we play sports."

"Which sports do you play?"

"I play volleyball," April says.

"And I run cross country," Maya looks in Jessica's direction and continues. "I swear, some women challenge me when it comes to sisterhood for all. But I try my best not to say anything bad about her. She's...got a great...competitive spirit? It inspires me."

April flashes her blue eyes my way. "When Maya doesn't like someone, she finds one good thing about them and repeats it."

"That's really admirable," I say. "I've got to do that about my freaking roommate."

"You don't like DJ?" April asks.

"He's...difficult," I say.

"You haven't even been his roommate for a full day," Maya points out.

"I know. Which has me worried about the rest of the year."

"What is it about him that you don't like?"

"It's like he gets off on making me mad."

"How did he make you mad?"

I let a breath out.

"He kind of...showed me his business today."

Their jaws hang open.

"He flashed you!?" April grits out. "How dare he! That's like harassment!"

"No, no. It was in the bathroom, I was washing my hands and he spun around...*sans* towel."

"I hate to be this girl, but I'm too curious. Is Jessica accurate in describing his, ah, reputation?"

I close my eyes, then open them. "I'm guessing he's got a big, long reputation."

"It's definitely not a narrow reputation," April chimes in.

"Yes," I admit. "It's definitely true, as my awkward shower encounter showcased today."

"Dammit," Maya says, pounding her fist on the table. "I hate that Jessica is right about him."

"Are you...interested in DJ?" I ask.

They look at each other and laugh. "Oh, God no," Maya says. "He's so far from my type it's not even funny."

"Are types really a thing?" April asks. "I'm not saying I'd sleep with him. But yes, he's über hot. What about you, Alex, do you like him?"

"I mean, he's objectively attractive, but he's not my type either. Yes, I do think types are a thing."

I feel my body stiffen. Somehow, I feel like all three of us are lying to ourselves right now. I opt to change the subject.

"So, do you guys have tattoos?"

"No, but I want to get one," Maya says. "What about you, April?"

"I think my father would literally kill me if I got a tattoo."

Maya leans back and sips her coffee, a strange grin coming across her face. "We should all get one together."

April pushes her tray back. "No way. You think I'm joking about my dad? I'm not. I would literally be disowned."

"Oh, come on, pretty girl. Don't let your dad control you. You're a free woman now." Maya waggles her eyebrows toward me. "What do you say?"

"Right now?" I ask.

"Not like we have anything else on the agenda today. Unless... you do?"

It's a very unorthodox proposal. I can't help but think how, not thirty minutes ago, I said a prayer and it got answered.

"If it's somewhere on the body no one can see," April says.

"Yes!" Maya yells.

"And if Alex gets one with us, I'll go."

I look at the two of them. Doe-eyed, sweet April. Self-assured, Tasmanian devil-level enthusiasm Maya. A warm feeling comes over me, from the inside.

My personal philosophy in life is that sometimes a thing might seem crazy to an outsider but it just feels right to you in your gut.

And you've got to go for it.

"I'm down," I say. "Let's do it!"

"Hell yeah!" Maya says. "That's the spirit."

At that very moment, DJ appears at our table, passing by from getting a second helping in the serving area.

"What are you all so hyped up about?"

"We're hyped up, DJ, because we just became best friends and we're going to get tattoos," I say.

"Bet you didn't see that coming, pretty boy," Maya winks.

"Pretty boy?"

"You're not exactly the tattoo type, let's be honest. You're the clean-cut all-American. Or am I wrong? Do you have any tattoos?"

Before DJ can answer, Jessica approaches from behind and grabs his elbow.

"Hey, so what are you doing right now?" Jessica glances at me out of the corner of her eye, then looks back at DJ. "Do you want to hang?"

"I'm a little bit busy today," DJ says, his eyes still focusing on me. I wonder if he's disappointed at me for not sitting at his table. Even though he *was* being a bit of a dick this morning, I technically ditched him.

"Busy? What are you doing? I thought afternoon practice wasn't until later?"

"Yeah, it's later…but I have to take a nap after getting up early today."

I can feel DJ's eyes still on me, and it causes the hair on the back of my neck to stand up.

"Surely you can spare some time to hang out with me, DJ?"

"Nah," DJ says. "Need that nap. Gotta go."

He leaves, and now I can feel Jessica's eyes on me again as she slowly walks away.

"Ugh, I've really got to get back to student services," I say. "I already tried to plead my case, but I don't think I made it clear how urgent this situation is."

"And you shall," Maya says with a smirk. "After we get that tattoo."

She pulls up her phone and shows us the Instagram profile of a tattoo artist in town.

"Ohh. She'd be perfect. I'll message her and see if she has an appointment. What do you guys want to get for our tattoo?"

"The sky's the limit, besties," I tell them as we walk out of the cafeteria arm in arm.

9

ALEX

Our spontaneous tattoo plans are put on hold because evidently the best tattoo artists book out at least a few days, even in a smaller town in Illinois. I explain to Maya and April that no matter what kind of tattoo we get, having a high level of artistry is super important. So we're willing to wait until she has something open up. I send her a message on Instagram, and we wait for her reply.

With the day now free, I head to the student services office to plead my case again and force them to figure out my situation.

Fred Makem, the student services officer from yesterday, is a peculiar-looking man in his forties with a handlebar mustache and big glasses. He looks like some sort of throwback from an era I'm not really sure existed. He listens again patiently to my roommate dilemma.

"You're one of the lucky ones," he says, when I'm finished.

"How am I lucky? I'm the only girl in an all-male dorm. I'm really going to have to shower there for an entire year?"

He leans back in his desk and throws a foam ball up in the air, then leans forward.

"Alright, I'm going to be straight with you, Alex, because you seem like a good person and I think you deserve the truth."

"Thank you."

"What do you know about how colleges admit students?"

My stomach knots. I'm worried about where this question is coming from. I have a bad feeling I'm about to get admin-splained.

"Uh, well, I know the average ACT score at Greene State is twenty-eight, and that's one of the main criteria for admission."

"Twenty-nine last year," he corrects, fondling his mustache. "Good though. And how big is each incoming class?"

"Around two thousand, right? I remember from my admissions tour that the total student body is just a hair over eight thousand."

"Good memory."

"What does this have to do with me being put into an all guy's dorm? I don't understand, Mr. Makem."

He clears his throat. "See, here's the thing. When the admissions department admits students, they have to accept a certain number without knowing how many will actually enroll. Say if we accept ten thousand, and of those two thousand enroll. Well, that's perfect! But, in reality, it's impossible to predict. We never know how many will truly enroll. So, say five thousand of the ten thousand enroll. What happens then?"

"That would be...a huge influx of new students," I say. "Where would they all live?"

He points one finger in the air. "Bingo. Last year, we had a record over-acceptance rate for our incoming students. Turns out, Greene State University is one of the top private colleges in the country. They actually call us the Harvard of the Midwest!"

I don't laugh. I'm waiting for him to get to the point. He goes on. "Miss Reyes, we're building new dorms as quickly as possible, but they won't be ready until January, at the earliest, for winter trimester. So, you're one of the lucky ones. At least, you *got* a room on campus. And I'm sorry to hear you've been having disagreements with your roommate. And as far as the all-male situation, that dorm will probably be co-ed next year. The school is trending female—over seventy percent of the student population is female."

This doesn't help me out at all. We're no closer to a solution than we were yesterday.

"Maybe just consider yourself a ground-breaking, progressive trailblazer who is integrating the genders of the dorms."

I sigh, not appreciating his patronizing tone.

"That all sounds nice, you know, *if* there were other girls in the dorm *this year*."

"Which there will be."

"Next year. Not this year."

"Right."

I squint. He's definitely trying to admin-splain me and make this problem go away easily.

"I just really think I'd be a better fit for some other living situation. I'm at a disadvantage when it comes to making friends and dorm parties, not to mention the problems with using the bathroom, which is going to be a constant stressor. You don't have *any other options?*"

"Well, you could go live off-campus at the hotel with some of the other incoming freshmen."

"Seriously?! That's a thing?"

"Remember how I mentioned you were one of the lucky ones? Well, some students will be bussing to and from school every day for classes. It's not perfect, but when you have a freshmen class that is five hundred over your infrastructure...let's just say heads are going to roll in admissions this year, and we're taking a much more statistical look at the process we use. Anyway, want me to book you a room at the motel?"

"I thought you said a hotel."

"Motel, hotel," He shrugs. "Similar thing." He points outside and I see a bus loading and unloading students. "There it is right now. Shuttle runs all day, seven to seven."

Though I'm left wondering how a guy like Fred Makem ends up with a big, corner office,

I thank him for his help, leave the office, and head outside to the bus. I show the driver my student ID and I get on to do some exploring.

Where I come from, 'motel' and 'hotel' have two very different connotations.

'Motels' are where my mom tried to take me to run away from my father when I was very little.

'Hotels' are where Aunt Mia took me on my first vacation to Hawaii and we stayed on the beach.

I want to see if those same definitions exist in Illinois as they do in San Francisco.

The shuttle heads down College Street and turns on to Red Road. Ten minutes later, we pull up in front of a local motel.

Emphasis on the "Mo."

There are a few pickup trucks in front of the place, and I

see a young female student with a Greene State U shirt unlocking her door.

"Hey, excuse me," I say. "Do you go to Greene State?"

She shrugs. "I guess. Why?"

"You guess? What does that mean? I'm Alex, by the way."

"Rachel," she says. "It doesn't really feel like it, living in this motel. Not exactly a true college experience."

"Do you have a roommate?"

She nods. "Haven't met her yet, but I supposedly do. Why are you out here? Did they put you here, too?"

"No, I just thought I would check it out. They accidentally placed me in the all-guys' dorm."

"Ooh la la. Lucky you. With all those men. I think I heard about you, come to think of it."

Jesus. How does everyone know about me already?

I shake off the ridiculousness of townie gossip and chat with Rachel for a little while. She's funny; I ask about her classes and find out we have Spanish together, so we exchange numbers before I bid her adieu. She isn't super psyched about living in a motel, but she's trying to stay positive.

I take a quick walk around the motel grounds. It doesn't seem so bad, until I find a used syringe on the ground behind the motel and I have flashbacks of walking through a neighborhood in San Francisco with Aunt Mia. She explained the drug epidemic and said she would always love me, but if she ever found out that I was doing drugs, she would be very disappointed in me. I never used those kinds of hard drugs, but had high school friends who did. It was shocking and sad to see how quickly, how hard, and how far they fell.

It's one of the reasons I chose Greene State in the

Midwest—to get away from San Francisco and the people I knew.

As I wait for the next shuttle bus back to campus, a short man with a leathery face approaches me.

"Need anything?" he asks in a gruff voice.

"Excuse me?"

"Coke. Heroin. Smack. I got you, young lady. You look sad—like you could use a little pick me up."

"Jesus," I say. Because of my tattoos, people make their mind up about me, and doing drugs is certainly one of those misguided assumptions.

Thankfully, the shuttle pulls up right then and I know that I'm never coming back to this place.

As I ride the bus back to campus, I grin at the text thread I'm on with April and Maya.

Maya: Bitches. After practice is over I want to have some fun. What are y'all up to?

April: Do y'all 'practice'? I thought all you do is run.

Maya: So funny I forget to laugh. Do you do anything at practice besides swat balls?

April: :D You wish you played volleyball. We should definitely switch sports.

Alex: I just got back from my exploration of alternative housing options. Totally unsuccessful but at least I know where to buy drugs and it's scary AF (and no, I don't do drugs!).

Maya: Oh, no! Sorry!

April: You can crash at our place any time, boo. We should make you a third key.

. . .

My heart warms, and I think, yes, it's true about that weird feeling I got earlier today in the café. I could sense the good energy coming from April and Maya.

Maybe my housing situation couldn't be worse, but you know what? I just met two great people, and Aunt Mia told me to pay close attention to who I meet the first week of school because they could end up being your best friends for life.

Alex: There's a mixer tonight in the quad near old Main. Want to go?

April: Yes! Sounds awesome. Are there refreshments?

Maya: Yes, there are! There's lemonade and some snacks. Let's go!

I grin. Even if I'm not going to make it into the female dorm this year, I definitely am feeling a sense of comradery with the two of them.

When I get back to campus, I take a much-needed walk around campus by myself, and I feel so much better.

Maybe I'll survive this after all, but in the interim, my walk inspired me with an idea.

I go back to Fred Makem's office.

"Ah, Miss Reyes! So good to see you again."

"I don't want to move out, but I demand you give me a daily stipend for the inconvenience. I'm going to have to shower at the gym...or something, because I don't feel safe being the only female in an all-male dorm, so it's the least you can do. Fifty dollars a day."

He blinks several times. "Miss Reyes, I must say I'm surprised. This is quite an, uh, unorthodox offer."

I smile. "Well, it's an unorthodox situation that the university has put me in because of the college's mistake." He takes off his glasses to clean them.

"Or," I continue. "I can come back here every day and give you updates about how so and so was staring at my breasts in the bathroom and making me feel very uncomfortable."

Mr. Makem puts his glasses back on and folds his hands on his desk. "Miss Reyes, you've got a stipend. I'll have my assistant work out the details."

I smile. "Thanks. You're the best, Mr. Makem."

As I get up and leave, I think, *if only I were this good at negotiations when it comes to DJ.*

10

DJ

After our Wednesday afternoon film session, I'm heading in the direction of Dalton with Luke and some of the other football guys, when I see this guy I went to high school with.

"Hey! Buddy!" he yells, waving at me from the quad.

"Who the fuck's that?" Luke asks.

"Guy I know from high school."

"Is he...all there?" Luke asks.

Jeff smiles widely as he makes a beeline for us.

Fuck, man.

You know that person you were nice to in high school math class that one time, and now they act like you are best friends forever?

That's Jeff. I saw him at high school parties back in Davenport, and something about him just never rubbed me the right way.

"Holy shit, you really did decide to come here!" he says as he approaches me from across the quad. "I should bow down!" he tells me, looking at Luke. "This guy? Football fucking legend!"

Jeff makes an awkward, half-bowing motion.

Jesus.

"Dude, please don't do that," I tell him.

Luke looks at the two of us. "Alright, well, you two do your thing. I'm going to head to the Alpha house."

"What's the Alpha house?" Jeff asks.

"I'm in a fraternity," Luke says. "The Alpha Delta Zetas."

"Oh," Jeff smacks his face with his palms. "The Alpha Z's! I was spending my time at the Lambda house. They do *not* like you guys. Do you guys have like a rivalry or something?"

I start to remember why Jeff has always bugged me—he's a little slow when it comes to social queues and it kind of weirds me out.

"Uh...I mean, I don't really think much about the Lambdas, to be honest." Luke shrugs. "They don't seem like bad guys, I just happen to be in a different fraternity."

"Oh," Jeff says, and he actually seems a little disappointed that there is no beef between the frats.

I grin. It's funny—Luke is the antithesis of every stereotype of a jock and a frat guy. Well, except for the part where he's athletic as hell and garnered interest from pro teams in both football and baseball. That's not exactly normal.

But Luke is all about varieties of experiences, like his study-abroad term in Buenos Aires.

For some reason, I expected Luke to be pushing his frat on me from day one. We are clearly bros, plus the fact that we have the amazing quarterback-wide receiver connection thing going on. But he hasn't even invited me to his house yet.

"Catch you guys," Luke says, and then adds over his shoulder. "Hey, Dalton! Don't be late tonight. Get those ladies out of your head, ya little twerp!"

I purse my lips. Alex distracted me for five minutes this morning, and I'll be hearing about it all season, apparently. Damn her.

"There's a mixer going on right now," Jeff says, pointing at the quad. "Let's go."

I shake my head but walk in the direction he's pointing because all of the people are mulling around the patio right near Dalton Dorm, so it's on the way.

"Right by my dorm, too," Jeff says.

My stomach rolls. Fucking A, he's in my dorm, too? I heave a sigh and remind myself he's probably a good guy, just a little on the awkward side.

"Who is that hottie?" he asks almost immediately as we approach the crowd, nudging me in Alex's direction. Okay, on this point, I can't blame him. She's a knockout. What with beautiful curves, raven hair, and dark eyes, every guy on the quad tonight is stealing a glance at her.

"Subtlety, my dude, subtlety. Just nudge me, don't point with your finger. That's just plain rude." I push his arm down. "C'mon, man."

"Do you know her?"

"That's my roommate," I shrug, then grab one of the lemonades sitting on the table for guests of the mixer. "For now, at least."

She's just too damn distracting. I know that's childish of me to say, but hey—at least I am in touch with the fact that she drives me completely bonkers in a way no other woman ever has. I'm man enough to admit the reality that if we're together in the same room all year, something is bound to go wrong eventually. I figure that maybe if I act as ridiculous as possible with her, she'll get the idea and get out...or at least stay away from me.

And what with her randomly appearing in the bathroom this morning while I was having my sing-and-shower routine, she's making it way too easy for me to mess with her. Very dangerous combination.

"No," Jeff grabs my arm. "*That's* the girl? You're shitting me. She's...she's..."

I swallow. "She's got a great personality, too, you know."

Jeff looks at me. "Who gives a shit about personality? Those tits, man."

I purse my lips. Yes, it's true. Plus, I know first-hand that her nipples turn hard when they're wet...and staring at my naked body.

But still, she *does* have a good personality. I won't deny that her appearance adds to her allure, but the way I'm drawn to her isn't just because of her looks. There are lots of pretty girls on campus, and the magnetism I feel around her is unparalleled.

For instance, I want to know what all of her tattoos mean?

No, no, no.

No more of that talk, Dalton.

"Damn, man! You're lucky as hell. You gonna take her to pound town?"

Jeff slaps my shoulder and massages it. God, this guy is so annoying. I bite my lower lip and glance at her as she smiles at the girls she is talking with.

I've seen her two friends around during preseason. Maya, a blond ball of energy, who runs cross country. She's led a cat-call at the football team as they've run by on more than one occasion. And then there's April, the tall, pretty volleyball chick.

Of course, I would love to have some fun with Alex. But that seriously will not be happening. Not now, and not ever.

I came here for the football, not the women.

"And by pound town, I mean, you know, take her on a few dates, romance her, and date her, of course. But there would be a trip to pound town at some point," Jeff adds.

All this talk about pounding and I need something to calm me down.

"Be right back, dude."

I run up to my room real quick and grab a water bottle full of vodka, then come back down.

As I sip on my fresh lemonade—with a little vodka—she makes her way over toward us with her two friends.

We all shake hands and smile and run through the introductions, ending on our awkward roommate situation, and I'm on autopilot while I stare at Alex.

It's not even that she's traditionally gorgeous. I think she is, but maybe I'm just hallucinating. There's something in the air with her, like this aura that goes with her wherever she moves. My entire body feels suddenly energized, as if from some radiating energy inside. Then she puts a hand on my shoulder, leans in and whispers something in my ear.

"Hey, April thinks you're kinda cute."

I nod, unsure what to do with that statement but accepting her comment while April chats with Jeff. Then I put my hand on her shoulder and gesture for her to lean in so I can whisper back.

"And DJ thinks *you're* cute. Stunning. That wasn't a lie."

Fuck. This was *not* in the plan.

You're supposed to be repelling her, you idiot!!

Maybe it's the vodka. No, my buzz wouldn't have kicked in so quickly.

Alex leans back and furrows her brow. "Does he go by DJ, too? I thought his name was Jeff. Is he...oh." A bolt of realization crosses her face. "Dammit. Really? Talking about yourself in third person?"

"It's a compliment."

Autopilot again. Fuck, fuck. Repel!!

She wipes the smile off her face and shakes her head. "Stop screwing with me. April really does think you're cute. She saw you jogging without your shirt on yesterday. I'm trying to be a good roommate and give you some help. You know, a cock assist."

"A cock assist?" I snort.

She shrugs. "You never heard that? It's like the opposite of a cockblock. My friends and I used to say that all the time in San Francisco."

I wiggle my eyebrows and lean in again to whisper. "Well, thanks for the *cock assist*. But I have to be honest. I want you. You're a damn temptress."

No! No!

She smirks. "Will you please stop it with that talk? I'm no temptress."

"I'll be the judge of that."

She squints skeptically. "You have no idea who I am. I'm damaged and weird. And when I have sex, I take it out on the guy. I'm crazy. Just trust me. Guys like you...don't want me. It won't end well." She looks at her drink. "Shoot. I said more than I wanted to. Must be the lemonade."

My heart starts to race. "You're trying to *deter* me from you by saying you've got emotional issues and use sex as a release? Honey, you better try a different strategy. Because you're making me picture us just going back to the room right now and working out this tension."

Her jaw hangs open.

"Or are you going to pretend like it's not there?" I add, challenging her.

She stares at me with her mouth part-way open for a few moments before she finally responds.

"I just met you. And we're so different, this would *not* be a good idea, so please stop. I saw your beautiful family walking out of Dalton with a *We'll Miss You, DJ!* sign. I hate to break it to you, but not all of us grew up in the Cleaver family."

My nostrils flare. "You think I grew up like...*Leave It to Beaver*?"

"You know that show. Beautiful mother who smiles. Handsome dad who plays catch with you. Fun, younger sister whom you play cards with...or something. I saw them."

I run a hand through my short hair. My fists clench. She knows nothing about my life, and, I'm actually offended.

"I know the show," I grit out. But as far as the snapshot image of me having a *perfect* family, she could not be more wrong.

"Okay, great," she says. "And my upbringing was a little more like the show *Shameless*. You ever see that one?"

I take a deep breath. Damn, I brought this on myself. This is what I wanted—to repel her.

Well, mission freaking accomplished. Even though those words coming out of my mouth, well, I was straight up hitting on her in a way I promised myself I wouldn't.

But if Alex wants to make assumptions about my upbringing? Well, then, she's not the one for me.

A blow-up at my roommate in a very public place would not be good for anyone.

"Hey, Jeff," I nudge him. "You want to run to the Alpha Zeta house? I hear they have a *real* party tonight."

He shrugs. "Sure."

"Nice talking with you, April and Maya," I say with a polite smile, and we get out of there.

∼

THE PARTY at the Alpha Z house involves beer pong, dancing on tables, and substantial drinking. When I come back to the room later that night, I'm really drunk for the first time in my college career. It feels great to go back to my own room.

There's this feeling of unparalleled freedom that stretches before me, and it goes on for four years.

Fucking freedom. I slap the *Dalton Dorm* sign at the top of the stairs as I unlock the door to the third floor. I think of Gramps every time I see the sign. R.I.P to that great man.

I check my phone and see if there's any texts from my sister. None from her, but there is one from my mom asking how everything is going. I text her back and remind myself that I'll call her tomorrow.

I bust the door open to room three twenty-nine, and Alex is nowhere to be seen.

"Thank God," I mutter, then flip on the lights. I've been craving a solid music-listening session. After trading my jeans for sweatpants, I turn my computer on and start playing my favorite new country rap song with Lil Nas X and Billy Ray Cyrus.

I sing along, and just as I'm getting to my favorite part, I hear an extra shriek in the room.

"Hey! What the fuck, DJ! I'm trying to sleep here!" Alex says, sitting up in her little tank top.

"Oh, good, you're here," I say. Whoops. I guess I somehow missed the fact that she was even in here. But that's no concern right now. My buzz tells me she needs to know about this song. "Do you like country rap? What do you think of this song?"

"What don't you understand about midnight being quiet hours!"

"Well, maybe you should get up. So we can have a talk," I say, swaying to the music in my chair. The beat feels so damn good.

She rubs her eyes. "Turn the fucking. Music. Off."

I lock eyes with her. I'm steely. "Why don't you. Make. Me."

Why doesn't she understand that this song is absolutely amazing?

I didn't think she would respond to my challenge, but she hops off the bed in her tank top, walks over, and stands beside me.

"What is this silly music anyway?" Her voice is still laced with annoyance.

"It's country-rap."

"They *combined* rap and country?"

She leans in front of me to see my computer screen close up. Her left hand lands on my leg, and I wonder if I'm drunkenly hallucinating, or if I'm actually getting a flirty vibe from her. On the inside, my entire body responds to her touch. On the outside, I stay as still as I can.

Too still?

"Do you have something against combining those two genres?" I ask.

She finds the volume control on my speaker and turns it down. "Some genres—some things—just aren't meant to be combined."

Reaching across my body, she grabs my headphones. In the process, her boobs nearly graze my face, and I pray she doesn't look down because I've got a full-throttle erection coming on.

Putting her hand on my shoulder, she hands me the

headphones. I steal a glance at the way her body is positioned and can't help thinking how perfectly arched her back is as her nighty rides all the way up her thighs.

I want her so badly, but I'm drunk and she's not, and what kind of a first hook-up move would that be?

"Temptress," I say in a low voice as my eyes run along her cream and coffee skin in the faint light. "I like you, Alex."

Her eyes widen, and I take the headphones from her.

"What did you say? I couldn't hear you."

I clear my throat and find my resolve, looking her in the eye. "I said you need to cut it out."

"Cut what out?"

"Oh, please," I scoff. The innocent gig just doesn't play well on her. "You're bent over in your night shirt or whatever, leaning over my desk with your tits hanging out. I'm an almost twenty-year-old *man*. You know exactly what you're doing. I'm exercising every ounce of self-control I have."

She rolls her eyes. "Shut up. I just rolled out of bed with no makeup on, I look like shit."

My eyebrows raise instantly. "If you look like shit, then why has *this* happened?"

I glance down at my legs where my cock is pressing against the sweatpants I changed into when I got back.

Alex claps her hand over her mouth, literally looking at me as if she did something wrong. "Dear God!"

"Alex..." I growl, and run my hand over her side.

"Wait," she says. "Why did you run away from me at the mixer today?"

I shrug. "Don't worry about it."

"I *am* worried about it."

"Well, don't."

"How drunk are you?"

"Why don't you taste me and find out."

I see my clear blue eyes reflected in her pupils. Her focus lowers to my lips. My hand wraps around her head and I don't know who makes the move, but I think we both do and we kiss and now I know she's the type of girl who wears cherry Chapstick to bed.

And I'm wondering if she's wrong that country and rap aren't meant to be combined. I think they are. And I think we're meant to share this room and kiss and do much more than that. Her pierced lip feels great against mine. She flicks her tongue in my mouth, and I haven't kissed a girl with a tongue piercing, and damn if that's not hot, and I wonder if she's got any other secret ones.

"Goddamn temptress," I mutter. "You taste amazing."

If it feels this good when Alex and I kiss, I think different things should go together all the time.

She pushes me away when we're done.

"We can't do this," she says.

"But we already did it," I respond.

She jumps in bed and slides under the covers. "Good night, DJ. Please keep the music down."

11

ALEX

The first light of dawn spills through the shades and I stare blankly up at the white ceiling from under the covers. DJ stirs and grumbles on his side of the room. He's on his stomach on top of the mattress, in just his briefs, face turned away from me as his body rises and falls with each breath.

My stomach grumbles with a combination of hunger, nerves, and lack of sleep. I grip the teddy bear my aunt gave me when I moved in with her, and I stew. I've had insomnia since I was fifteen, but I was ready to sleep last night.

I was just merrily dozing off when DJ bounced in and turned room three twenty-nine into his own personal late-night party place. I think about giving his bare back a slap to get even. It doesn't seem fair that he's able to sleep through the night and I'm not.

I get up from my bed and walk over to my desk.

It also doesn't seem fair that I'm dead set on staying hyper-focused on school, and I've been given the most distracting roommate situation ever. Why did I have to get assigned to live with the douchebag who is cocky enough to call me *temptress* and blatantly hit on me? Why couldn't they just put me with Mr. Short-no-name, who clenches up whenever I walk past him and is too shy to look me in the eye? That would have been preferable.

I pause as I watch him sleep. God, he is distracting, indeed.

And he calls *me* temptress? Oh, the irony. He's the tempting one. Though I would never give him the satisfaction of a nickname. Besides, what would the male version of *temptress* be? I screw my face up at the wall, thinking. Now I'm wondering why language is so sexist as to infer that *only* females can tempt. What bullshit. I'll just have to stick with my stupidly sexy roommate with deep blue eyes and abs that look like they were chiseled out of a Michelangelo sculpture—if Michelangelo sculpted guys who look like romance cover models, that is.

Somehow, I managed to summon the strength last night to pry my lips away from him and jump into bed before things got out of hand. I could feel my hands betraying my conscious mind, eagerly slipping up his skin. When his hands gently ran down my backside, he touched me with a lot more finesse than I had imagined. Still rough, but with a control I didn't see coming.

And no, I didn't spend time last night imagining how his body would feel on top of mine.

Okay, fine, I did. I'm a bad liar. Yes, I did spend time doing that last night. But not more than ten minutes or so.

We're *roommates*. I can't think of a more distracting way to kick off the term than to get into a tryst with my sexy roommate...whom the entire campus of girls want to be with. Come to think of it, his shirtless jog yesterday makes sense now. It was a mating call.

Although, last night all I could think about was giving into my craving and jumping into bed with him.

Thank God I was sober.

I have to get out of here and think about going for a walk around campus, but the early morning tweety birds are chirping and it's too early for any sort of physical activity, especially on zero sleep. So I grab my Kindle from my night stand and turn it on.

I begin reading Thucydides's *The History of the Peloponnesian War* to get a head start on class, but it's a very dry read and I keep getting distracted. Worries of what will happen when DJ wakes up pop into my head. We'll have to address what happened last night. No way around it. I chide myself for even getting up and going near him last night. A kiss was now going to make every second of this experience even more awkward than it already was.

Did I kiss him, or did he kiss me? I couldn't even tell. I wanted more, though. I wanted to straddle him on his chair and...

My heart pounds furiously. DJ's on his back now, still facing the wall away from me, on top of the covers, breathing deeply in his sleep. Seriously. His grey briefs are tight, , and I can see, well...*everything.*

I shake my head and return to my Kindle, deciding that I'll read something a little less dense. It is barely five thirty in the morning and classes don't even start until next Tuesday, anyhow.

I decide to read a love story, something to distract me. Bad decision but I'm already committed. The romance novel I settle on is sexy and hot and I've got the covers over me. I can't help but slide a hand down my hot skin and land it between my thighs when I get to the sexy bits. The book is steamy but my own mind is steamier right now, and my fantasy is quickly spiraling out of control. Maybe what I need is a little relief to the tension that's been building up inside me these last couple of days.

I do my best to control my breathing as I press into my clit with my middle and ring finger and curve my pelvis up. My free hand covers my mouth, and I keep one eye on DJ to make sure he's still sleeping.

I imagine what last night could have been. That gravelly smooth voice whispering in my ear as he rocks into me. *Is this how you like it, temptress? Slow, smooth and deep?*

I start to pant.

Could Mr. Perfect handle my cat scratching? I bet he likes it missionary only.

But I bet even *that* he does perfectly.

I look over at him and he clears his throat through his sleep. My entire body quivers with pleasure as I imagine riding him, using his abs for balance as I grip his cock. He's never been with a girl like this. He's never been with a girl like me.

"Oh!" A soft noise escapes my vocal cords, but I manage to stifle it so it's barely audible. My eyes bulge and I let my Kindle fall as I build closer to my orgasm. I'm getting close, and I shut my eyes and let a wave of pleasure rip across my skin and core.

When I flutter my eyes open, to my utter shock, DJ is staring at me.

"Good morning, sunshine," he says, his voice a full octave deeper than normal.

My eyes widen to saucers and my heart pounds like I've just been caught with my hand in the cookie jar.

"Uh, good morning," I say, my hand wet. I don't budge from under the covers.

He sits up in bed and scratches the back of his head.

"Shit, what happened last night, temptress?"

I clear my throat and sit up like I *didn't just imagine how DJ's hands would feel on my hips when I ride him.*

"Yeah, we should talk about that," I say.

He waves his hand. "Look, I'm sorry about the music. That was too loud, even by my obnoxious standards. Man, I was drunk as fuck. Those last shots really hit me hard."

"Shots?"

"Oh, yeah, I was doing shots of tequila at the Alpha Z house. I barely even remember what I played before I went to bed in this room. It's all hazy."

"Oh, you forgot what happened when you got back to the room," I squint, and a little ray of hope opens up inside me that maybe we can just forget about what happened. "So what *do* you remember about last night?"

He stands up, looks out the window, and stretches, and fuck him for being so goddamn attractive

"I just remember I came home, put on some music—I think—and then passed out hard. Damn, I slept like a rock last night."

I clear my throat. "So you really don't remember what happened when you got back?"

He turns around and he's doing some sort of yoga stretch routine in front of the window and I think it's just an excuse so I can see every defined muscle in his body. Part of me wants to tell him to put some damn pants on, but that would just start the same argument from yesterday that went nowhere. Plus, another part of me is quite entertained with his hungover state. He seems a little more vulnerable than usual.

"Did something happen last night? Besides me being a dick with the music?" he asks, scrunching up his face.

I swallow and I thank my lucky star.

He was so drunk he doesn't remember our kiss.

Oddly, I'm suddenly sad in a way because I was just wishing that it hadn't happened. And it hits me:

This is my get-out-of-jail-free card.

Our kiss? Never happened. If he doesn't remember it, then there's no reason for me to acknowledge it. That would only complicate this already rocky roommates' situation.

"Yeah, you just kept talking about country rap," I say. "That's all."

He looks off into the distance out our window, which looks down at the quad.

"Huh. Sorry about that."

"Wow. I didn't take you as someone who apologizes."

"I'm willing to admit when I'm wrong. Also, I'm a lot nicer when I'm hungover. It takes my edge off."

"Really? I'm an asshole when I'm hungover, which for your information is a rare occurrence because I'm not a big drinker. At least, until I get my coffee." I give him an up-and-down, and it pains me but now I have to say it. "Can you at least put some pants on?"

DJ looks down, as if he didn't know he didn't have pants on, then looks back at me.

"We've already had the 'no-pants' argument. I'm sticking to my stance."

I roll my eyes. "I'm serious. We need to set some rules while we're living together."

"Well, do *you* have pants on right now?"

"No."

"That makes you a hypocrite. Nice teddy bear, by the way." He flicks his chin in the direction of Franklyn the bear.

I ignore his teddy bear comment. "I'm under the covers, though."

His deep blue eyes sear into me.

"Okay, okay," I say. "You're right. We need some ground rules, and we both need to agree to them. So, first rule. Shirt and pants worn at all times. When we're not under the covers."

"Just pants. No shirt. I still like being shirtless in the dorm."

I sit up against the wall and fold my arms as he continues.

"Come on. It's still September. It will be hot here potentially through October. I'm compromising with the whole wearing pants thing. Also, you're welcome to join me in the whole no shirt thing, temptress," he winks.

I squint. *Does he* remember what happened last night?

On the other hand, he was relentlessly hitting on me all day yesterday, starting with the infamous shower incident. So it would actually be weird if he *stopped* hitting on me now.

"You would like that, wouldn't you?" I say, coyly.

He walks over to his closet and pulls out a pair of shorts.

"I would. You have a great body."

"Hey! Stop staring at my boobs."

"Is that...a piercing?" He squints.

I cover up. "Seriously."

"My bad. I just saw that piercing and now I'm curious."

"I have one nipple pierced. Good eye."

"Fuck me," he growls, drawing out the syllables.

My stomach tumbles with a surge of heat. I don't allow a grin to cross my face.

"You'd like that, wouldn't you?" I breathe, and it comes out way flirtier than I intended.

"Yes," he says, putting on socks and shoes. "I would."

I shrug, a little flustered. "You can't just...keep saying that!" I blurt out.

He doesn't seem fazed.

"First, *you're* being flirty, too. Don't act like this attraction isn't a two-way street. I'm not a dumbass. And second, Yes, I *can* keep saying that. I'm fine with apologizing when I'm a dick and I wake you up with late night music—total dick move, I can admit that. But you're gorgeous and I don't see a reason to pretend like you're not. Does that mean I'm going to do anything? Of course not. I think it's probably best if we don't, anyway."

"And I'm not interested, so there. You're not my type," I add, just for good measure.

"Oh? You have a type?"

"Don't you?"

"No. I just like who I like."

"Oh. Okay," I nod.

"What's your type?"

"Punk. Rocker. Inked. Probably plays in an indie band. You know the type."

"Got it. You like bad boys."

"Yes. Sure. Bad boys," I say sarcastically. I feel like the term is overused but I'll say it anyway.

"And I'm not bad enough for you?" His tone drips with sarcasm.

My spine tingles. "No. Just no, DJ. I don't find that funny."

He nods. "Alright. Well, then, back to our house rules. We've got one rule. Shirts optional, pants or shorts, required. What about hooking up?"

"What about hooking up? I told you, we're not—"

"Relax. I mean hooking up with other people. How are we going to bring them back here? Obviously, I'm not going to hook up when you're in the room. Unless you're into that."

I roll my eyes. "You've arrived at college and you're thinking about how to bring people back to the room?"

"Uh, yeah," he says. "Isn't that one of the main benefits of college? That you get to shack up with people?"

No, but since he obviously is thinking about it, we'll have to figure something out. "Fine. What were you thinking?"

DJ then shares his plan, proposing he can get the room Monday, Wednesday, Friday, and Sunday night.

"Like all night?! Where will I sleep?"

"Well, it doesn't have to be the whole night. Maybe like a few hours."

"A few hours?! How long do you need to..."

He wiggles his eyebrows. "To what?"

"To hook up," I say, and I can't stand the pang of jealousy that rolls through me.

"Well, I don't like to rush things. Also, I have classes in the morning on Tuesday and Thursday, so you can, you know, do your stuff those days if you want."

"What do you mean, 'do my stuff?'"

"I assume you'll have no trouble finding your bad boy rocker here."

"I'm not here to date and mess around. I'm here for school." Oh. My. God. I've got to make something of this...of myself. I don't have rich parents and a perfect family to support me.

"Well, that makes one of us. You're hot as fuck, so you'll get the pick of the litter, I'm sure."

"That's...actually a nice compliment."

"I know. You're welcome."

"Thank you." I clear my throat and stretch my arms up, leaning against the wall. "So that's your main priority in college? To mess around?"

"My priority is football, and staying close to family. Women aren't even in the top five, so quit your worrying."

"Why do you want to stick close to your family?"

He runs a hand through his hair, continuing on like he didn't even hear me. "So you're cool with that arrangement? You'll get the room Tuesday, Thursday, and Saturday nights if you want it? Saturday is a big concession, just so you know."

It's not lost on me that he ignored my question about his family. But I decide not to prod.

"So I don't understand. Where will I go those nights?"

"Well, you could sleep in the lobby for a little bit, then come in here after midnight, maybe."

"I don't like that." I shake my head. "But then again, I don't sleep anyway, so what's the point?"

"You don't sleep?"

"I have insomnia. I'm lucky to get a few hours here or there."

"Have you always had insomnia?"

"Since I was fifteen."

He cocks his head, seeing a little concerned. "Did it just randomly start?"

"My mom died from cancer when I was eight. It's been going on ever since."

"I'm sorry to hear that."

There's an awkward pause.

"It's fun being around you." He stands up, unscrews a bottle of water and takes a drink. "Being around you energizes me."

"It's because you want to fuck me," I blurt out.

He starts choking on the water, and a rare, sly smile crosses my face.

I hop out of bed and walk over to put a hand on his back.

A cloud of inspiration comes over me, and I realize it's true, I've never seen him vulnerable—and agreeable—like he is when he's hungover. I decide to capitalize on this by slinging with a new nickname that occurs to me. "Are you okay, Mr. Perfect?"

"No, I'm not okay. I think I need a full body rub down. Want to help me out?"

I sigh and listen to my stomach grumble. "I think I liked you better when you woke up and I felt like I was talking to a normal person for a few minutes."

"I'm very not normal."

"You look...normal, though."

"Don't judge a book by its cover. Normal is relative."

This time I walk over to the window and look outside with my back to him. He chugs the rest of his water, crushes the bottle and throws it in the recycle bin, then walks over to me and rests his chin on my shoulder.

"Cute," I say.

"Watson, like I said. Never judge a book by its cover. I'm not normal. There is not a fucking normal thing about me."

"You're right. No normal guy would rest his chin on a girl like this in a non-sexual way."

"Non-sexual?" he says, and I can feel his jaw moving against my shoulder while he speaks. It feels oddly soothing. "This is my favorite opening sex move. Does this not work on girls or something?"

I smile and a giggle escapes me as I turn around and push my hand into him. First, I wanted him to move away, but now I just leave it there at the top of his abs close to his chest. I can feel his heartbeat.

"There, I did it," he adds.

"Did what?"

"Made you laugh."

"Is that a big deal?"

"Yes. Because you have R.B.F. I heard someone making fun of you for it last night at the mixer."

"What's R.B.F?"

"Resting Bitch Face."

I giggle again.

"Twice in one day. I'm the fucking man."

I let my face fall back to neutral. My heart races and I'm touching him and why am I *still* touching his skin? I got the get-out-of-jail-free card from last night and now I'm already feeling how he makes my body buzz again.

"Bet you can't get three times," I say.

"It's early in the morning. Plus, I've always liked a good challenge." He looks down at my hand. "You like touching me, don't you?"

I pull it away. "No. Sorry, my mind is slow from not sleeping."

"Right. So slow that you're breaking the *one* rule we made." His eyes slide down my body so slowly, I swear it's as if he's touching me with his gaze. Down my arm...to my side...my hip...and landing on my ass. "You still don't have pants on. It pains me to remind you, by the way. If I were you, I would probably never make it to class on time because I'd be staring at my own ass in the mirror."

I burst out laughing and lean my head against him, then stand up straight.

"God," I mutter softly.

"Yep, that's three times! Another win."

He turns around and heads for the door. With his hand on the doorknob, he turns back. "You know, temptress, I don't care what those people say about your resting bitch face. You're a fun roommate. And there's one more rule we need. I think you and I both know what that is."

"Under no circumstances, do we ever, ever hook up. Or do anything with each other," I say. "A roommate truce. Is that what you were thinking?"

He nods. "Exactly. We're roommates. I don't want you turning into another crazy ex who keeps begging to fuck me because her new boyfriend sucks at it."

"Um, what?" I say. "Are you talking about Jessica?"

But he's already out the door.

12

DJ

This morning, Jeff and I head out on a run through the cornfields around Greenfield. Like I said, we were not the best of friends, but he wanted to go for a run today and we don't have a morning practice, so I obliged him.

I'm not sure if he's still drunk right now (I am), but I feel like I'm having one of those conversations that goes nowhere.

"April was hot, she totally wanted me, man." He pauses, as if thinking. "Right? Do you think she wanted me?"

I shake my head. "Dude, I don't know, I was drunk. You were drunk. April was drunk. Hard to tell."

I hate to break it to him that April was shooting me eyes. But Alex was all I could think about.

Still is, unfortunately, after that kiss.

"Fuck, man," he says. "Slow down. Who goes running at seven thirty after a night of drinking anyway?"

"I just feel tense," I say. "Running has always been a calming release for me. Once the hangovers kick in, our bodies will already be fighting the headache with endorphins from the run."

"It's aggressive. I dig it. But seriously, slow down. I think I'm still drunk."

I slow slightly. In early September we don't want to be out running past nine a.m. anyhow, since it will get oppressively hot by midday.

He blabs on about April and how hot she was and I tell him if he's so into her he should tell her he likes her. Then Jeff goes on about some Twitter post that he's all amped up about, something about someone posting something they shouldn't have ten years ago. Jeff clearly spends way too much time on Twitter. I'm not in the mood to shut him down, though, so I smile and nod and run and keep my thoughts to myself and let Jeff tire himself out talking.

My grandfather was a great man and he once told me you'll end up, for better or worse, like the five people you spend the most time with in your life. But Jeff's here, too, and he's an acquaintance by default. I need to choose new friends but I also don't very well want to be a dick and tell Jeff directly I'd like to hang out with other people. It's a fine line.

Yet getting settled into college is a huge change, and I'm a little too worried about my real life to be concerned with the digital world.

"Bro, why aren't you incensed about this? Isn't this bullshit? Geez, are you even listening?"

"Can you just shut up for two minutes, enjoy the run and stop bitching?" I retort as we run. The scenery of the great plains is beautiful. Right now, we're rolling past a grove of trees with an old railroad to our right while the sun rises up.

"Whoa, man! Shit. Someone woke up on the wrong side of the bed. Why you so tense, bro?"

"I'm fine, man," I say, gesturing for us to make a turn at the next country road and start our loop back to campus.

Part of me wants to confide in him, because he's right. I *am* tense. But it's none of Jeff's goddamn business that I'm so attracted to my roommate that I kissed her last night.

It's also none of his business that she pushed me away and leaped into bed faster than a speeding bullet, like I was some kind of venom that would poison her if our lips continued to touch. I still haven't washed my face today because I want to keep the taste of her cherry Chapstick on me, faded as it is. I might even give Katy Perry's song "Kissed a Girl" a new listen. And I hate Katy Perry.

Alex is taking over my thoughts and it's annoying is what it is.

I can understand a mild attraction. It's the *overwhelming* part of the attraction that makes no sense to me. Tall, leggy April at the frat house last night was hot. April's blonde-haired friend Maya was gorgeous and hilarious, too. She had me in stitches with her jokes about pop rocks and blowjobs and how she had perfected the art of combining the two.

Even though they are attractive, I'm just not into April and Maya the way I'm into Alex. With Alex, I imagine fucking her for hours and then lying in bed after, cuddling with her on my chest and finding out about every single one of her tattoos and piercings and filing them away in a mental file marked 'why Alex is how she is.' Then I want to fuck her again and tire her out and fall asleep to the sounds of the train horns blasting through the night and wrap her up so tightly that her insomnia falls away.

"Fuck," I mutter softly, through gritted teeth.

I've known Alex for two days and I'm already creating fantasies in my mind about where our relationship will go. True love fantasies that are completely, totally, destined for failure. I am completely insane.

Because you don't meet the girl you're going to marry on the first day of freshmen year. Well, sophomore year for me. And she definitely doesn't get assigned to your room. It's never this easy.

"Dude, you're definitely tense. What's going on?" Jeff asks.

"It's Alex," I finally admit.

"What about her?" His eyes widen. "Did you two hook up or something?"

"Hook up?" I snort and shake my head. "I mean, no."

My heart races. Fuck. I hesitate a bit.

We kissed and I lied to her this morning. I was drunk last night, but I was not *so* drunk last night that I would forget our kiss. Not as long as I lived. That kiss cut through my drunken state like a lightning bolt of sobriety. So rather than confront an awkward situation, I sidestepped it like a professional bullfighter. Genius.

"You did hook up with her!" Jeff says. "Holy shit!"

"No, no, no. We most certainly did *not* hook up," I underscore.

He laughs. "Bro, it's okay. You want to hit that on the down low. I understand. Ain't gotta lie to me. It's Jeff. NCHS Ironmen, bro!"

His calling out the name of our mascot just seems desperate. I don't reciprocate his high five.

"I didn't hook up with her. I'm serious."

"Of course, you didn't." He winks. "You dog, you. I got you."

I don't say anything to him. All I know is that this will be our final run together.

And I'm going to have to make Grandfather Dalton proud—I'm going to choose my friends consciously. Which means I'm going to stop associating let alone being friends with someone like Jeff. I don't like him, in general, or the way he talks about women. So I won't be talking with him any more than I have to.

We get back to the campus gym, shower off, and change. I play football in the fall, and I'll run track in the winter and spring terms when football is in the offseason, so I've got an athletic locker in the track area as well where I can store my things.

Jeff and I walk over to the quad, and on the way we run into a few other guys who were at the frat party last night: Finn, Nelson, Chris, and Grant. Together, we all walk in to the campus cafeteria, affectionately known to everyone on campus as The Oak Room.

I get some scrambled eggs, hash browns, and a pile of bacon and sit down.

A few minutes later I see Alex walk in. I almost invite her to sit with us, but I see some other girls waving to her and I figure I'll give her a break from the guys since she sees enough of us already at Dalton.

After some brief conversation, I decide that Nelson, Grant, Finn, and Chris are good guys and I want to be friends with them. They're not like Jeff, who seems to have some sort of ax to grind with everyone.

Nelson Manzo speaks softly in a deep voice, but when he does it's almost always something profound. Nelson is from Chicago and he shows off his Italian roots by having a *Godfather* quote for just about every situation. He also makes references to his great great-grandfather being the top hitman for Al Capone, and none of us are sure if he's actually joking or not.

Finn Cooney is from the south side of Chicago, but also Irish as fuck and apparently plays in an Irish-American folk band with his dad and two uncles. He's smart and a smooth talker and he runs the one, two, and four-hundred-yard dash in track, like me. Although he doesn't play football.

Chris is a curious nerd—or possibly artist—trapped in a jock's body. If you close your eyes and talk with him, you'd think you were talking to a teddy bear, not a six-foot-three, solid rock of muscle who was an all-state wrestling champion in high school and is a starting defensive linemen for the football team as a freshmen.

Shaggy-haired Grant Rhodes is from northern Minnesota and obsessed with snow and hunting and axes and anything outdoors. He loves Marcus Aurelius and knows he's going to major in philosophy. Good luck finding a job, buddy, I tell him. But he's not worried. He doesn't seem worried about anything. I give him the nickname the Woodsmen Zenmaster.

And then there's me, of course, from Davenport, Iowa.

I did get the handsome blue eyes and the height, though.

And I almost forgot…then there's Jeff with us. I honestly start to feel a little sorry for him because he's out of his element here and I think he knows it. It's not that we're excluding him, it's just that he's on a different wavelength from the five of us. It's like we've weirdly known each other our whole lives, even though we just met. I can easily picture myself getting into—and out of, hopefully—shenanigans with the four of them over the next four years.

Grant pokes his head behind me.

"We've got a few fine-looking young maidens here," Grant observes.

Finn cracks up. "Yes, some fair maidens, indeed. Bro, what is this, 1920? Fair maidens? Next thing you're going to start saying is how they're wearing 'trousers'."

Grant ignores Finn. "Look at them just...eating and smiling. So careless. So frivolous. So beautiful. Women eating and laughing has to be one of the best things in the world."

Nelson chimes in with his best *Godfather* voice, "Women and children can afford to be careless, Don. Men cannot. They are fair maidens, indeed, and it is our fate as men to care for them."

I squint. "Is that last part in the *Godfather,* too?"

Nelson slams his fist on the table. "Damn, you're good, Dalton. Usually I like to slip a few extra quotes past everyone."

We all laugh. I get up from the table for more bacon and chocolate milk, and I look over at the four of them, April with the red hair, Maya Pop Rocks, Alex, and one other girl I don't recognize.

Maya is cracking a joke and everyone is laughing except for Alex. Her smile is forced, and even hilarious Maya can't make her crack a smile.

I remind myself that I made her laugh three times before eight this morning and that makes me smile as I shovel a few more pieces of bacon on my plate. My eyes catch with Maya's, she smiles and nothing happens inside me.

Then Alex pokes her head up and my whole body shakes. I don't imagine this. It's like there is some extra dimension between us, telling us to be together.

"Grant is right," I say as I sit back down at our table. "Women are made for men and men are made for women and we make each other happy." I pause and see a couple of guys talking to each other a few tables over who are staring into each other's eyes quite closely. "Well, some men are made to make other men happy, too, I suppose. And women who make other women happy. Shit, what the fuck do I know?"

They all crack up except for Grant. "That's some wise shit right there, Dalton. Be cocky enough to make an assertion, but humble enough to admit when you're wrong. Hey, I don't care what those seniors were saying about you last night. You're alright."

"What were the seniors saying about me?"

He shrugs and sips some orange juice. "Just that they didn't want a stuck-up ass third-generation entitled rich boy who thinks his shit smells like roses in their frat."

"What the fuck? Who said that?" I fume.

"I don't know their names," Grant says. "But I *did* hear a couple of guys saying that."

"Bro, calm down," Jeff says, putting his hand on my shoulder from across the table. "Man, you really are tense. You'd think that fucking Tattoos McGhee last night would calm you down." He nods in Alex's direction and they all look.

"Holy shit," Finn leans in and raises his eyebrows toward me. "You slept with who?"

I close my eyes and massage my forehead. I'm not hungover but I'm also not *not* hungover.

"She's his roommate," Jeff adds. "She's got great tits."

My hand flies out and I grab Jeff by the collar of his stupid shirt—*who wears a collared shirt to fucking Thursday brunch?*—and I pull him in toward me.

"Will you. Shut. The fuck. Up. Motherfucker. Before I have to take you outside and punch you so hard they'll have to sew your jaw shut."

"Holy fuck, dude, I'm sorry," Jeff pleads, putting his hands up and out. We've tussled in high school for fun and he knows it will not be a fair fight...and that he will not win. It's not a question of strength, but a question of fuse. Once mine is blown, I'm a bomb that goes off. "You don't want people to know about that. But it's just the guys, here. Just the bros. Who are we going to tell?"

I glance around. There are tables of students sitting all around us, all within earshot. They're also staring because I've got him tightly by the collar. Jeff is a fucking idiot, and my grandfather was right when he said that when you let your friends get chosen by default, you can end up with a shitty friend who talks out of their ass, like Jeff here.

"The walls have fucking ears," I mutter. When I let him go, he breathes a sigh of relief and falls back in his seat.

I lean in and motion for the guys to get closer and I speak softly. "And I did not, I repeat, not, sleep with Alex. Not that I wouldn't try. I would definitely take anything I could get with her. I'd love to replace that teddy bear she sleeps with at night."

"She sleeps with a teddy bear? For real?" Chris asks.

I nod. "She does." Something tugs at me when I say those words. What about our kiss from last night? I ignore the feeling. She didn't want to talk about the kiss this morning. She'd rather pretend it never happened. If she wanted to do it again, she would be all over me. She knows how I feel. "Plus, I actually feel a little bad for her. One, she's in a dorm with all guys. Two, she's got *me* for a roommate. That's an even worse fate."

They all chuckle.

Three, it's hard for her to smile, I think as my gaze drifts to her again.

"Ha. I can't believe she sleeps with a teddy bear," Jeff snorts.

But when our eyes meet right now, I swear I see hers flicker with life. I get this fuzzy, anxious feeling in my gut.

I think we should just be friends.

But little do I know, before I could even try, that chance is about to get taken from me.

13

ALEX

Thursday afternoon is the day we decide the tattoo is really going to happen. Maya, April, and I head in Maya's car to Lake Storey. Summer is winding down, but it's a beautiful day and we want to catch some rays of sunshine.

A warm feeling comes over me as we get out of the car. I have new friends and I have a good feeling about them. They're good people and they're a lot different from me, too. I get the feeling that we'll all learn things about ourselves being in each other's orbit, and I like that opportunity.

They're amazed by stories that are mundane for me. I tell them about my life in San Francisco with my aunt and going to epic gay pride parades and getting a host of tattoos by age sixteen, but I leave out a few details like the story about how my parents died… that I'm too embarrassed to tell just yet.

They don't pry.

We're lying on the beach for a while, daydreaming, until April yells out, "Delta!"

Maya and I give her the same confused stare.

"What do you mean, Delta?"

"I just had a vision. We should all get matching triangle tattoos. Symbolizing change."

Maya and I look at each other and nod.

"I like it!" Maya says. "And we should get it on our wrist!"

"Love it. It's official! I'm in, too!" I say.

After some time at the beach, we go to the tattoo shop and tell the artist our design. The shop artist is a thirty-seven-year-old woman inked with double sleeves. I go first—a small tattoo is child's play for me—and then April's up.

"Is this going to hurt?" April asks.

"Oh, you'll be fine, honey," Maya says.

April lies down and closes her eyes. "I don't like needles. I'm not gonna look."

Maya distracts us by telling us about the pole dancing class she signed up for the day she turned eighteen.

"My boyfriend at the time didn't mind the new skills I picked up, either. It's more for me, though. It's a release and it's fun. When I'm at home, I like to take off my clothes, put on 80's music and dance like no one is watching."

"Well, to be fair, they aren't," I giggle.

"Sometimes, I leave the curtains open," she says in voice that sounds like Maya Rudolf, the hormone monster in *Big Mouth*. "Give the people a show!"

"What does your...oo...ow...father think?" April asks.

"It was my father's idea...well, okay, not his idea, exactly. It was my mom's idea and he supported it fully as a way to express my sexuality in a healthy way."

April tenses up. "Are you serious? He doesn't care?"

Maya shrugs. "I grew up in a very sex-positive household. My mom is a sex therapist and they have always talked openly about sex at the dinner table. We all have sexual urges, it's nothing to be ashamed about. We all just need to make sure we're being healthy and safe and consensual. So, yes, I do pole dancing and there's nothing wrong with that."

April and I make eye contact and sort of shrug. "I wouldn't mind trying out some pole dancing," she says. "We definitely didn't have that in my town, though."

Mabel, the tattoo artist, smiles gently at our conversation.

"Alright, I need you all to stop talking about poles," Maya says. "I haven't been laid in far too long."

"Long summer?" Mabel asks.

"Summer? Hell no. Long week."

"A week!? Oh, ow!" April cringes, and Mabel stops and asks if she's okay.

"The needle is fine. I was thinking about sex!"

"Do you not like sex?" Maya asks, seeming very concerned.

"I'm waiting for the perfect guy to come along," she says. "So you have a boyfriend back home whom you hooked up with before you got here, then?"

"Ex-boyfriend," she corrects. "He was fun. We weren't built to last though. But I'll always have a special place in my heart for Johnny B. Wood."

"What was his actual name?"

"That *was* his actual name. And, get this! He's going to carpentry school. Some stuff you just can't make up. But alas, we were not meant for true love. His wood was good, but we were not meant to be."

I crack a smile. "Sounds like a poem."

"Not a laugher, are you?" Maya asks.

"Not really." Although, I was this morning.

"This isn't me being cocky, but I'm just really funny. Having to get a word in edgewise with four big brothers will do that to a girl. Why don't you laugh?"

I feel my pulse elevating. "How do you find time to dance naked with four brothers in the house?" I ask, dodging the question.

Maya winks. "How did I find time to have sex with my Johnny B. Wood every single day senior year of high school? Where there's a will, there's a way."

"You're so open about your views," April interjects. "I'm jealous. I've..." she hesitates.

"You've what?" Maya asks. "Spit it out!"

"I've never had sex."

Maya's jaw drops to the floor, and she gets up and walks around. She is fired up.

"Honey. Honey. What?! What?! This is the twenty-first century, not the nineteenth! Oh, girl, I am so glad I met you. And you are gonna be so glad you met me."

She shrugs. "I think it's like, something I wanna wait for, you know? I'll meet the perfect guy and we'll date for a few months..."

"...and he'll pick roses for you and make a rose petal scavenger hunt and you'll ride into the sunset on a white horse." Maya shakes her head. "Not gonna happen, sister. You've got to be realistic about these things and enjoy the ride while it lasts. We could die tomorrow, you know."

They both turn to me at the same time, as if by instinct.

"Alex? You're the tie-breaker. What do you think?"

A rare, genuine smile crosses my face, because my "friends" in high school had no idea what real sisterhood was. They were gossipy and always trying to one-up each other in dress and conversation and everything, and now April and Maya are asking me, casually, but seriously, for my opinion.

Maya notices how I'm reflecting.

"There's that Alex smile! I knew that wasn't your real smile before."

"You're thinking hard," April says. "What's going through your mind?"

"My aunt always said what's good for the goose isn't necessarily good for the gander."

"What's a gander?" Maya asks.

"Basically, I mean that Maya, maybe you're happy having a healthy sex life and that's a priority for you and you know that about yourself." I turn to April. "And maybe you're happy waiting and that's okay, too. Or maybe you have a mental block about sex. I don't know. Do you have a block?"

April shrugs. "I don't think so. I just don't feel ready."

"Then you're not ready. Don't worry about it. Maya can coach you through things when you're ready. And you can learn vicariously through her experiences."

Mabel smiles. "You three are really funny. How many years have you known each other?"

"Since breakfast two days ago," I say.

She pauses her work. "Damn. Really? I wish I had friends like you when I was your age."

"Well, we can be your friend," Maya says, and pulls out her phone. "What are you doing later?"

Maya takes Mabel's number down and we chat some more until she finishes with April's tattoo.

Then Maya gets in the chair.

April is soft spoken but has intelligent blue eyes. "What about you?" April asks me. "You must be pretty happy with your situation."

I furrow my brow "What situation?"

"Oh, we didn't talk about this yet?" Maya chimes in. "When we went back to our dorm room today, these girls in our lobby were talking about hot guys they'd seen, and obviously DJ Dalton came up."

I roll my eyes. "Obviously."

"Well, according to them, DJ was bragging to some guys that you and him were sleeping together."

My heart drops down to my feet.

"DJ Dalton was *bragging* about sleeping with me?"

April nods. "Apparently someone overheard him at their table at brunch this morning talking about fucking his girl roommate with the piercings and the great tits and the teddy bear. All details aside, you're the only girl on campus with a guy roommate, so ipso facto, it had to be you he was talking about. And it had to be DJ doing the talking."

Rage bubbles up from every corner of my being, and I clench my fists.

"He *told* people about Franklyn? He's talking *shit* about me already?!"

"Hey, it's okay," Maya says, rubbing my back and trying to comfort me. "He's hot. I would totally do him in a second. We saw him at the café. He was probably just telling his guy friends. Guys are entitled to talk about things with their friends."

"We didn't sleep together, though," I say through gritted teeth. "He was talking about us sleeping together at the cafeteria when we saw him this morning? That little dick!"

"He was just making the whole thing up? You don't sleep with a teddy bear?" April asks.

"I do sleep with a teddy bear. That wasn't a lie."

"No shame in that," April says. "So do I."

"And you do have great tits," Maya says. "I'm a little jelly. Not gonna lie about that one."

I smile for a split second but I can't full out laugh because I'm so charged up about this DJ situation. "We didn't sleep together! Or anything close!" I hesitate. He doesn't remember the kiss, so we're just writing that off as 'never happened.' "DJ Dalton is a fucking liar."

The girls—and tattoo artist—nod.

"What a freak," Maya says. "So weird. Why would he need to make up rumors about sleeping with you?"

"That sucks he said that," April adds. "I'm sorry about your reputation."

I scoff. "My reputation?"

"Who cares, anyway?" Maya waves her hand in the air. "No one even knows who you are. And we're all friends, and we don't care. DJ Dalton can go fuck himself."

"It's not about my reputation. I don't care about that. What I *do* care about is that DJ was straight up about the two of us."

"Word," Maya says. "Fuck him."

"Yeah!" April seconds. "Fuck him! I mean, not literally, though. Because he's an ass. We've got your back, Al. And you *didn't* fuck him. But if you did, we'd also have your back."

I'm angry but I chuckle because April sounds funny when she's swearing. She's got a high voice and it's clear that she doesn't normally swear. It's also fun to see her amped up because she is very introverted most of the time. I'm extra appreciative of her kind spirit in this moment.

I think for a moment, then say, "He wants to start rumors about his roommate on the first weekend of freshmen year, before classes have even begun? You're right. I thought for a moment I might just have a roommate who was a fun, trustworthy guy. Not an asshole."

"So what are you gonna do?" Maya asks.

My chest tingles with anger. In high school I might have

tried to side-step this conflict. But I've got a new tattoo, and I like my college crew tribe, and this means war.

"I'm going to get him back."

"How?" April asks.

"The only way I know how."

14

ALEX

I take some time and process this new information I have about DJ. I took him for a cocky bastard, yes, but not for a liar, and I mull over whether or not I should confront him, or just sit on the information until the time is ripe.

Friday night he has to travel for a game—the games start before the academic year does—and I spend all day Saturday out with April and Maya exploring the town of Galesburg.

DJ isn't there when I get back to the room later on Saturday night. I see some of the other football players on my floor back home already, and I wonder if he came back then went out.

Sitting in my room, with the window open, I relish in the soft breeze blowing in.

Why, DJ, would you spread such a rumor?

I wanted to like you. I really did.

The room still carries the scent of him and his piney deodorant. I write in my journal for a little while, meditating on my mother's warning:

Tall, handsome, and rich, pick two.

I can hear roving bands of college students walking through the quad, obviously drunk. They are hooting and hollering and enjoying college like they should be.

I want to be out with them enjoying the first Saturday night on campus and be frivolous. But I'm no longer in the mood to be frivolous. I'm in the mood to be gloomy and embrace my gloominess for the night, and I decide that's okay. I'm not depressed or anything, it's just that everyone feels a little gloomy from time to time.

I pick up the phone and call Aunt Mia.

"Well, hello there, sunshine!" she says. "I was just thinking of you."

"Were you now?"

"Yes. I was wondering if you had your mailing address yet. Rudy sent you a postcard from Peru, and I thought I'd mail it to you."

My stomach clenches at the mention of my ex. It's only been about two months since Rudy left for his travels.

Yet that world seems so very far away now. Even though I've been at college for less than a week, it feels like months have passed.

I give Aunt Mia the address and decide to tell her about the roommate debacle since it seems like it truly won't get resolved.

She's very concerned. "Do you feel safe?"

"I do," I say, and that's the truth. "Oddly enough, I was alone here last night and I realized I feel safer when DJ is here, even if we don't necessarily see eye to eye on every little thing."

You know, like if he should be bragging to everyone on campus about hooking up with me.

"If you're safe and you're happy, that's what's important to me."

My heart warms, and I pull the phone away from my face so Aunt Mia can't hear the sniffle that escapes me.

"Thanks, Aunt Mia. I miss you."

"Not too much, I hope. You're going to be the family's little trauma research professional. God knows we need one of those."

I grin. "Classes haven't even started."

"But I can bet you did the reading already."

"Working on it tonight, actually."

"My gosh! It's Saturday!"

Sensing she's worried about my not taking time for myself, I tell her all about April and Maya and our escapades this week.

"That's amazing! You never know. Those could be the friends at your wedding one day."

"Well, we *did* get matching tattoos..."

She cackles with laughter. "Oh, Alex. I miss you."

A beat passes.

"Aunt Mia, can I ask you something?"

"Anything."

"When my mom said that you should stay away from a man who is tall, handsome, and rich, how serious was she?"

I hear Aunt Mia suck in an angsty breath through her teeth. "Have you found someone like that?"

"No, I'm not seeing anyone. I just want to know. I never got the chance to ask her, and I've always wondered if she really meant that."

There are a few moments of silence until Aunt Mia speaks again. "Honey, your mom and dad, well, they had their problems." *An insane understatement.* "But they loved each other in their own way. You're a beautiful, thoughtful, down-to-Earth young woman who deserves the best man she can get."

"So you're saying…"

"I'm saying you shouldn't let some advice that stuck in your head from when you were eight years old determine your future. You can be what you want to be. And you can learn from your parents' mistakes, grave as they were. You can be something new. They say history repeats itself. Well, I don't believe that. It might rhyme, but it doesn't repeat. There are exceptions to every guideline. One of the most important lessons I've learned in life is to trust my own judgment. And you, Alex, should trust yours. Eighteen is young, but it's also not."

"I'll be nineteen soon," I grin.

"That's the spirit. And it sounds like you've met two really good girlfriends. Be there for them, too, like you'd like them to help you when you're down."

I hear her inhale a deep breath, and a smile already crosses my face because I know what she's about to sing.

"This little light of mine…"

I grin and answer. I can't not sing back to Aunt Mia. "I'm gonna let it shine."

"I'm gonna put it out…"

"No! I'm gonna let it shine."

We both cackle in laughter at the inside joke dating back to the first year I lived with Aunt Mia.

"I love you, Aunt Mia."

"I love you, too, honey bunches of oats. Call me any time."

I hang up, grinning and feeling much better about school, my friends, and life. Everything except for DJ, really. I'm still so pissed and unsure about why he would make up a story that's a complete fabrication and brag about it to people on campus?

Okay, well, it's not a *complete* fabrication. We *did* kiss. But he didn't even remember that. So why would he brag to his friends about us? DJ does seem to have a dickish attitude, but he didn't seem like the type who would do something like that. For a moment I thought he was different then the stereotypical blue-eyed, brown haired, handsome, privileged young man with a rich family—I mean, he's got the dorm named after him. How many millions of dollars did his grandparents have for that to happen? I wouldn't be surprised if he's a trust fund baby. Another mark against him is that he'll apparently lie at any turn for his own benefit. I thought wrong.

Even though DJ is obviously a bad person, the room still feels empty without him. I hate the fact that I actually enjoy his stupid presence.

I try to read about Thucydides for classes again, but it's a dense read, and after I look at the words from the same page about nine times, I give up. I can't read this at seven thirty on a Saturday evening. I consider going out, being a functioning member of society and all, but I didn't sleep very well last night and I won't exactly be a social butterfly. Plus, at this time of the night I'd have to get ready and I don't feel like putting on makeup.

Instead, I pull out my Kindle and I realize I may be developing a bad habit of procrastinating my school reading, but allow it because school hasn't technically started so I'm not procrastinating something that hasn't happened yet, right? So I read a sexy romantic comedy and the scenes are hot and the writing is good, but it's a short story. At least I get carried away to another place for a time but I'm brought back when

I start a new book and the protagonist is lean with blue eyes and brown hair and DJ's stupid sexy face pops into my head. I can't get him out, though. He's really crossed a line with this whole lying about us hooking up thing.

I'm thankfully getting drowsy around midnight but then there's a knock on the door. I wonder why DJ would be knocking, so I quietly check the peep hole.

Adrenaline surges through me when I see Jessica, a beer in hand, wearing a black dress and has enough mascara on to supply a small community.

"Open up, DJ! I want to talk to you!"

I don't open the door, I just stand there quietly, hoping she didn't hear my steps on the carpet and thinks no one is here. Didn't we say I get the room on Saturday nights, anyhow?

I kind of thought Jessica was just a bitch before, and now I feel a little sorry for her. She's coming off as desperate.

The fact that she keeps showing up here without DJ being here makes me think DJ won't respond to her texts. He clearly doesn't seem into her, but she still sneaks into his dorm to try her luck? Geez. I better say a prayer for her.

I wait a few minutes, then dive back into bed. I'm just drifting off when I hear her fist on the door again.

Okay, now I'm mad.

I storm toward the door and swing it open, ready to give her a verbal tongue lashing about letting people sleep.

But when I open the door, it's DJ's friend Jeff, whom I met from the other night.

I can smell the alcohol on him, and he's so shitfaced he's actually swaying from side to side.

"Hey, so, can I, you know. Come in?" he asks. His speech is a little slurred.

My heart begins to pound. "Do I know you?" I feign like I forgot all about meeting him. Mistake.

"Of course, you know me. We met the other night at the mixer. Here, I'll just come in..."

"No. that's okay," I say, forcing the door closed. But Jeff is strong and keeps his foot in the door.

"Oh, come on, Alex. I've heard about you. DJ told me all about you on our run the other day."

Fire rages through my blood. "What did he tell you exactly?"

He snorts. "Just that you're, you know. Talented. In certain areas. And how you sleep with a teddy bear."

"What the fuck does that mean?" I belt out, and I can feel my blood pressure rising.

He licks his lips. "You know, how you have some special talents. Just let me in and let's have a little fun."

"No," I say firmly, then push him out of the door frame, then slam it and lock it, my heart racing.

I hear Jeff huff on the other side of the door.

It's almost one a.m. and DJ still isn't back. Why do I actually wish he was here?

I toss and turn, worried now about some asshole trying to sneak in my room. Eventually, I'm so exhausted from not sleeping well the past few nights anyway that I fall asleep on top of the covers...with the lights on.

Around eight a.m. the next morning I hear the key in the door and DJ comes in. He's got disheveled hair and rings under his eyes.

"Hey," he says as he walks in, then sits down to take his shoes off.

"Good night I take it?" I ask.

"Yeah. Got a little out of control there at the end. You?"

My stomach tumbles and my imagination wanders. I'm not even going to tell him how my night went.

"Where were you all night?"

"Got too drunk and fell asleep on the frat house couch."

I hate that relief pours through me.

"You weren't shacking up with someone?"

I try to ask the question as innocently as possible.

"Nah. Not worth bothering with anyone else because I have a special girl I'm wearing down."

"Oh? What's her name?"

He collapses on his bed with a thud, then looks at me.

"Alex."

I clench my fists and my skin tingles from the inside.

"I thought I'd give you a break last night," he adds. "You know, make you wonder if I was out with some girl..."

I sit up. "You know what? Screw you."

"Oh, come on, I'm just joking. Someone's in a sour mood tonight. I've got a cure for that. I swear I can help you."

"It's morning," I inform him, pointing at the sunlight streaming through the window.

"Oh. Right."

Just then, my phone buzzes with a text from Maya.

MAYA: Breakfast, biotch?

"I CAN'T HAVE this conversation right now," I say. Although DJ has no idea the full extent to which I've been imagining ripping into him verbally about him talking shit about me around campus.

"Good, me neither. Gonna get some sleep. Good night."

He turns over and I feel like I'd built up this argument to monumental proportions in my head, but instead it came out anticlimactic. I head down to the cafeteria, which is in the same building but on the first floor of Dalton Dorm.

I eat brunch with the girls, and halfway through Maya drops a bomb. She saw DJ out with a girl on the dance floor last night at the Alpha Z house.

"He was still dancing with her when we left the basement party. It was really late."

Jealousy flairs inside me.

He's out dancing with whoever, then telling others about how we were hooking up? How can I trust someone like that?

He's going to be a nuisance to me as I try to do the right things and keep my scholarship.

"Can I sleep at your place tonight?" I ask April and Maya since they're roommates.

"Sure," April says. "I brought an air mattress for when friends from home come for visits."

Maya shrugs, and wiggles her eyebrows. "Or we could just snuggle up." She gauges my reaction. "Kidding. I'm kidding. Unless you're into that kind of thing."

DJ IS there when I go back on Monday in the early afternoon. Shirt on, for once. He turns the music down when I walk in.

"Hey. Where have you been?"

"Oh, why do you ask? Are you worried about me? It wasn't like I saw you for two whole days or anything."

He shrugs, an unusual look crossing over his features. "I

just wanted to make sure you're okay. Are you? You look a little...disheveled."

I blink a few times, feeling disarmed. He's such a dick most of the time, that when he's genuinely nice, it catches me off guard.

My nostrils flare, though, and I remind myself that this is the same guy who gossips about me, and judging by his demeanor right now and yesterday morning, he has no problem whatsoever pretending to my face like he's not a rumor spreader.

"Oh, I just shacked up somewhere since Sunday nights are yours for the room, remember," I say nonchalantly as I put my backpack down.

"Oh," he says. "Where?"

"Don't worry about it," I say. "I wouldn't want you spreading rumors now, would I?"

"Why would I do that?" he says. "Roommate agreement. What happens here stays here. I thought about that—we should make that rule number three. In addition to wearing pants and dividing up the room by night."

"That's quite the idea," I say. "So what happens here stays here? You won't tell anyone?"

"Nah. Not a soul."

"Interesting. Starting now, obviously. Yeah, I'll think about it."

Liar, I think as I disrobe and change from jeans into yoga pants and from a hoodie into a tight tank top. I see him steal a glance, a confused look on his face, obviously unsure what to make of my attitude.

"Keep your eyes to yourself," I bat.

"My bad," he says, and I can tell he's battling himself to keep his eyes on his computer. "Temptress," he smirks.

"You are not allowed to call me that. It's not funny anymore."

"Yeah, sure, whatever," he says.

I sling my yoga mat over my back.

"I'm not joking about that. It's inappropriate and I won't stand for it."

"I only do it when we're alone, Alex. It's not like I'm out bragging to everyone about how hot you look like in yoga pants or something. It's just our private little thing. Where's the harm in that?"

My jaw drops. *Liar, liar, pants on fucking fire. You bragged to the whole freaking campus.*

But I know better than to play this card directly, if this is how he wants to roll.

I pause in front of him on the way out the door, standing right close to him.

"You, DJ, are *not* allowed to hit on me. *I don't like you.* Anything you've felt between us, it's all in your head. I am not your temptress. I am not anything. I'm your roommate, and you damn well better start being respectful."

His jaw drops.

"Really?"

"Really."

"Okay. Sorry. My bad, Alex. I...must have misread the signals."

"Yes. You misread the fuck out of them."

"My mistake. No more temptress talk."

I linger in front of his face for a few moments, ironically, *tempting* him to steal a glance at any part of me other than my eyes.

"That's more like it," I say coldly, and walk out of the room to head to yoga.

15

ALEX

The first week of classes fly by. Greene State utilizes trimesters instead of the more common semester system. Which means three-and-a-half classes per term is full time. Our classes reset in the fall, winter, and spring terms. Supposedly it allows us to 'go deeper into the subject areas' since we're not juggling as many classes at one time. So I'll be going deep into Theories of Personality, Freshmen Preceptorial, the required class, and Spanish 102, the language requirement I need to get out of the way.

On Friday after the first week of classes, I have an appointment with my advisor, Professor Z, as he's known.

"Holy shit, your advisor is Professor Z? He's so hot," April says as I walk with her on the way to my advisee appointment. "Give him an eye fucking for me, will you?"

She covers her mouth immediately after. "Oh. Did I just say that?"

"Yeah, you don't usually talk like that."

"Maya must be rubbing off on me."

"April...are you into older guys? Is that your thing?"

Her voice raises, and I wonder if I've hit a nerve. "Me, older guys? Don't be ridiculous."

"Oh, you only go for the ones your father approves of? I'm feeling like we're getting somewhere with your virginity thing."

She sighs. "You're a little too smart. Let's save the psychoanalysis for our next party. I have to focus on classes right now. Catch you later."

"Later."

I wave goodbye and she turns on the walkway toward her next class while I continue across campus. The September leaves have the slightest hint of changing color today, and the temperature is perfect for jeans, flip flops, and my favorite Zeppelin t-shirt.

April isn't the only one who finds Professor Z attractive. It's *common knowledge* that he's the hottest professor on campus, as Maya has reminded me several times already. He's also my psychology professor, and I will admit he looks damn good in the sports coat and jeans he rocks.

When I get to his room, he's standing with his back to me, staring at his bookshelf—his *huge* bookshelf. It takes up the entire wall of his office. Since he hasn't noticed me, I stand in the doorway for a moment admiring his handsomeness. He seems much too well built to be a professor...and is that a *tattoo* sticking out of his rolled-up sleeve? He covers that well with his coat. And what with his round-framed glasses, a tattoo on him seems like it's simply a relic from a more rebellious era in his life. It certainly makes him more intriguing, though.

I swallow and a pit of anxiety forms in my stomach, reminding me of the time I got sent to the principal's office in seventh grade for kissing a boy in the back of class.

Finally, I give a light knock even though I'm inside his office already, and he turns around with a slight smile.

"And I've seen you in class. You must be Alex. Come on in and have a seat."

He shakes my hand and sits down in his desk, and I sit in the easy chair across from him. He folds his arms and adjusts his glasses. Wow. Hello, there, Mr. Sexy Forearms.

"As you probably know, I've been assigned to be your general advisor. This is just the first, quick meetup where we'll discuss how you're getting along in school, and get to know you and what you're looking at studying. Once you have your specific major, you'll be transferred to an advisor in that area. Unless it's psychology, of course. That's my area."

My heart hammers. It's Professor Z's first year. I wonder how on Earth this gorgeous man is going to make it through even one year without some indecent proposals from students. In his glasses he's like a real-life version of Clark Kent.

"Actually, I really like psychology," I say, realizing I've been pausing for a few beats too long.

He scans something on his computer, then turns back to me. "Right. It looks like you've claimed psychology as your major. Tell me more about that."

"In high school I volunteered at a mental health clinic, and that's when I first started thinking about it as a career. I saw that so many of the problems the patients had seemed to be a product of their own mind, and how they dealt with trauma in the past."

He nods, listening. "By the way, I forgot to mention this at the beginning. Whatever we talk about together is bound to confidentiality by federal law. FERPA and all that. Not that anything personal will come up, but if it does, I'm here to help you and guide you along."

"Good to know," I say.

He clears his throat and looks at his computer. "Wow, impressive ACT score. And you're from San Francisco. We don't get too many west coasters here. How did you end up at Greene State U?"

"My aunt went here a long time ago. I've always had it in my mind that I would come here, and when I found out how good the psychology program is, that sealed it."

"Wow. Same," he says, leaning back. "I wanted to study under Professor Faulkner."

"Yes! I'm hoping to get into his death class during the winter term."

Professor Z raises an eyebrow. "He only instructs that class once every two years. It's three-hundred level. And you're a freshman. You might not have the prerequisites."

"Oh. Well...I'd love to get in. I don't want to have to wait until junior year. I'm sort of trying to get ahead of the curve here. I'd like to go to an Ivy League graduate school."

"Oh. For what purposes?"

"Research. I want to do trauma and neuroscience. I know you went to Yale, right? What does it take to get in there, for grad school?"

His face softens. "You want to go to Yale, do you now?"

I nod. "Yes."

"Just let's be clear. Although you've got a good ACT score, that doesn't do much for you when it comes to getting into an Ivy League. Doing some extraordinary research that you undertake while here and you've got to show them something you haven't seen, something that they haven't seen. Not trying to deter you in any way, I'm just stating that it's not going to be easy."

He shuffles some papers around on his desk, appearing to be looking for something.

"I can see why you want to get into Professor Faulkner's class. Getting on his radar freshmen year would be a big deal."

"I know," I say. "I've read just about everything of his I can get my hands on."

"I'll look into what I can do to get you into the course, Alex. But as it's my first year at Greene State too I don't have much pull around here. Yet."

He stops looking around his desk, and his eyes pan the massive bookshelf on the side of his room.

"How do you get pull as a professor?" I ask.

He brings his gaze back to me. "Research, of course. And lots of it. Publication of one of my papers in a major journal is what I'm gunning for this year. That's how you get tenure."

"Well, what are you researching right now?"

Grinning, he runs a hand through his hair. "I feel like you're interviewing me now. This is supposed to be your time."

"I'm curious."

He leans in. "I'm trying to find the most effective therapies for addiction and getting over traumatic life events."

My ears raise. "Oh? That's right up my alley, actually."

"You're familiar with trauma research?"

Whenever this sort of question comes up, I'm never quite sure how blunt to be. But I get a very relaxed, sincere vibe from Professor Z, so I decide to give him the story instead of glazing over it.

"I've read a lot of books on grief. Aunt Mia used to give me a book a week, and I would devour them in middle and high school." I take a deep breath and look him in the eye. "And I'm personally familiar with the subject. When I was seven, my father attempted to kill my mother in a murder suicide. He ended up killing himself but the wounds to my mom weren't fatal. We thought she would make it through, and then she passed away from cancer a year later."

His face goes white. "Oh my gosh. I'm so sorry to hear that."

"I was away traveling with my grandparents when my dad tried to kill my mom, and I never knew the full story of what happened until recently. My family likes to hide things. Anyway, after that I moved in with my aunt. She's been my guardian and she's amazing. I love her to pieces. But I've had to overcome a lot of trauma to get where I am."

His face tenses and he scrubs a hand across his jaw. "I'm very sorry for your loss," he says, looking me in the eye.

"Thank you."

We share a moment of silence and it doesn't feel forced or awkward.

He smiles. "So Alex, how is everything else going with you? How's school life the first week?"

"Well, it's alright. I'm making friends and everything."

"Great. Which dorm are you in?"

"Dalton."

He raises an eyebrow. "I thought Dalton was an all-male dorm."

"Yes. It is. I'm the only girl."

"Your roommate is a guy?"

I nod.

His forehead wrinkles. "I know we had a heavily skewed female-to-male ratio on campus, but I didn't think it had gotten to that point. How are you handling it?"

I shrug. "He's sort of an asshole, to be honest. From day

one, he was hitting on me and telling me I was the most stunning girl he'd ever seen."

"Wow. Sounds pretty over the top."

"Very." A smirk crosses my face.

"What was that look for? More to the story?"

I shake my head, and consider not telling him, but Professor Z seems nice and classy and obviously not creepy, so I figure what the hell? I might as well be an open book with him. I've been searching for an older mentor. Aunt Mia is amazing, but I don't want to worry her with every little romantic detail in my life. Plus, FERPA and all that. He literally *can't* repeat what we say or risk penalty of law.

"It's just ironic. I'm actually *very* attracted to him. But he acts so ridiculous toward me, I can't handle it. He even called me *temptress,* for goodness sake. Who *does* that?"

He laughs. "Seriously? He's not joking? This guy must be a piece of work. Oh, shoot, don't tell me who it is. I could be advising him. Please, don't tell me." He waves a hand in the air and continues. "Sometimes young men have a lot more maturing to do at that age than young women. Go easy on him if you can. He's not inappropriate, is he?"

A conniving grin crosses my face. If anything, *I'm* the inappropriate one.

"No, not really. When I'm clear that something is making me uncomfortable, he'll stop. And funny enough, I like it better when he sleeps in the room with me. I feel safe. But he—"

I falter and decide to draw the line of confiding in Professor Z at repeating the Greene State U gossip that DJ and I have slept together.

"He...?"

"But he's not even there that often," I say, adding fairly

random words to a sentence I considered ending in a much different way.

What I almost said was, 'But he *bragged to the entire campus about how we slept together. And that's not true.*'

"Well, keep me updated on that situation. Feel free to email me anytime, I'm here to help, especially if that situation gets out of hand—I'm an email addict, unfortunately, so I check it every day and weekends, too."

"Okay," I say, and a warmth comes over me. He's too young to be a father figure, and I'm not going to be Professor Z's femme fatale, but he is a nice guy for sure.

"Anyway," he goes on. "Back to research, before we have to part ways. I'm happy to hear that trauma psychology is an area of interest for you. And I'll feel out the situation as far as getting into Professor Faulkner's class as a freshman. But like I said, it's a small class and he generally takes extraordinary students only."

"Oh," I say, suddenly feeling dejected.

Professor Z leans in. "Now, sitting here conversing with you I have no doubt in my mind that you're extraordinary, Alex. But let me ask you something. Do *you* think you're extraordinary?"

I shrug. "I don't know. I think so."

Professor Z pounds his fist on the table and it gives me a startle. He's smiling good naturedly, and that comforts me. "Gosh, Alex! That's not going to cut it. That's not the attitude for you to have if you want to get into the Ivy Leagues. You've got to *bring it like you mean it*. As you think you'll become. Look at me."

I bring my eyes up to meet his.

"I'm a great judge of character. Trust me on that. I can see the intelligence behind your eyes. But I also see some timidity. And you know what? I was once like that. But when

I was a freshman at Greene State U, I had an amazing advisor and she helped me believe in myself. And when I got to Yale, do you know what I discovered? The people there were no smarter than you or I. They just *believed* they were smarter. *Believed* they were better. Start believing right now you're as smart as they are. Because you are. You got set back with a hell of an upbringing, yes. But it also sounds like your aunt kicks ass."

"Yes, she does," I say, feeling a ball of emotion rise in my throat.

"And I'll tell you this—you've got one thing I haven't seen from *any* of my students whom I've met so far. You've got this triple threat of maturity, drive, and the will to become something, and damned if I'm not impressed that it all comes from a selfless place."

I nod and process his words, feeling a flow of confidence ripple in me like I've never really felt before. My teachers in high school never believed I could get into Greene State University, let alone Yale. So it means a lot to hear this.

After a pause, Professor Z stands up and walks over to his bookshelf. He pulls out a book and hands it to me.

"How to Change Your Mind?" I ask, reading the title of the book. I flip it over and read the back of the book's jacket.

He nods. "Give this a read. When it comes down to it, it's all about trauma therapy."

The subject matter gives me a startle. "Trauma therapy through drugs?"

He nods. "There's a lot of evidence to show Psilocybin—the active ingredient in magic mushrooms—and LSD can help terminally ill cancer patients live a better life in their last months and years. And those drugs, combined with guided therapy, have helped ease severe PTSD in patients, as well."

I cringe a little, holding the book. "I'm not really into drug therapy. More about the homeopathic methods. I don't think another anti-depressant drug is exactly what we need."

"I used to agree with you one-hundred percent. Just read the book, and let me know what you think. Oh, and read this one, too. This is just for your confidence. Speak up in class, will ya? I'd like to hear what's going on in that head of yours. You've been sitting in the back all week. Maybe try the front, or the middle, for starters."

"Thanks."

We say our goodbyes and I walk out of his room feeling so refreshed.

Professor Z has the ability to do this to women, apparently. He's so damn nice and low-key authoritative, but without appearing to be—no, without *being* cocky. He's the kind of guy who makes you want to go find his mama and thank her for the way she raised her son.

I linger outside his open office door for a moment, glancing down at the two books in my hand, *How to Change Your Mind* and *Daring Greatly: How the Courage to be Vulnerable Transforms the Way we Live, Love, Parent, and Lead*.

I head into the office lounge of the psychology department and smile at the secretary, who is typing something at her desk. She's got permed black and grey hair and wears a pair of legit 50's-style glasses that turn up in the corners.

I look past her to a study room with a few tables, and I'm taken aback by a pair of intense, grey eyes smoldering into me.

A shudder runs through my body. He's sitting at a table, and he waves me over to him. I'm hypnotized, so I obey. The closer I come, the hotter he gets.

"Hey," he says in a low, gravelly voice. "I'm Grant."

My eyes widen. "I know. I'm Alex."

"Sit down. Rest a bit. You look stressed."

"I do?" Ack, do I look that bad? Now he's making me feel self-conscious, even though he's probably just trying to be nice.

"Yeah. You look like you've got a lot on your mind. Did you just have your first advising appointment?"

I sit. He's got shaggy brown hair, and a chiseled face.

"Yes. How'd you know?"

"Lucky guess. I'm about to have my appointment with Professor Z right now. Word on the street is he's a pretty cool guy, so I'm happy about that. What's your major?"

"Psychology. And I'll probably double in something else, but I'm not sure what yet. How about you?"

"Psychology. And I'll probably double in something else, but I'm not sure what yet."

I do a double-take at his near imitation of me, and he laughs.

"I'm serious. Not making fun of you. Great to meet another psych person. What interests you about psych?"

I grin. "What *doesn't* interest me about psychology? People fascinate me to no end."

"People are so strange." Grant leans in, like he's telling me a secret. "Sometimes, I like to go sit in the quad, late at night, just to people watch. Early morning, too."

"That's so weird." Not sure what to make of that little tidbit.

Grant laughs. "I'm kind of a weird guy, to be honest," he shrugs, then looks me over and smiles slightly. "What are you up to tonight?"

"Nothing."

"Want to go out with me?"

I open my mouth but hesitate. "Like a date?"

He grins. "Yes, like a date. I like talking to you."

"Alright." Why not? Maybe this will get my mind off of my asshole roommate and besides, I'm enjoying our conversation, too.

I give Grant my phone number and we make plans to hang out later tonight, then chat for a few minutes until he gets called into Professor Z's office.

"Wow. You're tall," I say when he stands up.

"I get that a lot. Helps me throw a baseball good and hard," he winks.

"You play for GSU?"

He nods. "Pitcher. And the weather's good up here, thanks for asking. See you tonight."

My stomach bubbles with anxiety as Grant walks away. Damn, he is one attractive, tall drink of water. Wide shoulders, lanky arms, big hands. No wonder he's a baseball pitcher.

I say goodbye to Grant and then head downstairs.

Just then, I get a text from DJ.

DJ: Hey, what are you up to tonight? Want to go over something roommate related.

I SIGH. Like how you're telling the whole campus about me? Yeah, I'm not ready for that conversation right now. Besides, I have a date with Grant tonight.

ALEX: Sorry. Busy tonight.
    DJ: With what?

16

DJ

We're taking a five a.m. bus to our football game tomorrow, so we get out early from practice on Friday afternoon to compensate.

After practice, I check my phone. I'm blowing up with texts and direct messages from a variety of ladies who somehow got my number. I don't even read them, I'm so uninterested.

Unfortunately, the one I want to text me back, Alex, still hasn't gotten back to me when I asked her what she was up to tonight.

In street clothes now, I knock on my dad's office door which is adjacent to the football locker room.

"Hey, Dad? I wanted to talk about some stuff."

"What's the sign on the door say?" His voice is steel.

"Greene State Football." I have a seat in the chair in front of his desk.

"What else?"

"Coach Sal Dalton's Office."

"Right. So on the field, I'm Coach Sal to you. Especially when you can't be on time for practice."

I blow out a loud breath. "Jesus," I mutter.

He furrows his brow. "Is that back talk, boy?"

I shut the door. "I was *one* minute late. And no one can hear us in here."

"It's a matter of principle. And habit."

"I've been early every day since. I had a record day in the weight room yesterday."

"Did you come in here to brag?"

I clench and unclench my fists. "No."

"Well, did you come in here to beg for your starting spot back? Because it's not happening."

I grit my teeth. "I came *in here* to ask why you haven't been talking to Mom or Felicity since they visited campus."

"Dennis, there are some things you'll only understand when you're older. Right now, your mom and I are having some issues. I make no secret of that."

"What about Felicity?"

For once, I actually see his face twitch. "I...I'll call her."

I stand up. "You know, when I was little and she and I would have silly fights, Mom would say, 'now, DJ, you only get *one* sister. So you damn well better treat her right.' Maybe you should heed that advice, too."

I put my hand on the doorknob. "See ya, Coach Sal."

When I get outside, I feel unbalanced, so I decide it's time for one of my solo thinking trips.

I take advantage of today's early release from practice, grab my car, and head out just before sunset to look for some solid spots to take photos. The leaves in central Illinois are just starting to change colors, and the rolling hills of trees across the landscape are beautiful.

I drive with just a light jacket, my camera, and a tripod.

Photography has always been my passion, and now that I've got the first week's assignments from my photography class, I want to jump right on it.

This week's assignment is super broad: Photograph the most beautiful thing you can find. I'm happy to have something to take my mind off the stresses of the week. My roommate seems to hate me now, for some reason I can't figure out, my father is distant as all hell, and I lost my starting spot on the football team. Even my sister is acting strange when I text her. Besides the first day of classes when I called her, she's been giving me one word answers and not returning my calls when I try to reach out.

So yes, beauty is a welcome topic for my mind.

Where do you find the most beauty? It's a valid question. One that men and women over the ages have wondered. Whoa, I'm going deep here. But really, there is beauty everywhere, I think. There is beauty in sadness and melancholy, just like the Elliot Moss album I've been listening to on repeat this week. How have I not discovered him before?

Once I make it safely to Bald Bluff overlooking the Mississippi River, I take my wireless headphones out of my pack, turn on the album, and just sit, looking out over the river. Something about the water puts me at ease. It's not trying to fool you, not trying to be something it's not. The river just flows in the direction God intended, the way gravity dictates. When you try to thwart the laws of nature, that's when you get into trouble.

Thwart the laws of nature.

That phrase makes my heart flutter because I've been avoiding Alex all week. I crashed on Grant and Finn's couch two nights just because I knew she was there. Whatever. She hates me anyway. But honestly—the two nights I "slept" with her in our room, I wasn't doing much sleeping. How was I supposed to, hearing her gentle breathing five feet from me?

Now *that's* beauty. Alex's soft breaths. The silence in between her inhales that takes just a little too long, so much so that I wonder if she's okay. But she always is.

I push the thoughts of Alex down and remember that I didn't drive all the way out here just to think about her; I could have thought about her any place. But now the Mississippi River makes me think of Alex and I huff a silent curse, wondering now if I'll always associate the Mighty Mississippi with the unattainable.

Instead, I reset the Elliot Moss Album to my favorite song "Boomerang." The next three songs after that are bomb and play incredibly well one after the other. I close my eyes and remember how things went the last time I let myself fall head over heels for a girl in my sophomore year of high school. Jessica stomped on my heart so bad, I don't like to let myself think about it. But like my high school counselor said, if you don't think about it, you can't get over it. Don't repress it.

I look around before I pull out a joint I packed, then walk a little over the side to an area where no one can see or smell me, light it, and take a few puffs. It's a small one and it gives me a nice little buzz. I don't like to get stoned out of my mind or anything, but I don't think there's much wrong with a few puffs now and then. Especially since it's legal now in Illinois.

I take a few pictures with my phone camera, mostly of the sun setting over the Mississippi River, and see how they come out. They look beautiful, but the photos never do the real thing justice. I snap a few more using the old-fashioned film camera around my neck.

Down on a rocky ledge on a level below me, I spot a

couple making out in between catching glimpses of the sunset. As it lowers, its glow spins orange, red and even violet. I want to snap pictures of the couple because they'd make great silhouette figures. I haven't seen them before, but I wouldn't be surprised if they were juniors and seniors at Greene State. They can't decide if they want to kiss each other or watch the sunset, so they take turns doing both.

They take no pictures of themselves, and I wonder if they are some of those anti-Instagram people because the sunset is damn beautiful.

I take another puff of my joint so it's about done and put it in my pocket. I never understood those people who call themselves environmentalists but then toss their cigarette butts outside. So I've got to walk the walk.

As the sun becomes a half-sphere over the horizon, I snap a few pictures and know I definitely picked a lucky day to come out here to do this. I don't know if it's the most beautiful thing I've seen all week, but it's up there at the top.

When the orb disappears, the couple down below packs up and I'm disappointed in them now. Don't they know that the afterglow is the best part?

My grandfather used to chuckle at the people packing up their bags so quickly after the sun goes down. Racing to get home; for what, exactly? To sit at home and watch their TVs?

The couple acknowledges me with curt nods as they walk past me to their car. No doubt they're surprised to see me and wondering if I was here watching them the whole time.

"Afterglow," I say, pointing westward.

"Yeah, looks nice," the girl says while her boyfriend stares at her. She's a gorgeous redhead, and I wonder if their motivation to get home so soon doesn't have to do with that.

Their car rumbles to a start, and I take a picture with their crappy 2004 Blue Saturn Ion in the corner, rumbling away from the beautiful sunset. I wonder how their little romance will turn out.

~

When I get back to the room, Alex is flopped on her bed with earphones, watching some movie on her laptop. Her eyes flit quickly to me as I enter, and then she goes back to whatever she's watching.

I try desperately not to stare at her, but my eyes want to flow over her as sure as the Mississippi River wants to flow south.

I came on so strong with her the first week that I earned a *talking to* from her. So it's time to tone it down, live and let live and all that. And the more I think about it, the more I realize a hook up with my roommate truly will make things more complicated than both of us need things to be during this first term.

I pass by her to set my things on my desk, which is nearest the window. Peeling my eyeballs away from her is almost impossible, and when I turn around in my chair to unzip my backpack and take out my headphones, I pause and watch her again.

My heart races just looking at her. It's the soft flesh of her upper thighs. The way her butt carves out space for her shorts. And that *carelessness,* that *frivolousness* she has while she lies there. She's absolutely unaware of what she's doing.

Right?

A part of me wants to get my camera out and snap a candid picture of her for me, *this* is the most beautiful thing I've seen all week.

But I've got more brains than to start snapping photos without her permission.

And anyhow, I'm not sure my professor would understand the beauty in her simplicity.

Hell, I don't even understand why she drives me as nuts as she does. There's essentially a two-to-one girl-to-guy ratio on this campus, so it's not as if I don't have other options when it comes to women. I have many other options, in fact. And these are *less complicated* options than my damn roommate.

"Hey," she says, unsmiling, pulling out an earbud.

"Hey," I say back softly, focusing on actually pulling my camera and headphones out of my backpack. For a moment I wonder if she's going to call me out for staring at her.

"Where have you been tonight?" She pulls her body up and twists her legs around so she's facing me.

I shrug, relief pouring through me that she didn't call me out. "Just went for a drive. Tried to get some pictures for photography class."

Her eyes shift. "I didn't know you were into photography."

"It's always been a side interest of mine."

"Can I see the pictures you took?"

"I would show you, but they're on old-fashioned film. Our professor is working with us on darkroom techniques, so we've a better understanding of the process when we work with digital—the same philosophy on developing photos still applies. I can show you a few shots of the water I took with my phone, though."

Her face lights up. "The water? Which water?"

Getting up, she comes over next to me and we both sit with our legs dangling off the bed. She leans her shoulder against my shoulder so I can show her the pictures on my phone.

How pathetic am I? That little lean, just that touch of warmth she gives me sends a bolt of electricity straight to my cock. I take a deep breath and play it cool.

"The Mississippi River. I know you said you're from San Francisco. How much time have you spent in the Midwest?" I ask as I pull up a couple of photos of the river with the sun setting over it.

Her mouth widens to an O. "Jesus. I've heard about it, but I didn't realize it was so damn big!"

I press my lips together, holding back a snicker.

Alex presses her hand against my chest. "Don't you dare say 'that's what she said.'"

I show her another pic of the river, and I can't resist.

"I mean, if you think that's big, just wait until you see it in person."

Her eyes roll at my double entendre.

"What? I'm serious! The pictures do *not* do the Mississippi River justice."

I run through all of the pictures, including the ones of the couple kissing as the golden rays of the sun sets.

Her sigh does something to me. "I do miss the water. That was probably my favorite thing about living on the coast."

When she pulls her body away from mine, since we're done looking at the pictures, I miss her warmth.

"I'd love to take you down there some time and show you around. It's not too far from here."

Alex stands up and gets off of my bed. To say she frowns would be an exaggeration. "I don't think that'd be a good idea."

"Why not?"

She shakes her head and puts her laptop away. "Just wouldn't."

I sit on my bed and ease my back against the wall. "What about you? How's your week been, anyway? I basically haven't seen you."

She shifts her body, sitting up and stretching. "Haven't seen much of you either."

"I have practice every afternoon. It's been nice weather to get those workouts in. You?"

"Just tons of studying. I've been holed up in the library most nights trying to stay ahead of my reading. I like having just three classes, but it sucks having to read one-hundred pages of a dense text in a week."

"Yeah, you've got that two-hundred level psychology class, right? What's it called?"

"Theories of Personality with Professor Ziemson. It's a wonderful class."

"I thought you had to take Intro to Psychology first, in order to get in that class?"

"I took Psychology AP in high school."

Her phone buzzes and she checks it.

"Going out tonight?" I ask.

"Maybe. I might go out with this guy...Grant. You know him? He plays baseball. Pitcher."

"Uh, yeah. I do actually." I swallow, jealousy riding up my throat.

She glares at me. "Super nice guy. Very down to Earth." The way she voices the words, they sound like an accusation.

"What's that supposed to mean?"

She walks over to her dresser and pulls out a couple of items of clothing.

"Take it as you want. *He* doesn't call me temptress. He's just, you know, nice."

"I was joking."

Her eyes zoom in on me like lasers.

"A little," I continue, knowing now she's not one to be toyed with.

"No you weren't," she smirks, then starts to take off her tank top and stops, doing a little rolling motion with her finger. "Eyes, please. Close them."

Inhaling a deep breath, I close my eyes. "You know this is a very progressive school. The bathrooms are even all unisex. I don't get what the big deal is. But I'll still close my eyes if it makes you more comfortable."

I hear soft breaths and her delicate motions as she squeezes out of her shorts and tank top. And what about bra? Is that a *snap* I hear?

Holy shit. Is she taking off her panties right now?

Is she going panty-less to a date with *Grant?*

I like that guy, but we're going to have to have a talk about bro code. He *knows* Alex is my roommate and that I like her.

"Okay, you can open your eyes now."

She wears a short skirt and a halter top that shows a healthy amount of midriff. I swallow. She looks terrific, and I can quite clearly make out the single nipple ring. She's traffic-stopping gorgeous.

"How do I look?" she asks, and does a twirl for me.

My gut clenches at the thought of her going out with some other guy. Plus, Grant is cool as hell. I can't even deny that. I like him...except for this little maneuver he's pulling. He should have at least *asked* me if he was going to ask her out. On the other hand, it's not like I staked a claim to her or something. None of the guys even know about the kiss.

Well, except for Jeff—who is coming to his own ridiculous conclusions about the two of us no matter what I say.

I keep my expression stoic. "You don't look half bad," I say, ignoring the butterflies rumbling through my body.

And then a little smirk crosses my face. Because even if we never have anything again—Alex and I will always have that kiss. That drunken, passionate, sloppy, hot kiss.

"What are you smiling about?" she asks.

"Nothing. Have fun on your date. Where are you guys going?"

"We're grabbing a drink at Mac's."

"Do you have an ID?"

"No."

"So how are you going to drink?"

She shrugs. "I mean, I don't really care if I do or not, I'll just have a Coke. Honestly it's more just to hang with Grant."

Another tug at my stomach. "Have fun."

She walks out looking hot as fuck, and I clench my fists, wanting to have a little talk about boundaries with my good friend Grant.

17

DJ

After Alex leaves, I head to the co-ed dorms in the quad where I meet up with my friend Finn. When I open the door to his room, he's got his electric guitar out and he's playing quietly and singing.

"Yo, dude, what's up? Where do I recognize that song from?"

"You probably don't. It's from a 2000 one-hit-wonder band."

"Try me. Play it again."

He plays it, and I smirk a little at the lyrics. And the subject matter of the song.

The song is called "I'm Going to Steal your Girlfriend" and it's by this band I am indeed familiar with called Lucky Boys Confusion, a local band from Chicago.

"Someone going out with your girl or something?" I ask, somewhat jokingly.

"Kind of. I mean, she's not *my* girl. Yet. But I will make her mine. Soon enough. We all know doing long-distance relationships with a guy from back home will be a disaster soon enough."

I nod. "Yeah. And I can relate. Grant sniped in on my girl, too."

"You wanted to get with Alex?" he says. "I thought you said you didn't want her?"

"I *said* she was my roommate and she was hot," I say.

"Yes, but you didn't say you wanted her," he points out. "If you do like her, you better tell Grant. He's a big fan of Alex."

Just then, there's a knock at the door, and April and Maya appear in the door with a paper bag.

"Hey, Finny!" Maya says.

Nicely done, Finn.

"Maya runs track with me, and April is her roommate," Finn informs me.

"Hey Maya! Hello, April."

"April has a boyfriend back home," Maya says. "I see the way you're looking at her. No, DJ."

"Uh, I was just saying hello."

April and I exchange a confused look. "Sorry," she says. "My roommate's a little bit protective."

The girls unpack their paper bag, which includes vodka, orange juice, and cups.

"Damn. You came to party tonight," Finn says.

"So, would everyone like a vodka with orange juice?" April asks. "We should start this Friday night off the right way."

I sigh, thinking of the five a.m. bus ride I've got to take tomorrow. But I'm not starting, so I suppose it doesn't matter.

Finn goes to turn the guitar off, but Maya pokes him. "Play a song for us."

Finn shakes his head. "Nah. You don't wanna hear me."

"I do," April says. "We could hear you singing a song

from outside the window when we were walking here. Which song was that?"

Finn has a soft spot for shy girls, obviously, which is actually sweet coming from one of the most boisterous guys on campus.

"You want to hear the one I was just singing?"

April and Maya both nod enthusiastically, and Maya hands out a round of drinks.

Finn shrugs, then plays "I'm Going to Steal Your Girlfriend." Again.

Well, for me, that is, and it sounds just as good the second time.

He looks at April while he sings, and she is blushing like mad.

As soon as he's done, she takes a big swig of her drink, and says, "Hey, I'll be right back. My boyfriend just called and I need to get back to him."

She leaves, and Maya sighs. "I feel sorry for them."

"You mean for April , because she has a shitty boyfriend?" I ask.

Maya nods. "Yes. And because that boy is still a virgin. Poor guy."

April comes back in a few moments later. "Sorry! Matt is a bit of a psychopath sometimes."

We all stare at her.

"Like, in a cute way, you know?" she adds.

We all take an awkward, long sip of our drink.

We chat and drink in the room, and it's a lot of fun. I like April and Maya, too, but something's missing and I know what it is: Alex.

I've taken a liking to having her around. I like her presence and her awkwardness and I like her perfume, too. It's vanilla and fresh scented.

My gut clenches thinking about Alex on a date with Grant.

At the same time, I realize that Finn is right. I need to take a chill pill and realize it's not like I've got a claim staked on her or anything like that. This is the first couple weeks of college, and it's like the Wild West of dating.

After we finish our drinks, Maya suggests a shot of whisky and we all take one. The smell of the drinks bring me back to the night when Alex and I had our kiss.

It seems almost surreal now that I tasted her lips on mine, I think about the way her soft body felt pressed up against me, and how much more of her I wanted.

Needed.

She needed me, too. I could feel it on her lips. But she's restraining herself for a reason I can't figure out.

Now she's on a date with fucking Grant.

"Hey," I say. "I've got an idea. You guys want to go hit the bars?"

"Why not?" Maya says, and unbeknownst to them, I lead us directly on a secret mission to the bar where Grant and Alex are.

18

ALEX

I meet Grant in the quad, and we stroll over to Mac's Bar, a hole-in-the-wall place on Cherry Street just off campus with good enough food and, most importantly, drinks.

Grant pulls my seat out like a gentleman and orders us each a gin and tonic. They don't ask for our IDs and I wonder if it's because they don't want to learn that we *are* underage, or because Grant looks like he could be thirty.

Either way, I sit across from him at the bar table and we chat about the psychology department, about Professor Z, and getting settled into classes. Grant informs me that there is indeed a female version of Professor Z, a Spanish professor named Professor Flores. The conversation flows.

So it makes no sense that after two drinks with him, my annoying roommate and his friend keeps popping into my head.

Okay, it makes some sense. Grant might be hot, but I don't know that DJ wouldn't beat him in a hottest male contest.

DJ stretching in front of the window and turning around.

DJ violating the no-shirt rule.

DJ, and I pause, because I have to remind myself that he's the DJ of gossip, as well, and that helps me to take my mind off of him.

For about a minute.

I need a moment to compose myself because my mind has gone down a rabbit hole that I'm not sure I can pull myself out of.

I excuse myself to go to the bathroom, thankfully it's a single-use restroom, so I can give myself a pep talk. I splash a little bit of water on my face and look at myself in the mirror.

"Alex, get a hold of yourself. DJ equals liar. Grant equals tall, smart, nice guy who pulls out your chair. DJ equals hot, sexy guy you have gotten very turned on by when you kissed him. Grant equals baseball player with a brain. DJ equals..."

I'm about to go on when there's a banging on the door.

"You done yet?"

Chills roll through me when I recognize the low voice. *Are you fucking kidding me?*

Gathering my composure, I take a deep breath, and then unlock the door. "What are you doing in th..."

DJ's eyes stop when they connect with mine. "Oh. It's you."

"Impatient much?"

There is actually a tinge of guilt on his face. "I was very patient. I waited for a full two minutes before I banged on the door."

He stands, somewhat menacingly with his arm pressing into the door frame.

"Were you...talking to yourself in here?"

"Psst. No."

"What did I hear in the bathroom then?"

"Nothing.

To get past him, I'll have to go under his arm, but I don't want to drop to that level.

"So...are you going to let me pass?"

"How's your date going?" he asks, ignoring my question.

"Great." I furrow my brow. "Wait, what are *you* doing here?"

He shrugs. "Me and the gang decided to hit the bars tonight."

I look past him and see Finn, Maya, and April, who are of course talking to Grant.

I put my hands on my hips, not quite fuming, but let's just say I'm not *not* angry. "What the hell? I see you every night in the room and now I see you out at the bars, too? Are you stalking me, or something?"

He smiles. "My bad. Thought you said you were going to Big Brew."

"Bullshit. You knew I was coming here. Why are you creepily stalking me? Don't you get enough of me when I'm in the room?"

"Oh, Alex," he grins. "I could never get enough of you."

I'm flooded with warmth, yet I have an urge to slap him. But when I think about that, I think about touching him and that *turns me on*. How ludicrous.

I inhale his musk, and it's a cologne and whisky mixture and so very *male*.

I fight the desire to erase all distance between us and kiss him again, just like I did when he was drunk the first night.

I remind myself *that'll never happen again.*

"You're a dick," I say instead. "Now, will you please get

out of my way so I may join my date?"

"Of course," he says, stepping aside.

I get back to the table and say hi to everyone, and Grant shoots me a look that says *yep, I guess this date between just the two of us is over* and shrugs. I definitely wanted some more alone time with him to see how things would go. But at the same time, I'm somewhat relieved, because deep in my bones, I can't get rid of this attraction to DJ.

Plus, the way Grant looks at Maya makes me wonder if there's something beyond friendship going on with the two of them.

DJ comes back just then asking, "What'd I miss?"

I shrug. "Oh, you know. Just my date being over."

"Aw, man. I'm really sorry about that," DJ says. "My bad."

I shake my head at him and punch him playfully. "You're not sorry."

He grips my hand when it lands against his chest. "You better not touch me, Alex. You're going to make me think maybe you *don't* hate me for some random reason."

I lean in and whisper. "You *know* why I hate you. Liar."

He gives me a confused look. "No, I don't, actually. Why don't you enlighten me."

I purse my lips together. Wow, is he that bold so as to play dumb with me?

"Nah," I say. "You can figure it out for yourself."

Dick.

And it hits me, he's still trying to play me like he hasn't spread a rumor all over campus that we're hooking up?

I feel like I've just let rumor-spreading go by the wayside. I still need to come up with some sort of revenge game plan. I can't just let this thing go like it's no big deal. Especially when DJ is straight up denying it's ever happened.

19

ALEX

The next week, I spend most of my time at the library and we blessedly manage to keep things civil. But every time I'm in the room with DJ, I feel this tension rising. Or maybe it's my body heat. But he's respectful, and stops being as ridiculous as he was the first few days. Every time I miss him calling me by my special nickname, all I have to do is remind myself that I'm likely dealing with a sociopathic liar here who will gossip about me and my teddy bear, my tits, and make up lies behind my back. And I feel fine reveling in that I'm much better off not paying attention to him.

I was a little worried that he might be one of the types who goes out every single night, but during class time he's actually quite disciplined.

The next couple of weeks of classes roll by without much incident. DJ has pretty much relented his romantic assault on me.

Nevertheless, there are times when we can't avoid seeing each other in our underwear, but he keeps his head turned away. Yes, I steal a couple of glances—but I feel like if there's already campus gossip out there about us fucking, I deserve to know what I *would* be working with. But we both become experts at not showing each other full nudity.

By the first Friday in October, the leaves are just starting to get that gorgeous early fall yellow-red hue. It's a beautifully warm night, and I'm ready to go out and enjoy the night with April and Maya. I put on my loud blue and green floral wrap dress, being sure to get ready early enough that DJ won't run into me. He usually gets back from his afternoon workout and dinner past seven on Friday, so that's not too hard.

I head out to the patio outside the Gizmo, our late-night food place on campus.

Everyone has been saying to enjoy any warm weather because it won't stay this nice all year in Galesburg. So that's just what April, Maya, and I are intending on doing tonight. We're dressing up and going bar hopping. I've got a fake ID and so do they.

Fun fact about me: I know it makes me sound like I'm twelve years old, but I enjoy lollipops. So I pull my favorite flavor out of my purse and enjoy it while I'm waiting for April and Maya to come meet me on the way to the bars.

There are dozens of people out on the patio tonight eating dinner and there's a great buzz in the air. I suck on my lollipop, lean back in my chair, and enjoy the warm, early evening sun on my skin.

A few minutes later, I hear April's voice.

"Dear God, what are you doing?" She sounds genuinely concerned.

I spin my head to the side. "Oh, hey. Just waiting on you guys. What does it look like I'm doing?"

"You look like you're broadcasting your blowjob skills to

the entire damn campus," Maya grins. "Are you trying to steal my thunder or something?"

I squint, and the lollipop makes a *pop* sound as I pull it out of my mouth.

"No idea what you're talking about."

April shakes her head, backs up, and takes a picture of me, then shows me.

"This is what you look like right now. Hot as hell in the bright sun in that sexy dress, tonguing a lollipop."

"I like to enjoy the flavor, though. I'm not a biter."

"I'll believe that when I see it," Maya laughs. April folds her arms, letting me look closer at the photo.

"Okay, I see what you're saying. But I just like lollipops. Is there something so wrong about that?"

April nods her head toward a table of guys who are seated in front of me. As soon as I look their way, they twist their faces back toward each other.

Maya nods. "Yeah, girl. They were staring at you." She puts a hand on my shoulder. "Don't act like it's a bad thing. You just look very sexy. I'm not even usually into girls, and *I'm* getting a little aroused staring at you."

"Usually?"

She sighs. "Yeah, you know. If the night is right, I morph into someone who's a little more sexually fluid. I've got a little sapiosexual in me, which means I sometimes get aroused from intelligence alone."

"So you weren't joking about cuddling with me?"

She smiles. "There's nothing wrong with a little platonic cuddling. Humans need to touch each other. It's important."

April sighs. "Just make sure you don't do that in front of DJ."

"What does that mean?"

"I mean, that he's going to think you're trying to turn

him on and flirt with him if you're flirting with another girl in front of him! Plus, Maya's right. I've never kissed a girl, but we could see you from far away...sucking on that thing. If you do that in front of DJ when you two are alone, it's going to drive him absolutely bonkers."

"Hm. Bonkers you say?"

"Oh, yeah. I mean, the fact that you won't let him have you will drive him up a wall," Maya adds. "I don't care if he's a liar or tells people your secrets. I would just take advantage of a good thing while you've got it. A little friends with benefits action never hurt anyone."

April shakes her head. "That's a silly idea. He blabbed to the campus about her stuffed animal, he'll blab all the details of your sexual exploits. You can't trust him, period. Don't do it, Al," she advises. "Plus, you're rooming with him. Once you cross that line, I mean, just no! This has disaster written all over it. And remember when we got tattoos, you said you were going to get back at him. You haven't really done that. But it's been a month. Maybe you're going to let it go? Personally, I don't forget that kind of thing."

When I stand up, I notice another table of guys checking us out. I wave, and they spin back around and pretend like nothing happened.

"So what are you going to do?" Maya asks.

I shrug. I've got the devil on one shoulder and an angel on the other. "I'm finally going to give him the *Maya* tease treatment."

"Yes!" Maya exclaims.

"Oh my. Here we go," April chimes in. "I've got a bad feeling about this."

20

DJ

"She's the hottest girl in the school. No question," Finn comments as we chill, lazing on the grass of the quad on this sunny Sunday afternoon. We've got books out to study, but we're basically just enjoying relaxing. Grant runs cross country in the fall, and Chris is in soccer, so Sundays are the only free afternoon in the fall term for them to rest without guilt.

And it doesn't feel like we've only known each other barely a month or so. On the contrary, we already have the dynamic of old friends. Finn's the over-the-top, inappropriate one who has no filter. Nelson is the one whom we're never sure if he's high, the next Elon Musk-level genius, or both. Chris is the overly thoughtful jock. Grant is the wild one who probably was a shaman in another life. And then there's me, the supposedly NFL-ordained football star who isn't getting any playing time from his own father.

"Maybe she is to you, but let's not forget that beauty is a subjective quality," Nelson adds.

We all turn our heads toward him with curiosity. Nelson has a photographic memory, and always seems to be on a totally different level of thought then the three of us. It's fun to hang around someone with such a different mind.

"Maybe beauty is sometimes subjective," Grant says, "But I know energies and she's a magnet."

"You know energies?" Chris challenges. "What does that even mean?"

"I told you, they're real. When we put negative thought vibrations into the world—"

"We attract negative thought vibrations," I say, finishing his sentence.

Like I said, we're basically old friends from another life. I chuckle, picturing us chatting at the retirement home some day, having the exact same debate about who the most attractive woman in the home is.

"I've seen those three girls hanging out a lot together," Finn says. "Maya Pop Rocks the hot blonde, Alex the tattooed hottie, and April the..."

"Quiet one," Nelson says. "I have dance class with her. Jesus, is she a good dancer."

"Fellas," I say. "You know what we need?"

"I need to head back and rub one out," Finn surmises.

"No, dude! I told you no porn. It's bad energy," Grant chides.

"Bad *energy*? What the fuck does that even mean? Plus, where the fuck else can I get my rocks off? I've got a lot of pent-up energy and it's starting to get to me. Come on, fellas, back me up?" Finn looks to me and Nelson for support.

"Can't help you," I say. "I can't whack it in my room. What if Alex comes in? God help me."

"Yeah, God help you because she might just get turned on," Chris snickers.

Grant rolls his eyes, propping himself up on his elbows. "My dudes, this is the problem with porn. That shit does not, I repeat *not*, happen like that in real life. I hate to break it to you guys, but your hot stepmom is frankly not going to find you on the couch and blow you for no reason."

After we stop ourselves from laughing, Grant adds, "You laugh but it's true. You've thought about it. You've wished it might happen. I'm sorry your parents never told you about the hard-earned facts of life."

"Well, there's no chance in hell of me and Alex hooking up," I clarify. "So I'd rather just avoid the situation entirely. I agree, Finn. She's stupidly attractive. When she's in the room and I try to study? No chance."

"But you know her class schedule, don't you? You could totally pull it off," Finn says.

"Pull what off?"

He winks. "You know, procrasturbate when you're trying not to study."

I shake my head. "I just don't know...a class could get cancelled, she could walk in. Never."

Grant squints at Finn. "Bro, are you jerking it when I'm in calculus? That's gross."

Finn throws his hands up. "Just because you've decided to repress your sexuality doesn't mean I've got to follow in your footsteps. If I want to make believe that I'm getting with Professor Rachel Flores, then so be it."

"Ah, Professor Flores," Nelson says whimsically.

We all sort of stare off into the clouds in fantasy. Professor Flores is the twenty-eight-year-old, very attractive professor of English Literature. Judging by his expression, even Grant the realist seems to wish this fantasy could come true.

Finn clears his throat and pokes me. "Seriously, dude. I saw Alex checking you out in the café the other day. I think she likes you."

"Not a cold chance in hell. She told me off the other day. And she's not really my type."

"Bullshit," Nelson says. "You said you're super attracted to smart girls."

"That's true, but—"

"I've got her in Preceptorial," Chris adds. "She's one of the few people in that class who actually reads the material and makes original comments. Don't get me started on Jessica Pearson who's the Teaching Assistant. I thought you had to be smart to be an assistant."

"Oh, fuck me, I've got her in calc and she asked me to tutor her. She has no idea what is going on in class. God Almighty is she hot, though," Grant says.

My gut clenches up. "Guys, you know what Jessica did to me, right?"

They all shake their head, so I tell them about our twisted history.

"That's good you're staying away from her and not answering her texts. She's bad energy." Grant looks around at all of us. "I'm serious about the porn slash masturbation shit being dark energy. And I'll bet you weak fucks couldn't go a week without choking your chickens."

"So what are you saying?" I ask.

"One week. No whacking it. Think you all can pull it off?"

"Ha," Chris laughs. "No whack week. I like a challenge. I'm in."

"Pinky swear this shit," Grant says, putting his hand out, and then looks at all of us. "I'm fucking serious."

We all put our hands into the middle and outstretch that awkward last finger. "And no fucking lying," I add. "I trust you boys. This is the honor fucking system."

"Honor code," Finn adds gruffly. "Update in the WhatsApp Chat group when you go down."

"What's the prize?" Chris asks.

We all look at each other.

"Twenty bucks," I say. "We all throw twenty bucks in and someone takes the pot."

"Someone will crack," Nelson says, his voice full of certainty. "Someone will definitely crack. I wouldn't be surprised if it's you, DJ."

IT'S A JUVENILE CONTEST, sure. But as I walk back to my room and bid Chris and Nelson, who are roommates right next to my room, adieu, I feel full of resolve. Of all of the people in the contest, I have the best motivation to follow through.

I absolutely can't do anything in my room, for starters. Just the thought of Alex walking in and catching me has me absolutely mortified. Maybe if we still had the same sexual vibe we had the first few days, I would think differently. But for the last two weeks or so, it's like she's put up a wall between us. She gives me one-word answers to my questions and spends as much time as possible out in the co-ed dorms with her friends, April and Maya.

So when I open the door on Sunday evening after dinner, it's quite the sight. Alex is in her yoga clothes, has her mat out in the middle of the room, and there are scented candles lit. The lights are off and the room is darkly lit. She's got earbuds in and her eyes are closed. She keeps them closed, staying concentrated as I quietly open the door.

She moves into downward dog, and blows out a deep, loud exhale, that sounds way too much like a moan.

"Mmmmmm," she breathes as she swings her ass unknowingly toward me as I stand just inside the door. She doesn't even hear me close it.

I stare, wide-eyed. A minute or two passes, and I just watch her while she goes through her practice. I feel bad because once I pass by her, I'll surely interrupt her.

Okay, and yeah, I like watching her.

It's incredibly arousing.

But my stomach coils and my cock twitches and I realize I'm having urges I shouldn't have. *Again.*

Finally, I walk past her to my desk and plop my backpack down. She opens her eyes slowly, seeming incredibly relaxed. She pulls her earbuds off.

"Oh, hey," she says with an air of nonchalance. "You're back."

"I don't mean to interrupt your session," I say. "I can go read in the lobby or something."

"No, it's okay," she says softly. "Actually, I think I could use your help."

She's in warrior two position now, with her arms outstretched.

Yes, I know yoga positions. My high school coach had us practice yoga for injury prevention.

"Oh?"

"Yeah. I've been having some trouble with a couple of positions. Can you give me a hand?"

Her black hair is tied up in a ponytail behind her head as she moves into downward dog again.

"Uh, sure. What do you need?"

"Come over here and stand beside me."

"Okay."

I walk over to her. Damn, her scent is arousing. I even enjoy the smell of just the slightest bit of sweat she emits.

"Good. Now, can you just press into the small of my back a little? I need some pressure there. It keeps poking out. My posture is getting bad. Too much sitting at the library, you know? All this studying."

"Course I can do that."

I press into small of her back and she pushes her body into my hand.

"Harder," she whispers. "And a little lower, right on my spine there. Oh yeah, that's the spot. I love it."

I swallow and press harder. My dick twitches again, and I want to pinch myself to see if this is really happening.

"I can always go harder if you want," I whisper in her ear.

"Mmmmm," she says. "No, that's good. That's perfect."

"So you don't like it extra hard?"

"Um, what?"

Fuck. Abort stupid, non-funny pun.

I backtrack. "I mean, it's good not to overstretch. Better to be conservative and just do a little bit every day."

She wiggles out of the posture and I let her go.

"Oh boy, I feel so much better after that. Luckily you caught me toward the end of my session."

Thank the good Lord.

"Oh, you don't say."

"Yep," she smiles, and proceeds to turn around and take off her top. I sit back on my desk and I don't look...because I am a gentleman.

"Hey, can you blow that candle out on your desk and hand it to me?" she asks.

Without thinking, I grab the candle, blow it out and walk it over to her. And then I realize she's just in her sports bra.

She watches my eyes as I hand her the candle. It's like

she's testing whether I can keep my eyes fixed on her. I decide to call her out.

"So we're back to instigating the shirts optional rule in the room?"

"Oh, I didn't know you were abiding by that rule to start with," she answers innocently. "Since you always sleep without a shirt."

"Didn't think you noticed."

"Oh, please. Don't act like I'm checking you out. It's impossible not to notice each other in this room."

She takes the candle but doesn't blow out the other one on her desk. The only other light in the room is the soft glow of the campus lights from the patio flowing through our blinds.

We stand inches from each other and I flash back to that beautiful night we shared together weeks ago. I can't help but smirk as I look her right in the gorgeous dark brown eyes. In my peripheral vision I can see her soft red lips. I wonder if she's still wearing the same cherry Chapstick.

"It is indeed impossible to notice each other here. Unless we avoid each other."

She squints. "What are you trying to say?"

"I'm saying in the past two weeks, I feel like you've been a ghost. Whenever I get back, you seem to run right out."

"Same for you. I'm always here in the afternoons and you're never here."

"That's because, unlike you, I work out in the *gym*. Not this room."

"There's no yoga class on Sunday nights! Can you believe that?"

I cross my arms. "Yes. I can. Greene State is a smallish school. And there *is* a class before dinner. Just not *after* dinner."

"I need to do yoga Sunday nights. It sets me up for a good week, mentally."

"Have you been having mental problems the last few weeks?"

She rolls her eyes and goes to grab a bathrobe.

"You're such an asshole, you know that?"

"I'm not being an asshole. I'm being serious. I've had mental problems before. I don't laugh about this stuff."

She's about to run out of the room to go shower, but she turns. "I can't tell if you're being serious right now."

"I am being quite serious," I say.

She takes a deep breath. "I wish I could believe you," she says, and she squints. "Can you toss me that bra on my bed. Hands are full."

Seriously? Okay, she's definitely fucking with me.

I swallow, then grab her bra, a shade of light purple.

"Your roommate, at your service," I say, putting it over her shoulder. "School colors even with your bra. I dig the spirit."

"Sometimes I do wonder to myself what would happen if you weren't such an asshole. Maybe we might actually..." her gaze trails off with her words. "You know," she says, and then leaves.

"Uh, no, actually, I don't know," I say when she's out of earshot.

I CHECK the texts from our group chat:

FINN: Still in, baby. Had a close call, though
    Chris: Close call? Wtf does that mean?
    Grant: He ran into Professor Flores in the library.

Finn: Seriously, what kind of school is this where you run into professors on SUNDAY NIGHT in the LIBRARY?

Grant: It's a liberal arts school, douchenozzle. The faculty is very engaged with the student body.

Nelson: Aren't you guys roommates? Can't you just insult each other in person? Do you have to do this over text?

Finn: Don't worry we're doing that, too. We're filtering everything for you guys.

DJ: I had a close call, too.

HOLDING the phone in my hand, I hesitate. I have a pang in my gut and it's telling me that maybe me and Alex are roommates and what happens here should stay here. The guys are great friends, but maybe they don't need to know about her eccentric Sunday night yoga and candle thing she's doing tonight. Maybe that something is just between us.

Another text comes in.

FINN: ??? DUDE?

I PAUSE, twisting my face up and wondering if I should tell them. The answer comes across, clear as day.

DJ: Yeah - I saw Professor Flores coming out of the library too, total babe.

YEAH, it's a lie. And the whole point of the contest is the honor system. But I decide that from here on out, what happens with me and Alex is just between us. No more blabbing to Jeff or the guys, even about something tiny like a stuffed animal or yoga on a Sunday night.

I take a deep breath. I am certainly charged up from seeing her little yoga routine, though. Tossing my phone aside, I relight the unlit candle, sit cross-legged on top of Alex's yoga mat, and close my eyes.

I just keep my body still and watch my thoughts come and go for a while, I'm not sure how long. At some point I hear Alex come back inside. She doesn't say anything, but she sits down with her back to me on the yoga mat. Her back is warm pressed up against mine like that.

We don't say a word, just sit like that, propped up against each other for the longest time, until I finally get up and go to bed.

21

ALEX

Professor Z speaks, and the class hangs on his every word. In addition to his terrific content, there's something hypnotic about his voice.

"Conscious mind is reasoning will. Subconscious mind is instinctive desire—the result of past reasoning will. The subconscious mind draws just and accurate inferences from premises furnished from outside sources. Where the premise is true, the subconscious mind reaches a faultless conclusion. But where the premise is in error, the whole structure falls."

I nod, thoughtful, and do my very best to comprehend what Professor Ziemson is saying, but there are a couple of problems.

One, I did the reading on this section in our psych textbooks last night and it was a little out there, even for my tastes.

Two, Professor Nathaniel Ziemson looks way too young to actually understand the things he apparently understands.

Maya leans into my chair in the back of the lecture hall.

"I heard he's dating Professor Flores," she says, frowning.

"Oh? Who says that?"

She shrugs. "Not sure. The walls? It makes sense, though. They're the two hottest professors. Why shouldn't they get together?"

"Oh, I don't know, just because two people are hot doesn't mean they should get together, does it?"

Maya shakes her head disapprovingly at me.

"Look, just because we're into October and you haven't found your ideal 'study partner with benefits' doesn't mean everything is about sex and dating. Maybe Professor Flores and Professor Z don't even know each other."

Maya's eyes twinkle. "So are you saying I might have a shot with Professor Z?"

I sigh, and I want to tell her she's crazy, but what do I know anymore? Clearly Maya likes an intelligent man and I don't blame her. "I mean, at this point, I'd love some study tips myself for the quiz this Friday."

"Quiz? Oh, no. If I was with Professor Z I would be going full out research."

Before I get the chance to ask her what she means by research, Professor Z appears next to us on the stairs.

"Hi, ladies."

"Hi," Maya chokes out.

I flash a smile. "Yes?"

"I see you two are still discussing the in-class writing assignment I just explained. Did you have some questions before you get started writing?"

Whoops.

Maya squints thoughtfully at the chalkboard below. All it says is:

. . .

Conscious Will vs. Subconscious Desire

"Yes, would you sort of rephrase the way you explained the assignment? There were a lot of, ahem, complicated words and I'm not sure I got them all," Maya says.

Professor Z smiles slightly and adjusts his glasses.

"Complicated words, eh?"

Maya nods, and Professor Z leans in, lowering his voice. "Look, Maya. And you, too, Alex. I read what you two turned in last week for the writing assignment. You're both incredibly intelligent young women. Don't give me this 'complicated words so I couldn't understand the assignment' routine. If you were chatting and didn't hear me, just tell me that. I appreciate honesty. Not bullshit."

"Yes, sir," I swallow.

He waves his hand. "You don't have to call me sir. Just handwrite two pages right now about how your conscious will and subconscious desires interact in your daily life. Don't overthink it."

Maya wiggles her eyebrows. "And what if it's my subconscious desire to call you sir?"

His focused grey eyes aren't fazed. Professor Z just taps the piece of blank white paper in front of her. "Write about it. What would Sigmund Freud say? This is just a free writing exercise. I won't be judging your content, just that you truthfully engaged in the exercise."

He walks away, and I notice a couple of girls to our left steal a glimpse of him, too.

Focus, Alex. So I begin to write.

. . .

Lately, I've felt this subconscious urge to be with my roommate. And it's making me afraid to get drunk. Didn't someone once say 'a sober person's thoughts are a drunk person's words, and a sober person's words are a drunk person's actions?' Well, I find that to be true and for this reason I've stopped drinking when I'm around him because I'm worried I'll lose control.

Last night, I thought we were having a 'moment' aka he was genuinely being nice to me, lighting candles while I was doing yoga, and then I remembered how he blabbed to the whole campus about how we had slept together when we weren't sleeping together and I wondered why he would do that?

But the thing is, we're totally different people. He's this blue-eyed, corn-fed Midwest boy with a picture-perfect family and I'm this mutt from San Francisco with a whole lot of baggage. He's not my type, I swear. I like inked guys in bands and he's not that. But this urge to be with him must be coming from somewhere deep down, right?

I look over at Maya and she's staring at Professor Z. I wonder what she's writing down.

"So what did you write about?" Maya asks.

I tell her I wrote about DJ and wondered why I am still attracted to him in spite of the fact that he's an asshole and not good for me.

"Well, that's easy," she says. "You're around him all the time. It's just nature. If you're around a sexy boy, you're going to want to be with him in all the ways you can."

I think about how I felt last night when he put his hands on my back to readjust me and my stomach folds over itself.

"But I can't trust him."

"You're sure?"

"He gossiped about me when it wasn't even true."

"If only there was a way you could test him."

"How?"

I grin. The plan is really devious and it's so not me, but I can't help thinking it would work to find out if DJ has changed.

"So I started 'The Maya Plan' the other night he was definitely curious about my yoga. I could tell he was trying to keep his eyes off me. Maybe If I continue being ridiculous and tempting him, and he's a big mouth, he'll brag about it to his friends that I'm hitting on him."

"Holy shit, that's true."

"Can you keep tabs on Grant and see if DJ says anything to him?"

"Of course." She cocks her head and squints. "Wait. What are you going to do to him exactly?"

I whisper my plan in her ear.

"Oh my gosh. You are devious. You might also be a genius."

22

DJ

"I'm out," Finn says as he rolls up on our table in the cafeteria and drops his tray down. "Out of the contest."

We all crack up. "You're out already?!" I exclaim. "Bro, we started the contest not twenty-four hours ago."

Finn snorts. "Yeah, well, Professor Flores called me into her office after class today, totally unprompted. She said I looked like such a lost young man and she had a great book for me."

"So did she give you...some special advice?" Grant waggles his eyebrows.

Finn sighs. "At one point, she had to get on a ladder in her room to reach a book on her shelf—you know what a book nerd she is, her office is basically filled to the brim with all sorts of books—and she asked me to spot her. *Spot her.* Dude, she was wearing a *skirt*. She practically made me cup her ass. Honestly—what would you do?"

"Man, I think you've got a sexual harassment claim against her. You should start documenting this stuff," Nelson says, and we all die laughing.

"Hey, that is *not* funny," Finn adds. "Do not make light of a serious issue. So yeah, after third period I had to go back and crank one out. I'm being honest, what would you have done?"

"If Professor Flores got on a step-ladder and put her ass in my face?" I say.

"In a skirt, dude! Eye-level!" Finn reiterates, pointing to his eye, then looks around at us. "Wait, did one of you pay her off or something?"

We all laugh again. "No, dude. Honor code, remember?" Grant shakes his head.

"Which book did she give you?" Chris asks.

"Eh, some book called..." he looks in his backpack. "*The Sun Also Rises.*"

"Nice," Nelson comments. "Love that book."

"Really, you like it?" Finn comments. "I tried to read it and it's just about people drinking wine and talking shit. I don't really get it."

"Yeah, it's like, relatable," Chris says, and I crack a smile at that.

"Speaking of great literature." Grant leans in and hands each of us a little pamphlet from his pocket. "Wednesday evening, I'm doing a live reading in the poetry slam at the Gizmo. I want you guys to come. Professor Flores is organizing it."

"Well, I know Finn will come for sure," I joke.

Finn pokes me, shaking his head. "Sorry we're not all Mr. Fucking Perfect over here. All the self-control in the world. And living with Alex 'with the great ass'. I don't know how you do it."

His gaze wanders over to Alex and the rest of our posse's eyes follow.

I suck in a deep breath and think about telling them

how good she looked yesterday when she asked for an 'adjustment' of her yoga form, but I hold off.

"Yes, it's true, she does have a great ass," I agree. They all nod in agreement.

"Fuck. Well, if you're gonna make a move, you better do it soon," Chris says, wiggling his eyebrows. "The seniors have spotted her. They're moving in."

I feel my blood pressure shoot up when I see Herman Blank, senior and captain of the track team, sitting next to Alex and her two best girlfriends while they eat, and blatantly hitting on them. I clench my fists under the table. Herman seems like a phony to me and I can't put my finger on why.

Watching him with Alex certainly gets my blood boiling. I can't deny he's a smooth talker.

I turn away from them, as I see him take out his phone and put a number from one of the girls. I have to look away.

"Plenty of fish in the sea, Deej," Grant says, putting a hand on my shoulder. "Marisa Nagle keeps checking you out. She's gorgeous."

"Marisa who?"

"Don't everyone look at the same time, you idiots. But at the table behind me and to our right—she's been checking you out multiple times, Deej."

"How can you see that? It's behind you."

He knocks a hand on the table. "Life is all about awareness, man. You have to know your surroundings. Besides, she's in my Translation of Poetry class. Smart girl. And cute."

One at a time, we take a surreptitious glance in Marisa's direction.

"Sounds more like your type," Finn says.

"Nah," Grant says. "I couldn't do it with her. She's too nice. I'd corrupt the shit out of her."

"What's wrong with corrupting her?" Finn says. "Someone's got to do it. Might as well be a classy guy like you."

Grant takes a sip of his chocolate milk and shrugs. "It's not even that, man. I've got my eyes peeled for someone else. Anyway, I'm serious, Deej. She's thoughtful. And I know you like the thinkers. I can introduce you to her on Wednesday night."

I steal another glance at Alex. Herman Blank stands up, puts his hand on her arm, and waves goodbye to them, holding his phone in his hand.

"Fuck the Lambdas," I mutter softly.

All four of my friends nod in agreement. The fact that Herman Blank is a Lambda is not lost on them. We went to a party at their house last week and they seemed desperate, and a little creepy. We've decided not to go back there. If we pledge any fraternity when pledge season starts—winter at Greene State—it would be the Alpha Z house. They seem to care less about being cool and more about just having fun.

"You should definitely introduce me to Marisa," I say, looking Grant in the eye. While I finish eating, though, I swear I can feel Alex's eyes on me.

"Good," Grant says. "I know she's your roommate, and I know you like her. But this is freshmen year. We should be exploring. And look at the signals, man. She's flirting with seniors and taking down numbers. Plus, I got into a 'types' discussion with her friend April who confirmed Alex is into bad, tattooed boys. And your nickname with that group of girls? Mr. Perfect. You can't win them all, man."

"Rub it in, why don't you." I nod, solemnly, and clear my throat. My feelings are betraying me, anyway. I should not feel any sense of jealousy from Alex's interactions with men.

I'm not *allowed* to feel that. Isn't that toxic masculinity, anyway?

But that kiss we had. I keep going back to it.

I felt something in my bones when I touched her lips. And as drunk as I was, I wasn't hallucinating that.

"And we'll definitely hit up the poetry read."

"We should throw a dorm party afterward," Chris adds. "Something low-key, maybe. It *is* on a Wednesday, after all. Wouldn't want to overdo it on a school night, right?"

ON WEDNESDAY AFTERNOON, I head back to the room after class before practice at four p.m. Today as I head back up the Dalton stairs to the room, I get what we men affectionately refer to as a NRB, or a No Reason Boner.

It's nothing to be ashamed of. Just nature working its course on a healthy man. And the thing is, when you don't snap the radish for a while, it's bound to happen. And I know...we've only been in the midst of this *contest* for a few days. But I've got one right now, and I'm fairly certain it's due to the images of Alex from last Sunday when she *happened to be* doing yoga when I walked in. I take a deep breath as I take my room key out of my pocket and look down at the erection pressing up against my blue jeans. If this wasn't the time that she was gone every day, I would probably pull the tuck-and-under maneuver, but since I'm going to be alone, there's no need for that. I'll just let this rocket fly its course.

So I open the door, and my body flushes and my eyes widen when I see Alex standing at the window, headphones on, dancing and humming and—*my God, what is she wearing?*

Or rather, it's not what she's *wearing* that makes me freeze in my boots, but what she's *not* wearing.

She's just got on one long white oversized t-shirt that falls just over the curve of her butt, no bra as I can clearly see from the back, and a black thong on. She sways back and forth in front of the window, then spins around and clenches up when she sees me.

"Oh my God, DJ, what are you doing here?" she says, taking her headphones off.

I swing my backpack around and hold it in front of my crotch. *Nope, definitely no bra.*

This is the opposite of what I need to get rid of my *NRB (pronounced nerb, by the way).*

Although, now my NRB has transformed into a BFGR—boner for good reason.

And, honestly, yes, her ass looks incredible and she just gave me a pretty view of it. But the thing that turns me on the most? Her voice.

"Uh, I live here?" I say. "You're doing some afternoon dancing?"

"I was just tidying up the room a little bit and I got distracted. So embarrassing that you saw me dancing like that."

Her face red, she goes back to her desk area and sits with her knees to the side on the chair, headphones around her neck.

"I think it's fun to see you dancing like you thought no one is watching," I say, and head to my desk to drop my backpack. "Do you do that a lot?"

"Oh, I'm just charged up today," she says as she nonchalantly sorts a stack of notecards into a little shoebox with different categories. I open my laptop and proceed to pull up a video so I can pretend like I'm unaware that she is basically naked. "I had a great morning. Did a ton of studying. So I'm ahead of the curve for the week."

I squint skeptically, the way she hesitates at the word *studying*.

"Studying?"

She giggles. "Oh, yeah. Do you know Herman Blank? He's a senior. He took Theories of Personality last year, so he was helping me out with some stuff."

She looks up and gauges my reaction. "Don't you run track with Herman?"

"I will in the winter, yes. Obviously football is going on right now, so I can only do the occasional workout. I don't really know him too well, though."

Aside from his reputation as a creep, I want to add.

Her eyes sparkle with a hint of mischief. "What are you staring at?"

"Nothing."

She gets up and grabs a piece of candy from her desk. "Liar."

I keep my eyes on her as she brings a chair over to me, turns it around and places it six inches from me, and kneels on it.

"I feel like you've had something on your mind lately. You've been avoiding me," she says.

I slide my body under the desk so as to hide my crotch. But in doing so, I have to twist a little awkwardly to chat with her.

"You're violating the pants rule," I say, looking over my shoulder at her.

"Well, I'm cleaning. I was vacuuming and dusting and I don't want to get my pants dirty, obviously. And this is just more comfortable." Her smile is so mischievous.

I clear my throat, and it comes out a low rumbly growl.

"I've been abiding by the pants rule. I think you should, too. Unless you want..."

Her eyes lock on me, and it's like she's *daring* me to look away from her dark brown irises and stare at her tits, through her baggy white t-shirt that only says the word 'misfit' on it. Then she takes the wrapper off the piece of candy she has in her hand—a yellow lollipop—and wraps her lips around it.

"Unless what?"

"What are you doing?"

"Mmm," she says. "I think this is my favorite flavor. It really does taste like yellow cake batter, like they say. So, anyway, what are you watching?"

She puts a hand on my shoulder and looks at the screen, ignoring my question. "Soothing nature scenes, eh? Well, that looks interesting. Why are you looking those up, though? You stressed?" Her hand squeezes my shoulder, and it might as well have a direct line to my heart. What in the hell is going on?

"Wow. You *have* been working out, haven't you?"

I can't take it anymore. I flip my laptop closed and jump to my feet.

"Okay, Alex, what the fuck? What the hell are you doing?"

"What? I'm not allowed to be nice to you?"

"You're never this nice to me. Plus, I can see your nipples."

She seems to shudder a little at that comment, and she stands up. "Well, you wouldn't see them if you weren't staring at my tits."

I put my hands up. "I don't know what you want from me. I've tried to make this roommate situation work. I feel bad that you've got to put up with all these guys on the floor, their stares and their occasional inappropriate comments. But I know you're smart. And you know what you're doing right now."

She puts her hands on her hips. "Yeah. I'm cleaning my room, so I tossed this raggedy old shirt on. That's what I always do. You just happened to walk in right now."

"You're skirting the issue. You're just acting weird."

"No, I'm not."

"So leaning on my shoulder and commenting on my workouts is what you do with all the guys?"

"Herman was telling me about your workouts. They sound intense. I was kind of impressed. That's all."

"Oh, fucking Herman," I react, and then regret it instantly.

"Do you not like Herman?"

"He's fine. He's a good guy."

"You don't like him, though. Why?"

Her eyes drive down, land on my crotch, and jump back up to my face, her expression wide.

Boner revealed.

"You're—"

Before she can finish her sentence, I jump to the ground and do the one fail-safe maneuver for getting rid of a Rocky Swellington: pushups.

I crank out twenty, thirty, fifty, and a couple of minutes later I collapse in a breathless heap. When I stand, her arms are folded sternly.

"Uh, what the fuck was that?" she asks.

"Just decided to do some pushups. I do them every day."

"In the middle of our conversation?"

My heart is still cranking when I stand up.

"I'm a fucking weirdo, okay? You know that."

"You are."

"I've got to get dressed for football practice." Changing the subject, and glaring at her, because this conversation is going nowhere.

"So change."

"We're done with the rules, then?"

"I'm honestly surprised you even paid attention to them at all."

"I was trying to be respectful."

She lowers her voice and a wry smile crosses her face. "Maybe I actually like it when you break the rules."

I bite my lower lip and summon all of my self control. "Excuse me. I need to get to my dresser," I say, then repeat, "Time to change."

She hesitates for a moment, then steps aside.

"Thank you," I say. She stays on my side of the room, though, while I take my shoes and shirt off.

"You need something?"

"I've got my dusting kit out. I can clean your space, too...if you want."

"Sure," I say. She goes to grab her lemony fresh spray and dusting kit and moves in front of me to my dresser.

I never knew that dusting—fucking *dusting*—could be this hot, but I'm seriously on my last nerve. I try to ignore her, and throw on my workout sweats over my boxers quickly and then reach into the top drawer for some socks. She backs up into me—right into my dick—which somehow didn't get fully soft even after all those pushups.

"Oh. Pardon me."

She flashes her big brown eyes at me, and giggles. "I knew it."

I lose it.

Fuck this.

The little touch of her ass on my cock. I'm done letting her get away with this.

I spin her around and pin her into my dresser, hand on her hip. My swollen cock pressed into her thigh. My sweats are made of thin material and I make sure she understands exactly what she's doing to me.

"You've got to cut this out," I growl. "Temptress."

"I honestly don't know what you're talking about." Now I know she's playing a game here and I'm not totally sure why.

"Are you shitting me? Please. I know you're not this naïve."

She giggles. "Okay, I *think* something is going on here. But it also was sort of an accident."

"So I'm not imagining it. You *are* fucking with me. Right now, and the yoga the other night—"

"I didn't plan for you to find me in here like this, if that's what you're asking. Honestly, I thought about *not* cleaning in my usual cleaning clothes just in case you walked in. But then I thought, fuck that, I'm not going to change up my habits just because you're in the room. This is my raggedy cleaning shirt. And that was my Sunday night yoga." Her hand slides down my bare stomach. Her breasts press into me, and the only thing separating me from her flesh is a very thin layer of cotton.

"And you have nice abs. Such a good boy. *Mr. Perfect.*"

The way she whispers it my ear, I realize something I didn't before: *she means it as an insult.*

"Too bad you're a bad boy chaser," I say, and I resist the urge to talk shit about Herman Blank and ask her if that giggle meant she was doing more than just *studying* with him this afternoon.

Fuck. An afternoon delight? Really?

The thought of them together allows me to peel myself away from her.

"I'm not fucking perfect," I grit out. "So you need to stop thinking that right now."

She gets in my face. "What do you mean? Every Tuesday night. *'Hi, Mom, sending you lots of love.'*"

I furrow my brow. "I do call my mom every Tuesday. So what?! Are you seriously making fun of me for telling my mom I love her?!"

"Uh, no, that's not what I meant. I just meant…"

My skin flushes with desire and anger, too, and I feel my inhibitions float away.

"Shit. I'm sorry. That came out really bad. I didn't mean it."

She's crossed the line.

"You know what? Fuck you, Alex. You're sitting here, making judgments about me and the way you think I am."

She scoffs. "You have a freaking dorm named after your family! You're loaded, DJ. Everyone knows it."

"So that's what I am to you? Just a spoiled, stuck-up rich boy? Mr. Perfect?"

"You're a good boy," she says. "And you know it. And I didn't mean it was bad that you said you loved your mom, I just meant—"

She stops midsentence.

"Just meant what?"

"Forget it. I don't want to get into it."

"Well, you're really leaving me hanging here. I'm waiting to figure out why you just insulted my mother."

I can tell she's uncomfortable. Her body language is hunched. "Sorry. I didn't mean to say that. It came out wrong."

I shake my head. "One second you're bragging about

your 'study session' with Herman Blank, the next you're 'accidentally' grinding your ass into my cock and dusting down my desk, and the next you're insulting my mother." God, this girl was confusing as hell, what is up with her anyway?

"I *said* I was sorry!" Her eyes soften just a little. "Sorry. I mean it."

I search her face for answers, because I get the distinct feeling she's not saying something on the tip of her tongue.

"I don't care that you want to act weird around me," I say. "I like weirdos. I love misfits. But you don't know a damn thing about me and my life. So stop making assumptions, and stop calling me perfect. You have no fucking clue what you're talking about. And you're just plain wrong."

"Okay," she acquiesces. "Are you still going to call me temptress?"

"The difference between the nickname for me and you is that yours is fucking one-hundred percent accurate."

"But I'm not trying to. I swear."

"Go stand in front of any guy on campus in that shirt, with your hard nipples, sucking on a lemon sucker with red lipstick on—yes, I noticed—and see what reactions you get. And tell me they're not tempted. Then I'll stop calling you fucking temptress."

I wait for some snide comment as I'm accustomed to with Alex by now. She always seems to need to get the last word in.

"Okay," is all she says as I walk out of the room.

I think Grant may be right. Maybe there is an upside to no sexual activity, if one channels it correctly.

Or at least that's what I try to tell myself as I crush the football workout.

23

ALEX

Maya swings her legs sitting on DJ's bed. After DJ and I got in a fight...would I call it a fight? An argument, perhaps. I called her over and explained the story to her. I'm curled up in a ball on my bed, wrapping my hands around my knees.

The argument we had was surface level, and I didn't tell him the full truth. I feel bad about that. And DJ is right, in a way. I *did* make an assumption about him having a great family. But I stare at the picture on his desk and wonder how I could be wrong. He took down the picture that Jessica was in, and put one up of him, his sister, mother, and father all wearing white and jumping up in the air on a perfect beach with blue in the background. Staring at that, I'm reminded of the ideal childhood I never had.

Not many people here know my full story, though. It's so embarrassing, I don't like telling it. I don't want to be that girl with an air of tragedy following her around everywhere she goes. That's what I was in high school.

Maya shakes her head. "You need to get a little self-awareness. And cut these guys some slack."

"Are you just saying that because you have five brothers?"

"No! I'm saying that because your expectations are ridiculous. I understand what you mean about not wanting to change up your routine of cleaning your room in a t-shirt and a thong, but that definitely sends a message to a guy."

I sigh. "I was thinking about Professor Z's lecture."

"Speaking of getting turned on."

"No, not in that way. About the subconscious and the conscious mind. I think I might be subconsciously doing things to attract DJ."

"Damn right you are! You were dancing in the window! And you said you pulled out a sucker, too. I'm honestly impressed with this man's mental fortitude not to try and hook up with you."

"I told him we were off limits and it's true. I can't have a guy who kisses and tells."

Maya shrugs. "How do you know for sure he'll kiss and tell?"

"He spread the rumor about us sleeping together in the first place. Once a liar, always a liar."

"Well, first, that means everyone already *thinks* you're sleeping together anyway. Second, why isn't everyone gossiping about you doing yoga in the room? Wouldn't he have bragged about that?"

"Good point." Unfortunately, Maya has me thinking. What the heck was I doing anyway? Even though I don't think the nasty t-shirt I wear to clean in is anything to get excited about.

"And he also would definitely tell everyone about this afternoon."

"Maybe." Ugh, she's racking up the points here.

"No, he *definitely* would. If he's the type who blabs about you to others."

"Who would he brag to?"

"Grant. Nelson, Chris, Finn. That's his crew. And I'm good friends with Grant. I could ask him?"

"Good friends, eh?" I wiggle my eyebrows.

"Puh-lease. Grant and I would not hook-up. He's just a friend."

"Yeah, A good guy with incredibly sexy, shaggy hair. And those gray eyes. They're always smoldering. It's intense."

"Well if you like his eyes so much why don't *you* ask him out?"

"I did, remember? And we didn't mesh."

Because I keep picturing DJ.

"I'm playing the field right now. So is Grant. So it's better that we don't get with each other right now anyway."

I gasp. "Oh! Does that mean you're *saving* him? Like you'll hook up with him after you're done with—"

"You can say it. My slutty phase. It's true." Maya owns up to her actions. At least you know where she stands.

"That's not what I meant, exactly. Experimental phase."

"I prefer slutty phase, personally. Call a spade a spade. But yes, we can call it 'exploratory' if you prefer."

"I do." At this point I'll just agree with her.

"Fine, then. And Grant—he's a wild man." She looks at her watch. "Oh, crap. Speaking of Grant...I promised him I'd go to his poetry read tonight. It starts in ten minutes. Go with me?"

WHEN I HEAD down to the Gizmo where they're doing the live poetry reading, the lights are already dimmed and I can hear Professor Flores giving an introduction for the first reader. Everyone claps, and she heads up on stage.

April waves me over to one of two seats she has saved. There's a solid crowd here for a poetry read, maybe forty or fifty people filling out the chairs all the way to the back. It's mostly freshmen in the audience, including DJ's posse. I see Herman Blank sitting in the back as I spin my head. He gives me a smile and a nod.

After the first reader, I see Maya striding toward us. She smiles as she takes the last open seat, and as the second reader begins her poem, I wonder what it is that makes people like April and Maya so different.

Her poem is about the ability to enjoy pleasure, and it gets me thinking.

What makes some people able to simply enjoy some bodily pleasures of life while others feel as though they aren't allowed to feel those things? Religious guilt, perhaps? Something else?

I wonder about the origin of hardship, wrongdoing and strife. The first time I remember strife was the very first memory I had. I was helping my mother as she was cooking for my father but she was nervous and I didn't even know what the word nervous meant when I was four. But I knew my mother was nervous and I didn't understand why.

I swallow and clap without thinking when she finishes her poem because I'm lost in my own little internal world right now.

My palms sweat and another memory flashes in my mind. The time I walked home early from school because I didn't want to go to church at the end of the day. Since I attended a Catholic school, we sometimes had church at the end of the day. But I thought church was boring being seven years old, and I thought I would outsmart the system.

Little did I know my own mother was at home thinking she was outsmarting the system, too, sleeping with a man who wasn't my father while my father was at work in Salt Lake.

I walked through the back door, which was unlocked, and heard the screams coming from upstairs. I went upstairs to check and make sure everyone was alright because the voices scared me.

I'll never get the image I saw out of my brain.

The crowd claps again and Professor Flores takes the mic to introduce the next poet. I zone back in.

"This is Grant," Maya says, smacking me and April on the shoulder.

"I know," April and I say in unison.

Like you could miss him, anyway. As I watch the spot from where Grant stood up, my eyes catch on DJ's for a split second, and I avert mine back to the stage. The two of them look almost like they could be brothers.

I tune in for this round. Grant smiles briefly, and then his expression fades, he's in the moment. I like the fact that he's taking this seriously. Too many people try to turn life into a joke.

"I'm Grant Taylor, and this is my poem. It's called, 'Like Fucking Champs'." He clears his throat and begins.

I come from the back woods back hills and the land of open back doors.

I grew up where country road J met F and you know the first names of the owners of the stores.

Lots of people talk about the Northwoods like they're some summer camp for fun

But come winter those city folk gotta run and hide or they're done

Thing is, November, December, January—that's when the real butterflies cocoon

When you run from the pain and the cold you might as well head to Cancún

You ain't really lived until you seen the Mighty Mississippi freeze

My grandmother used to say that's what gives us Great Lakes people our humility

I say give a man like me an ax and a gun and that's what makes me cocky

People say it ain't easy where I'm from in the North

But to be honest that's just jealousy I can put up with some scary shit

Now at Greene State U we've got a crew and we're in this metamorphosis together

Let's Kafka this year ya'll and we'll brew this stormy, shitty, cold weather

LIKE FUCKING CHAMPS!

HE SHOUTS THE LAST PART, and it gets applause from the audience.

"Wow," Maya says. "Not what I was expecting."

"Yeah," April agrees. "That was actually sort of interesting."

Professor Flores tells us we're going to take a quick, five-minute break and there will be more action when she comes back. She goes back and sits down next to Professor Z, and I wonder what the chances are that the two young, quite attractive professors are hooking up with each other. They seem quite flirty together.

I grab a juice from the juice bar and sit back down, and when we start back up, Professor Z is now the emcee. He asks if there are any volunteers from the audience not on the list, but who would like to come up and share something.

There's some commotion in the DJ and Grant posse, and next thing I know DJ is standing up and heading for the spotlight under the mic.

Like Grant, DJ looks damn serious when he gets to the mic.

"I...don't usually like doing these things. But I'm trying this new thing at Greene State U called radical acceptance. And I wrote this thing down during the first few acts...anyway. Here goes. I'm calling this poem, *Things that aren't true.*"

"THEY CALL ME MR. PERFECT."

HE LOOKS at me with ice cold eyes and a chill rolls through my spine.

"I AM DJ Dalton the third, keeper of the perfect family and great old money fortunes.

The man behind the perfect deep blue eyes with the chiseled abs and on the football team.

I grew up in a gold-plated mansion in Central Illinois and when I shit, it came out diamonds. Still does. Because I'm DJ fucking Dalton the third."

. . .

A FEW PEOPLE LAUGH. He acknowledges it and continues. I already feel nervous, like he's talking directly to me.

"IT'S TRUE. No problems, no bullies on the bus, no drippy faucets in my family.

No siree. No affairs no failures no finding my mother face down on the couch calling the doctor on speed dial. No money problems no sister with depression no girls ever turned me down. No talking about any of this because these are all things that don't exist. These are all things that aren't true. We're a solution-oriented family, not problem-oriented. No denial no hatred no name calling no screaming parents and definitely, above all, no fucking money problems.

BECAUSE I'M DJ Dalton the third. And I'm the keeper of the perfect family and great old money fortunes.

THANK YOU."

"WELL...*THAT* WAS EVEN MORE INTERESTING," April says, reluctantly clapping.

"That didn't even sound so much like poetry as much like getting shit off his chest," I remark.

"It's free verse," Maya says. "Well done, DJ!"

He spins around and sees us, but I avoid eye contact with him.

I feel rotten all of a sudden, especially if all that stuff he just said has even an ounce of truth.

After the show, I hover around where the boys are standing, but they've got their backs to me and I wonder if they're avoiding me. But there's no way DJ doesn't see me.

A girl I know from class, Marisa, waves and bobs up to me.

"Alex, from Preceptorial, right?" she says.

"That's me."

"Cool! What a fun night, right?! God, that one poem DJ Dalton did! That was so hot."

"Hot?" I echo.

"I mean, have you *seen* DJ do his football workouts? Uh, sorry. I shouldn't be talking about this. It probably makes me seem superficial. But he's also got an interesting brain, you know?"

"You've seen him doing his workouts?" The degree of his celebrity dumbfounds me.

She nods enthusiastically. "Oh yeah. I time my visits to the gym in the afternoon so I can be on the treadmill, looking out of the window when they're on the track. Ohh, I see an in."

Marisa zooms in between Chris, the big guy, and Nelson, the lanky one, and gives DJ a hug. I should be happy for him, because it actually *was* a decent poem to come up with right on the spot like that. But the only true feeling that rings through me is jealousy.

"Girl, how come you didn't get up there?" I spin around to the sound of Herman's voice and offer him a smile.

"Oh, hey. I don't know. I just didn't feel like it, I guess."

"Well, you should. Use that great brain of yours."

"Maybe some time."

"What are you doing tonight?"

"I don't know. Going to bed?"

"Lame. Why don't you come to the Lambda house? We're having a party."

"Really? On a Wednesday?"

"It's a smaller gathering. Only a few cool people are invited."

"I see."

I glance over at DJ who seems involved in a vigorous discussion with Marisa.

"Alright," I say. "I'll come."

I can feel DJ's eyes on me as I walk through the door. It's eerie. Herman puts his hand on the small of my back and it feels like a foreign object.

There's a wall constructed between me and DJ, and I can't help but think it's getting taller. I wonder about the origin of our strife and wrongdoing and even though it was weeks ago, I keep picturing him bragging to his friends about hooking up with me, and I can't get over it.

Herman's not the man I want to be with now. I want DJ and I've known that for a while, but how can I just let him get away with his lunchroom gossip? Knowing him as I do now, I find it hard to believe he did that. It's time I confront him … I just need to figure out how.

24

DJ

"Sun's out, guns out, bros," I say as we start the warmup for our light track workout Friday afternoon.

With my dad being ridiculous and keeping me out of the starting lineup for games, I threw one in his face and ditched the last half of practice to come do a fall workout with the track team. Yeah, he's pissed, but what I'm doing with the track team today will be a better workout than standing on the sidelines, anyhow.

We're only doing a few four hundreds for speed, making use of the terrific fall weather. It won't last forever. We see the cross-country team doing their full-blown workout and we give them a respectful nod. Personally, I'm so fucking glad I'm a sprinter and I don't have to run their treacherous sixty-mile weeks.

During the warmup, Herman Blank and I jog together, then stand on the grass to stretch. Yes, we still have grass, not artificial turf. And I'm glad for that. No one else is around today except for Herman, me, and a mid-distance runner named Luis who opted not to join the cross-country team this year. A few athletes are playing hookie, Finn included, since the workout is optional. I chum up to Herman because I want information that only he can give me since Alex won't.

"So, man. Has Alex been treating you like a king?" I prod.

We glance at the girls' track runners on the other end of the track as they wind down their warm-up. They look cute in their Spandex and sports bras. At my high school, the girls weren't allowed to run with just sports bras.

He chuckles. "Man, I've been breaking her down. She doesn't break easily. And I don't mean because she's thick, you know? She's hard-headed." He taps his head.

"Oh, for sure," I say, just to agree with him. On the inside, relief pours through me that they haven't slept together, at least I don't think. It's not that I care if Alex sleeps with someone. She's a free person and can do what she wants. But for the love of God, *not him*. "So you're breaking her down?" I prod further.

He leans in and slaps me on the back as we jog up to the starting line of the four hundred, "You know what we say in the Lambda house. Break 'em down, pass 'em around. Ninety-nine bottles of beer on the wall. Or women...or something."

"Oh? Is that what you guys say?" I say, playing dumb. Actually, I think that really sucks. All I can think of is would I talk about my sister like that?

My suspicion of Herman's douchebaggery is confirmed.

He nods. "Oh, yeah. We can see the skanky ones from miles away. Her and her friend April—such skanks. And, *we*, man. That's what *we* say. I know you're feeling us, so I can't wait for you to rush Lambda in the winter."

"Oh, yeah," I say, not really sure what I'm saying *yeah* to, because I'm not sure fraternity life is really for me. And even if it was, there would be no way on Earth I'd join the Lambdas. "So how do you know they're skanks?" I feign interest, like I could actually learn something from the guy.

"It's the *look*, man. You can just tell, you know? Ever heard of Malcom Gladwell's book *Blink*? It's like in the facial expressions or whatever. Guys like me just know. We just know, DJ."

"I'll have to check that one out." I nod like I'm agreeing, even though since Grant and Finn's room is in the same dorm as April, right down the hall, I can officially confirm she's *not* a sleeper-arounder. Not that there's anything wrong with that, I think.

"What about that other girl..." I feign like I'm trying to remember her name. "Maya, that's it. Oh shit, she's on the track team, too. You think she's a good candidate?"

"Maya Waters. Yeah, dude, we fucking scouted her. Hot. So hot. But unfortunately, she's a prude, man. For *sure*. A total tease."

And I'm officially done paying attention to any opinions that come out of Herman's mouth.

I smile on the inside, because this is an old trick my grandfather taught me. Ask a question you already know the answer to, smile, nod, and listen to the person's answer. A true man will simply admit he doesn't know. But an insecure man, or an idiot for lack of a better word, will try and answer, simply to appear smart.

Playing dumb is a skill. I thank Grandpa Dalton for that one, and take a quick glance at the clouds rolling across the blue Midwest sky.

When my gaze wanders down, I see Maya and the rest of the girl sprinters finishing up their stretching routine. Maya is a wonder of a specimen of womanhood. Everything about her simply looks average, in a way. Well, maybe that's because she doesn't like to show off. I've already noticed how she likes to dress down during class and wear glasses, hoodies when it's chilly enough, and baggier clothes. Her green eyes flit up toward us as her crew starts to walk our way toward the start line. If I didn't know better, from what Grant has relayed about her to me, in confidence, she would look completely, totally innocent, and not the sex-positive high-sex-drive girl I know she is. You really never can judge a book by its cover, even though we all do.

I wonder if they're having the same conversation that we are, but about guys.

"Yeah," I say to feign agreement with Herman again. "You're definitely right about that. Total prude."

"When you join the Lambda house, you'll be instructed in all of our ways, man," he smiles, then leans in and lowers his voice. "You'll fuck so many girls. Trust me on that. Not even an issue anymore."

Luis, who is also a Lambda but is a sophomore, looks uncomfortable.

"So many girls, so little time," Herman says. "I'm going to break-in Alex this weekend. Just you wait. We're having our barn dance party tomorrow night and it is a panty-dropper. Garun-fucking-teed. Something about flannel shirts, bales of hay, and country music just gets girls wet. Did you hear that? Panty—"

"I heard you, man," I say as we walk up to the starting line. Every extra second I spend with Herman, he annoys me even more. "So what time are we going to take these in? Fifty-eight seconds per four-hundred?"

He squints. "Fifty-eight?? Bro, this is the off-season. We can chill. Not like coach is here. How about sixty-five?"

"Sixty-five? If I'm going to run a sixty-five second four-hundred on speed day, I might as well just stay in my bed and jerk my chicken, Herman." I slap him on the back, and he eyes my hand suspiciously, like he thinks I just rubbed my cock on his back. I wish I had.

"What's the matter, man?" I wink. "I washed my hands after I waxed the carrot this afternoon."

"Oh, dude, fuck. Gross." He gags a little, and puts his hand over his mouth. "Why you gotta put that image in my head, man? Come on."

Luis doesn't say anything, just shrugs and takes his spot at the starting line. I like his style.

Little does Herman know, I haven't been on a date with rosy palm and her five sisters all week. But I'll let him think whatever he wants.

"So, fifty-five seconds, it is."

"What?! Fifty-five? I thought you said—"

Before I can listen to him, I hit my stopwatch and take off running. He starts after me and so does Luis.

I feel charged up as we roll into the turn for the first two-hundred, and when I roll through the four-hundred-meter mark, I'm on fire and barely out of breath.

Well, that's a slight exaggeration. But I'm strong through four-hundred. Much stronger than Herman and Luis, who double over in a pant once they cross the four-hundred-meter mark a few steps behind me.

Maya claps as I cross the finish line.

"Not bad, champ, not bad."

I roll my eyes. "Champ?"

"You don't like it? Would you prefer blue-eyed snake?"

"Blue-eyed snake? I don't get it."

"I can kind of see...everything in that Spandex."

I look down. "But my snake's not blue-eyed."

She shrugs aggressively. "Come on, Deej. Work with me here. I'm trying to be nice for once."

"Are y'all doing the same workout?"

She squints skeptically. "You say 'y'all'? I didn't think they said 'y'all' in Illinois."

"It's rural here. And besides," I smirk. "I'll say whatever the fuck I want to say."

She throws her hands up. "Wow! Well, okay. I surrender. And yes, we're doing the same workout. Three four-hundreds for speed."

"What are you running yours at?"

"These girls are doing sixty-nine, but I'm doing fifty-eight. I'm a little jealous of them." She wiggles her eyebrows and lowers her voice just enough so that that no one else can hear besides me. "In more ways than one, just to be clear. I wish I could take it a little easier on this workout, but I also think there's a good sex joke in there."

I crack up. "Do you wish you could take it easy?"

She shakes her head. "No, you're right. I want it fast and hard and..." she wiggles her body. "I'm gonna have to give G—" she stops and clears her throat. "You ready to run?"

"Wait a minute. Did you just imply Grant is your go-to hookup buddy?"

"That is absolutely not true!" she yells, and everyone looks over at us. "Sorry. Sorry. Don't tell anyone. Don't tell him I mentioned this. Fuck, we're just friends. Why are we talking about me? How are you and Marisa?"

I don't answer because there is no me and Marisa, and that's a silly question. I wave us to the start line, and Herman and Luis join us again.

"Maya's running fifty-eight," I say, to rub it in that a girl is running faster than him. I'm not sure if he just likes showing up and being lazy or what.

"Yeah, well, I'm running this one in fifty-seven."

Says the guy who just clocked in ten seconds behind me on the first lap.

"Of course, you are. Ready, set..."

The dirty little cheater takes off in front me and gets a head start, and Luis and Maya follow his lead.

"...Go," I say, and start myself.

We come around the halfway point faster than last time. Herman is trying to impress Maya with his speed. Luis is...also trying to impress Maya?

As we round the turn, I have to swing wide to keep my speed up because Herman hogs the inside track. Maya rides his right shoulder, letting him block the wind. Smart girl.

And also, *fast girl*. She's still hanging right there with Herman and me.

As we come around to the stretch for the last hundred meters, the race opens up. For some reason, we're all sprinting like this is the most important race of the season. I'm neck and neck with Herman, Maya still drafting off him. Luis fades back.

And then she makes a move on the last fifty meters, and I try to run for it, too.

We leave Herman in the dust, and the last twenty-five meters we're so close I don't know who's winning, so I turn my head to see in the last five meters.

She doesn't turn. And she beats me by the slimmest of margins.

This time, I'm out of breath. We all are.

"Holy fuck, you're fast," I say to Maya, after catching my breath.

"Fast girl, eh? Well, lucky for you, I take that as a compliment."

"Want to take this next one in sixty-nine?" I ask.

She fake-gasps. "I couldn't do that. Alex has a crush on —" Her eyes widen and she covers her mouth. "Just kidding! I'm delirious! Looks like I ran this one too fast! Bye!"

Herman comes over to me and we watch Maya run to the locker room. "What did I tell you? Weird, weird girl. Total prude. Anyway, I'm going to head out."

"We've got one more, though."

Herman shrugs. "Eh, my right knee is a little tender. I'll let you take this one home with Luis. See you tomorrow?"

"Yeah, I wanted to ask. What kind of music do you do?"

"Country, dude. All country."

I cringe, but I nod. "See you tomorrow, man."

25

ALEX

Saturday is the barn dance at the Lambda Phi house. According to Herman and the rest of the Lambdas, it's the best party of the term.

I have my doubts, but we're still going.

On Saturday while DJ is at his game, I put my things in a bag and head over to April and Maya's dorm where I can shower and get ready in peace. Plus, I can enlist April and Maya for the biggest decision I've made all day.

"So, denim shorts and cowgirl boots with this red and white flannel," I ask, holding the flannel out, "or this sexy red and yellow floral wrap dress?"

April folds her arms and mulls it over. "How is the wrap dress barn dance-themed?"

I shrug. "It makes my butt look the best."

"Oh. Well, yeah, I'd go with that wrap, then."

Maya walks in, naked but with a towel wrapped around her head. "Yeah, I would definitely do a wrap. Everyone's going to be in denim shorts and flannel, so you'll stand out."

"Seriously, you don't think I'll get made fun of for not going with the theme?"

"Everyone is going to be too drunk within an hour of the party to even remember the theme anyway. Lambda is one of only two wet fraternities on campus."

"What does 'wet fraternity' mean?"

"It means they are allowed to serve alcohol at parties. Not all frats have that privilege. I was talking to some of the sophomore and junior girls on the track team. They all say this is the second drunkest party of the year because everyone still has that 'beginning of school' vibe, doesn't care about their reputation, are desperate for pledges, and of course, the free booze."

"What's the first drunkest?" April asks.

"That would be Spring Island, which happens at the Alpha house."

"I've barely heard of the Alphas," I say as I wiggle into my dress.

Maya shrugs as she puts on a skirt. "Yeah, they're low key. My friend Skylar who is a senior and totally legit likes them, though. And they are on social probation because their Spring Island party last year got so out of hand. Happens just about every year, apparently. Since the party is in mid-May, everyone brings their friends from high school whose college classes are done with, and it gets out of hand. Like, very out of hand."

"Do we know any Alphas?" April asks as she touches up her hair.

"The Alphas are like the cool guys who we know but don't feel the need to bring up the fact that they're in a frat every ten minutes."

"Unlike the Lambdas," I say.

Maya nods. "Luke, the teaching assistant from our psych class, for example, he's an Alpha Z. Total nerd. Well, he plays baseball, too. But also a nerd."

"Hot hands Luke is an Alpha Z? Dang. We'll have to check out a party there sometime soon."

I squeeze into my dress and take a glance at myself in the mirror.

"Holy boob game," April says. "Herman is going to freak when he sees you tonight."

"Really?"

"Oh, yeah. You're good at hiding your body during the week."

I shrug. "Jeans and hoodies to class are just so comfortable. Plus, it's not like I'm trying to pick guys up in class or something. I'm here to learn."

Maya puts a hand on my shoulder. "Well, you're about to learn what happens tonight when you bring your milkshake to the yard. Jesus. I'll keep an eye on you tonight. We all will. Are you and Herman, like…talking? What's your status with him?"

"Yeah. Talking. We've shacked up a couple of times, but nothing's really happened. We cuddled out a little bit and then fell asleep. Didn't even kiss. I just wasn't feeling it."

"I see." Maya goes to her fridge and pulls out sliced limes, a bottle of tequila, and some Coke. "Just taking it slow?"

April and I both take ice-filled cups from Maya. The girl has her pregame game on lockdown.

I shrug. "I like him well enough, but I just don't know if I like him like that, you know? I mean, he's a cool guy and all. I'll dance with him tonight, for sure. We're pretty casual, though. Do you have your eye on anyone tonight?"

"Maya's in love with—"

"Shush, April! Sorry, roommate secrets. Not that we keep things from you. But…April only knows this one by accident."

"Yeah, because I walked in on you two doing it at midnight in the stacks."

Maya blushes, uncanny for her.

"Is it Grant?"

"Look, let's not talk about me," she says, her face bright red. "On paper, I am single and mingling tonight, despite anything you may hear otherwise. Also, Grant and I weren't doing "it." We were reading poetry down there."

April grins. "And you don't read poetry with any other guys. I think you like Grant because he *refuses* to sleep with you. What do you think about that theory, Alex?"

I put my hands up, then raise an eyebrow toward Maya. "So...you read poetry in the stacks with guys you *really* like?"

"Ugh. Can we not talk about this? We're just friends. I *told* you."

We head into the lobby of their dorm room and join another group of girls who are also pregaming, drinking whisky. I recognize one of them, Marisa, and she's being overly nice to me, so I know something is up. At least, I think there is.

"So you're the famous DJ Dalton's roommate," she says.

"Guilty as charged."

"How do you do it? Spending all that time with those boys in Dalton Dorm?"

"I tend to spend a lot of time here. That's the key."

She sips her drink. "I would, too. But, my God, they really put you with the number-one thirst trap in Dalton, didn't they? Ha, that's so funny, DJ's last name is Dalton. What a coincidence."

"Not a coincidence. The dorm is named after his grandfather."

"Oh, wow. I had no idea. So is he..." Marisa stops midsentence and bites her lip.

"Yes?"

"I shouldn't say. It's impolite."

I sigh. I always know someone is from the Midwest, as many students are here, when they have to preface a question they really want to know the answer to with 'it's impolite, but...'.

"Just tell me."

"Is DJ seeing anyone that you know of?"

Marisa's two friends look at me with renewed interest.

I shake my head. "Not that I know of."

"What about you guys? Seeing him in that room all the time must be quite the experience. Did you two...you know?"

The grip on my glass tightens, and I gesture for April to refill my glass.

"Where are you all going out tonight?" Maya asks, deftly changing the subject.

"We're going to the barn dance," Marisa's friend Carrie says.

"Ah, we should have known by your clothing," April says.

We make small talk, and I notice that Marisa keeps stealing glances at me.

Finally, we get up to leave, and Marisa touches my arm and pulls me to the end of the person-train as we walk the five minutes across the concrete path from the quad to the Lambda house.

"Hey, sorry about that back there," she says. Marisa is dark-haired and dark eyed like me, with long eyelashes. "I didn't mean to ask you personal stuff in front of everyone. It's just that I heard through the grapevine you were hooking up with DJ. I kind of like him, but I don't want to step on any toes...especially if you're already dating him."

My skin tingles, the anger I felt a couple of weeks ago but had somewhat forgotten rising back to the surface.

"It's fine. There is absolutely, positively, nothing going on between me and DJ."

"Oh, good," she says. "I mean, if that's what you want. I feel a lot better now about everything. He and I have been texting." She giggles, and a sideways smile crosses her face as we turn the corner around the basketball courts. We can already hear the buzz of music coming from Lambda. "We have a Snapchat streak going."

My heart drops at that. It's such a silly, childish thing to be jealous of. A secondary reaction kicks in, and I feel angry at the simple fact that I feel any jealousy for him at all. But I can't stop the feeling.

Luckily my phone buzzes with a text from Herman and it's enough to distract me.

HERMAN: *You have no idea what's in store for you tonight. You ready?*

I SILENTLY ROLL MY EYES. The thing about Herman is he's delusional and cocky. Like he thinks he's a big badass, but I still haven't made up my mind if he is or if he's just pretending he's badass and gets the world to believe him just because he's a senior now. TBD.

"Oh, here he is now!" Marisa presses a button to answer her FaceTime. "Heyyy, D. What's up."

My heart drops further. *D.* She has a nickname for him. One that I don't have.

"Hey, Marisa," he says with a smile and a decent Spanish

accent. Damn. I didn't know DJ spoke Spanish. "Dang, you look sexy tonight! Yum."

She blushes. "Aww, stop."

"No, seriously—not many girls can make a pair of overalls look that sexy. What are you up to?"

"We're heading over to the Lambda house. You?"

"Nice! I'm with my squad in the quad playing some drinking games. We'll be heading over there shortly, as well."

"Who's in your squad?" she asks, flipping her hair. Keeping the phone at the perfect fucking angle. I hate that she *does* make those overalls look good.

"The usual suspects. Me, Grant, Nelson, Chris, Finn."

"Arrrrghhh!" I hear Finn's voice yelling into the phone. "What's up, Marisa!"

She smiles and waves. "All good."

"Who's in your squad tonight?" he asks. "Oh, the usual three. Me, Katie, and Carrie. And I'm with your roommate, too!"

She flips the phone so he can see me, and I offer a curt smile. "Hey, DJ," I say.

He pauses, and gives me an up and down. For a moment, I flash back to him telling me how stunning I look.

"Well, hello roommate. Are you enjoying your night so far?"

"Very much so," I say feeling melancholy right now, to the point that I'm not sure I want to go anymore.

He hesitates like he's going to add something, but then his eyes shift, and he just says, "Well, I guess I'll see you out on the dance floor."

"Maybe," I say, doing my best to muster a wry smile.

Marisa waves goodbye and blows him a kiss, then hangs up.

The two of us are trailing behind the rest of the group who are waiting for us now, close to the house. The walls vibrate from the outside with music. It's going to be loud inside and I decide it's now or never to ask my question.

"Hey, so, Marisa, question."

"Yeah?"

"What about you and DJ? Have you guys...you know?"

She smiles slyly. "Hooked up? No. Haven't even kissed."

Relief pours through me and I hate the fact that I care.

"Oh. I see."

Her smile goes crooked and she bites the side of her lip. "I'm hoping to change that tonight, though."

It's everything you would expect from a fraternity dance party: Top 40 music, lots of free drinks, and a smallish but fun dance area on the first floor of the house.

DJ's short-sleeve button down is just about half open at this point, and Marisa is grinding on him like she's at the high school prom and it's the last dance. She's good at letting her inhibitions go to dance like that. She has no idea that I'm staring at her every move.

I feel inspired all of a sudden, and I take my moves to the next level.

"Shit, girl, damn," Herman says. "Shake that thang."

He puts his hands on my hips and they feel tentative, like he's not sure about something but I can tell he's turned on because he's hard and pressing into my ass. A thin layer of cotton is all that separates us right now.

Then my eyes catch DJ's. His hands are wrapped around Marisa's midsection and he's biting his lower lip, staring at me.

He looks brooding. His clear blue eyes seem brown in the shadows. He runs his tongue around his lips, his gaze never leaving mine, and I feel a chill roll over me, and I have to avert my eyes from him.

Feeling charged up, a new song comes on and I drop it low and into Herman.

"Oh, yeah. Yeah, girl," he says.

I flash my eyes up toward DJ again, and he's still staring at me while his hands are on Marisa's hips. He's gaping at me, really. The crazy thing is that it turns me on, despite, or maybe even because of, the anger stirring inside me. My body heats and I feel Herman's hands, and I wish they were DJ's. Why the fuck does he have to be so hot and also a big fat liar? It's not fair.

Marisa's hands are on her knees as she bends down, pressing her ass into DJ's crotch. I do the same with Herman, and mouth the words, *this should be you* over to DJ...

And I mean it.

God, I'm messed up. There's something seriously wrong with me.

Could have been you, Deej. I could have even put up with your cockiness. Actually, I thought it was quite funny. Lying, however, I do not do.

"Drop It Low" ends and the next song is slower. Marisa whispers something to DJ and he nods and heads out of the dance area.

I tell Herman I want to get some air, then follow DJ as he walks out the door to the open-air concrete patio behind the house.

He's talking with Chris and Grant when I roll up, and as soon as I get there, he walks away, not making eye contact with me.

I two-step to catch up with him and tap him on the shoulder.

"Yeah?" he says, and half turns. "What do you want?"

I freeze up. "Where are you going?"

He scrunches up his face, a little angrily. "Is that any of your business?"

I soften my expression, but don't say anything.

Come on, are you going to act like we weren't both just eye fucking each other on the dance floor?

When I don't say anything, he finally answers. "I'm going to check on Marisa. She said she was going upstairs to the rooms to do some shots, and she hasn't come back."

"It's been five minutes."

"A lot can happen in five minutes. And—to be honest with you—I think the Lambdas are fucking shady. I've heard some weird stories, and I'm getting a really creeped-out vibe here. I don't trust her alone for two minutes up there."

"Really? I thought you liked hanging out with these guys." His confession baffles me and worries me a bit since I'm here with Herman.

"I did—for the first week. And then I got to know them. Thing is, you never know who you can trust for the first few weeks of college. Fucking Jeff wants to rush Lambda. *Jeff.* If that's not representative of a creepy fraternity, I don't know what is."

"I think they're good guys. A little awkward, maybe," I respond, trying to see the best in them. But I totally see what he's saying.

"Good. I'm happy for you. Seems like we're both having fun here. Anyway, I've got to go. Have a good night."

He turns again and walks away briskly.

Part of me feels slighted, but then again, what is DJ supposed to do? Stay and appease me? Not like I've given any indication that I'm interested. I catch a glimpse of him going up the steps two at a time with those long legs of his. Anxiety fills me and I head to the bar for another sex on the beach.

"Nice and strong."

"You're the boss," the guy making the drinks says.

I take another healthy sip. It's damn strong, alright. I check my phone, and I have a text from Maya that says she's upstairs, so I head up to the room number she tells me.

"Hey there! This is where the real party is," she says when I open the door. April sits on a couch next to Finn, and they're passing a pipe around, and the room is pungent with the smell of weed. "Want to smoke a little bit? Or are you too drunk?"

I shrug. "It's been a little while. But I'll partake, sure."

Finn is in the middle of telling some story that I can't follow, but April seems to be riveted by.

"Uh, who's room is this?" I ask.

Maya takes a hit and hands me the pipe, then shrugs. "No idea. I just needed a room to get out of that cramped dance floor. Not my thing. I saw you grinding out there. You've got some moves, shorty."

"Thanks. Wait, so you just commandeered this room?"

"As far as I'm concerned, this house and the booze are free game."

Finn and April burst into raucous laughter, and Maya and I just look a little awkwardly at them.

Maya's phone buzzes with a text and she reads it.

"Oh, wow. That's interesting."

"What's interesting?"

She hesitates, opening her mouth and then closing it, which gets me even more interested.

"Tell me," I say.

"Carrie from my floor just texted me...apparently, DJ just brought Marisa back."

I swallow and try to hold myself back. "Really?"

"I mean, what would you get from this text? 'DJ brought Marisa home tonight. Lucky girl, I guess.'" She shows me the text.

The pesky pangs of anger come back, roiling in my stomach. I have to hold back the wash of emotion that comes over me. I thought—I honestly thought—DJ and I had a moment out there on the dance floor. Fucked up as that may be.

I know he was dancing with Marisa and I was dancing with Herman, but I swear I felt it in my gut this visceral connection to him.

My gut has been deceiving me lately. Must be my dysfunctional head. Some fleeting thought comes across me and I wonder what Professor Z would have to say about my subconscious given my fucked-up past.

The mixed messages I'm sending are driving me nuts, so I can't imagine what DJ thinks...probably that I'm certifiable.

"Good," I say. "Good for them. I'm going to go hit the dance floor again. You want to go?"

She waves her hand. "No, thanks. I'm good. It's like one a.m. I like this chill environment anyway. More my scene."

I get up and head out the door. On the way out, a guy I don't know gives me a confused look.

"Uh, were you just in that room?"

I'm not sure why he's even asking that. I was obviously in that room and he saw me come out.

"No," I say, and the clear, blatant lie makes him hesitate enough that I have time to head out into the hall and down the stairs. I hear the same guy yelling *what the fuck are you doing in my room?'* and I smile. Maya is a fucking badass and I love her. After hanging out with her for just a couple of weeks, I'm already aware of one of her superpowers: to talk herself into—or out of—any situation she wants.

The weed hits me and the music sounds even better than normal as I walk down the stairs. I'm drunk and I'm high and I'm upset.

Fuck DJ. I almost want to cry. Fuck him and his lies. One tear slides down my cheek and I wipe it away as the song "Save a Horse Ride a Cowboy" comes on.

I spot Herman alone on the dance floor, bobbing to himself. He looks a little silly and awkward, but maybe I'm too harsh on him. Maybe I should ignore that feeling in my gut that tells me he's not my type.

His eyes catch with mine just as some girl comes and tries to grind on him, but he makes a *no* gesture and dances his way over to me.

"Come on, girl," he says. "Time to save a cowboy."

Everything that comes out of his mouth is corny, but at least he won't flaunt another girl right in front of me and then go home with her. The way I see it, that is some next-level shit.

"Thanks for saving the dance for me," I say.

"Always, baby," he says.

We grind it out to Big & Rich and I feel this part of my soul rise to the surface that hadn't been there before. I'm not like April—who is still holding out on her boyfriend—and I'm also not like Maya who needs it every day. I'm an in-between girl, and I need some relief tonight.

After the song, Herman goes over and gets another round of drinks at the bar—not sure if he knows how drunk I am—and then kisses me on the lips.

"So you want to go finish this last round in my room?" he asks.

My heart pounds and DJ flashes through my mind —*again*.

I grind my teeth. *Fuck him. Fuck DJ Dalton and the horse of privilege he rode in on.*

"Absolutely," I say. "I'd love to."

The party barely registers as we head up to Herman's room on the third floor.

He turns the lights down low, and points to his couch.

"Ready to have a good time?"

"Good time?"

"Yeah. Heh. You know. What kind of drugs are you into?"

My stomach lurches with anxiety. "I'm sorry, Herman," I say. "I can't do this."

I had a bad feeling when I came inside, but party drugs are the last straw for me. I've seen them destroy too many lives and I don't plan to start with them. Before he can say anything, I run down the stairs and out of the house, and shoot Maya a text asking if I can stay with them tonight.

26

ALEX

My head throbs the next morning when I walk back to my room.

Although nothing happened last night, this is indeed what's known around campus as the walk of shame. Going home in a hip-hugging dress and black CFM heels at seven a.m. definitely has certain connotations.

I unlock the door to the dorm floor and a rush of relief hits me. *Home free, and no one has seen me.* I just don't want to get the rumor mill started up again.

Then my anxiety hits me full force when I see who is standing at the door of our room, fiddling with his keys. He looks at me, says nothing, then puts the key in the door and opens it.

My whole body tingles as I walk into the room, closing the door he leaves open for me.

He's still got his clothes on from last night, too. Jeans and a flannel. I'm about to be worried about how hungover I look, but when I see the rings under DJ's eyes I feel less concerned about my own reflection.

"Late night?" I ask. And as soon as the question comes out, it sounds stupid. But I feel I need to say *something*.

DJ kneels down and opens the minifridge. "Yeah. You could say that. Water?"

"Yes, please."

He hands me a bottle of water, then chugs half of his bottle. I sip mine, and we both sit down on our twin beds and face each other, almost like we're both thinking the exact same thing.

"So how did your night end up?" I ask, trying to be nonchalant. But I think we both know it's a little game we're playing at this point.

"Not good," he says.

"Oh?"

His eyes float up to meet mine. "Marisa got alcohol poisoning—we think—and so Grant and I had to carry her back to her room. And then called an ambulance. We stayed with her in the hospital last night."

Adrenaline rushes through me as I run past the slightly blurry timeline of events last night. Relief that he didn't spend the night with her. Such illogical relief.

"Oh? She had too much to drink?" *Nonchalant*.

"Remember when I said I didn't trust her alone upstairs for two seconds with the Lambdas? Well. It's been confirmed. She was up there for two fucking minutes. Doesn't even remember what she drank or how it happened. We don't know if she was slipped something funny, or if she just did too many shots."

He runs a hand through his head. "Fuck the Lambdas. Fuck those fuckers."

"They're not all bad," I say, and even as the words come out, I wonder why I'm defending them. I barely know them, really.

"I suppose there is a small chance she was the one instigating the shot-taking or whatever. But I can't wash them of all blame. Fuck them. Last night, after Grant and I took Marisa to the hospital, we went back to their house after the party and asked who the fuck had been drinking with her. No one knew. Bunch of liars. All of them."

DJ stands up and starts pacing around the room, clenching and unclenching his fists. My heart pounds wildly, and I vaguely recall some sort of commotion going down on the second floor while I was with Herman. He said it was nothing to worry about, just his brothers arguing over something.

He stops at the window, staring out over the campus. He unbuttons his flannel and tosses it on the chair to his desk, then runs his hands through his hair and blows out a loud exhale.

"Where were you last night?" he says evenly, without turning around.

"Herman wanted to do drugs with me. So I just crashed with the girls."

"Oh, shit."

"Yeah." I stand up. "Can we please talk about what happened on the dance floor?"

"So you're not going to answer my question?" I can see he's hurt, suspecting the unsaid.

"I think we should talk first about the fact that you couldn't stop eye fucking me all night at the Lambda house."

He opens the window and lets a soft breeze flow into the room.

"Oh, please. The eye-fucking game we were doing on the dance floor last night was child's play compared to what you've been putting me through these last two weeks." He turns around and focuses on me. "Doing downward dog when you know I'll be coming in the room. Having me adjust your posture. Deep-throating a lollipop in my face. Cleaning the room in your fucking underpants when I can clearly see how hard your nipples are." He steps closer toward me.

"So what are you trying to insinuate?" I say, refusing to back down. *That I don't know what the fuck I want? Well, you're right.*

"These can't *all* be coincidences. Not possible. I think you're playing me for a fool. I think you get off on teasing me. And that's some fucked-up shit right there."

Maybe it's the fact that I'm still slightly drunk, but I feel my temper finally blow over. But I don't disagree.

I step up to him and pop my hip. "Well, maybe," I say, slowly, "you shouldn't make up fucking *lies* about sleeping together with your roommate."

He scrunches up his face and jerks his head to the side. "When did I say that?"

"The first goddamn weekend we were on campus." I wanted him to figure this out for himself but that could take forever apparently.

He looks down and away, as if trying to remember, then looks back at me. "I never said that."

My body stiffens.

"Wait. So you're saying what everyone—*and I do mean everyone*—was saying was just a straight lie?"

"Where'd you hear it from? Who made this up?" he says, and I sense him getting angry. If he's a liar, he's damn convincing.

"April and Maya told me," I say. "Everyone in the dorm was talking about it. They said you were bragging in the cafeteria about it. And everyone even knew about my stuffed animal, too."

He does the look down and away again, squinting, and then his expression widens. "Oh, fuck!" he says.

"Aha! You *did* say it!"

"No, I most certainly did not," he says this with such conviction I'm thrown off a bit.

"Then why did you just go 'oh, fuck'?"

"Because I remember the conversation you are talking about." He sneers and clenches his fist. "Fucking Jeff!"

"What's Jeff got to do with it?"

"He told everyone that I hooked up with you. I was telling him how gorgeous you are, and he took that to mean I had 'definitely already hit that.'" He does his best impression of Jeff's voice.

I cringe. "Is that really how it happened?"

DJ nods. "So that's why you've been such a bitch lately. It all makes sense now! You thought I was bragging about you."

"Don't call me a bitch," I say, my stomach sinking. I don't know what to believe now, but I think I may have misinterpreted the whole situation.

"Well, what would you call it? I can't talk to you for two seconds without you getting all up in arms about anything. Fucking *anything*." His jaw opens even farther and his eyes light up. "Holy shit. That's what this is all about! You've just been trying to fuck with me! Fucking Jeff! What an asshole for putting us through this. There's something really off about him."

Something else registers that he said, as just an off-comment.

I was telling Jeff how gorgeous you are.

How nonchalantly he said it made it all the more sweet.

My phone buzzes with a text from April. She and Maya are going to the café to get breakfast.

"Look, I'm still drunk," I say, not totally false, but with this new bombshell I need to get away and think...and I'm hungry. Spinning around and pulling yoga pants and a t-shirt out of my dresser, I say to him, "We can finish talking later."

"Where were you last night?" he asks again.

"I just crashed at Maya's," I say as I take my dress off. I can feel his eyes on me this time. I turn around, in bra and panties. At least they're my sexy ones.

"Stop staring," I say.

He folds his arms. "And what if I don't? What are you gonna do about it now?"

Sparks fly through me, and I try to swallow them down. I say nothing. My brain is a little slow, and I'm still slightly buzzed.

He looks at me while he takes off his jeans, only in his briefs, leaving little to the imagination.

"Stop staring," he smirks, biting his lower lip.

I shake my head as I pull my yoga pants on. "Look, you need to be a gentleman. It's only right. Respect the pants-on rule."

He turns his head a little to the side, then lets out a hearty laugh and slaps his knee.

"A gentleman. That's what you want? Really? Be honest now, Alex."

I nod, ignoring the warmth growing in my belly right now, holding my shirt in my hand.

He grabs a towel from his dresser, puts it over his shoulders, and strides over so he's a few feet from me.

He grips the ends of it with both hands and smirks.

Is he flexing right now? Fuck, he looks hot. I think even

April might go for him right now. Maya definitely would. I take a mental snapshot of him.

It's true—despite my trying to the contrary, I want him.

He licks his lips and smirks, and his voice comes out in a low rumble. "Do you have any idea how hard it is to be a gentleman, living in this room with you?"

I swallow. "Is it?"

Without taking his eyes off me, he slides his briefs down, then goes back to holding both ends of the towel.

He twists his tongue in his teeth.

"Yes. It is."

My pounding heart is in the eye of the storm right now and I know he's testing me, gauging my reaction. Following my eyes to see if I look like I did the first time in the shower.

I do my damndest not to look down. But my eyes want to travel downward.

I relent, and despite knowing he'll never forget, I glance down.

His cock is big, and so hard he could use it for a towel rack instead of his shoulders.

He takes another step toward me, and I flash my eyes up to him again.

"Does this make you uncomfortable?" he says flatly.

"I-I don't know what to say to that."

"Do you like it?"

I swallow. "I don't think I should answer that. What are you doing, DJ?"

"Since you're having a hard time getting the picture, I'm *showing* you. I'm as much of a gentleman as anyone on campus. But I'm only a man, too. It's like I'm lightning and you're the rod."

"Ironic that I'm the rod," I point out, and he breaks into

laughter, then takes a step toward me, but with his body facing the door.

"Regardless of what you think, I *have* been keeping it toned down these past few weeks. Because I felt sorry for you. You're on a floor of fifty-nine horndogs and you're the only female. Well, guess what? Any sympathy I have for you has come to an end."

I put my shirt on while a flood of anxiety washes over me.

He turns over his shoulder before he walks out. "The rules are done. No pants. No shirts when I want. And you are the temptress again."

"You can't call me that," I spit out. "It's sexist."

"How is the word *temptress* sexist?"

"Because there isn't a male equivalent."

"Yes, there is. Incubus."

I squint. "Seriously? Incubus means male temptress? I thought that was just a band."

"Look it up. I'm going to shower," he says and walks out.

It's impossible not to steal a glimpse at his naked ass. Let's just say it's evident he works out.

All of a sudden I'm worried and I can't put my finger on the precise reason. It was that look in DJ's eye when he was staring me down. And…walking naked through the dorm room? That's not something guys do, even normally here.

Before I go down to breakfast, I Google the term incubus.

Sure enough, he's right.

Incubus: *n. a male demon believed to have sexual intercourse with sleeping women.*

. . .

2ND DEFINITION: a cause of distress or anxiety.

As accurate a definition as I've ever read. When I turn the corner of our hall, I can hear DJ's singing blasting out from the shower.

He's singing an Incubus song: "Nice to Know You."

27

DJ

Friday afternoon, I sit on the second floor of the library, my eyes drifting up from my books and my notes, looking out the window to watch students as they meander across the campus sidewalks. My phone buzzes with a call from my mom, the second today, and I think about breaking my ironclad rule of no phone calls during my study time. But if I do it right now, I'll set a precedent and I can't be doing that. I slide it back into my backpack and put it on silent. I'll call her as soon as I'm done with this study session.

Now that we've rung in the month of October at Greene State U, it is now officially hoodie season. I'm honestly surprised there's not a holiday to bring in the occasion. We should have a drink to mourn the fact that short shorts and tank tops are no longer viable clothing options. Now those beautiful bodies on campus go under cloth until what —next May?

And, sadly, this means I'm slightly less apt to parade around our floor shirtless.

That's right, just slightly.

I love the Midwest and the people here, but I've got to be honest: when I nearly have to bust out my winter jacket on October third, I kind of wish I had gone to school in San Diego.

At least the leaves are changing and the orange-red hues here are one of a kind as they begin their transformation to brown and falling off the trees.

It's also a week of rediscovery. Number one, midterms are coming up next week, so I've got to reread a few books in order to form a coherent thesis statement for next week's paper. Number two, I've got Incubus's best album on repeat, and I now realize why my sister puts this in her top ten of all time. One of those things that you don't appreciate is a certain album or song until you hit a certain age.

Number three, Alex and I are certainly rediscovering how to navigate this new situation where she *doesn't* hold a grudge against me for no particular reason. But the thing is, now *I* hold a grudge against her for holding one against me. I don't like passive-aggressive people, and I don't understand why, if she thought I was the biggest, most gossiping bastard in the world, she didn't just *confront* me.

I'm also a little shocked that someone on campus didn't tell me they thought Alex and I had hooked up. I guess it's just one of those *everybody's talking behind your back, but not to your face* situations.

Grant and Finn said they had heard some variation of the rumor, but since they knew the true story from me, they figured it was just people talking trash.

Thanks a lot, Jeff, and thanks a fucking lot, rumor mill.

Gossip ruined my chance with the coolest girl on campus. We had some momentum at the beginning of the year, but we lost it. Momentum really is everything in a relationship.

I hear someone cough in the library, and I stare at the books sprawled out in front of me in the cubby hole I'm using to study. They really shouldn't put windows here. It's so distracting, and when I'm studying I envy the hell out of the people who are not.

I stare at the assignment we've all got to do for our freshmen Preceptorial class. We're supposed to pick a theme having to do with hedonism in twentieth-century literature based on one of the stories we've read, and compare that to modern-day life. I've been rereading the books and trying to decide which I'll choose: *Pimp*, a true-life warning story about one of the greatest pimps ever, *House of Mirth*, an early twentieth-century story written by Edith Wharton, and *Dubliners*, a collection of short stories written by James Joyce.

I stare at the books for another few minutes, and decide that this beautiful fall afternoon is not the day for this.

Due to some miracle having to do with a major soccer tournament the college is hosting this weekend, we don't even have practice this afternoon, either. We just had a light workout this morning.

When I get back to the room, Alex is sitting at her desk browsing the Internet, and as soon as I come in she closes whatever she was listening to on her computer—I couldn't quite hear it.

"Hey," I say as I walk in and set my bag down.

"Hey." She stands up as I plop onto my desk and pull out my phone. "Do you have a few minutes we can...talk?"

My gut wrenches. I'm a typical guy, and when a girl asks me if I can *talk*, it's instinctual—I clam up.

"Sure but I need to make a call real quick."

I dial my mom's number and she picks up after one ring.

"Hey, Momma! How are you?"

"Hey, DJ. Thanks for calling back. How's college going?"

I hear shakiness in her voice. "It's fine. What's going on? Everything alright?"

She clears her throat. "It's just that...well, you know your sister has had problems in the past."

The bottom falls out of my stomach. "What happened to Felicity?"

I see Alex's ears perk up.

"It's just that, well, her boyfriend broke up with her and she didn't take it well. She had another episode."

My blood boils. I fume and I want to get in the car and drive back to Davenport and beat this guy up.

"Is she stable?"

"Seems to be. Just wanted to let you know."

"Can I talk to her?"

"Probably not right now. We had to take her to the hospital. But your dad..."

I can hear the tears in her voice. "I haven't spoken with him in a few weeks. We're having some issues. I thought you should know. I think this might be affecting Felicity."

"Okay." I say, trying to take in all of this information at once. I've been so focused on workouts and classes lately, maybe I haven't been keeping as close of tabs on my mom as I should. "And how are you doing?"

"Oh, me? I'm holding up, DJ. Hanging in there."

Fuck. Hanging in there is code for *pills*.

"I'll come back tonight," I say.

"No, no, no. Absolutely not," she says. "We'll be fine. You need to do your thing at school. I just wanted to update you and not keep you in the dark."

I rub my thumb and forefinger against my forehead.

"When can I speak with Felicity?"

"She'll hopefully be out of the hospital tomorrow. She

was very weak today. She said to say hi, but she wasn't in the mood to talk."

"Mom, if *anything* changes, you call me, okay? I'm sorry I didn't pick up earlier today. I'll put my phone back on ring so I don't miss it. It's midterms and I've been trying to stay focused and get studying in."

"That's good, honey. You do everything you need to."

"I love you, Mom."

"Love you, too, honey. Goodbye."

I hang up and inhale a deep breath. Alex is staring at me with worried eyes. "Everything okay?"

I offer a false smile. "It's fine."

She comes over to my bed and sits next to me. "Doesn't sound too fine. Want to talk about it?"

My shoulders drop. "Trouble on the home front. I knew this would happen."

"What do you mean?"

I look at Alex, and a wave of heat hits me. I take a deep breath and blow it out, then turn to her.

"Do you want to go for a drive with me?"

"Where to?"

I shrug. "Anywhere. Let's just go. It's a nice fall day."

She hesitates.

"I don't really care where we go. Just that it's with you. We can talk in the car. It's a little stuffy in here sometimes, you know?" I brush her hair behind her ear. "Oh, come on. Don't say no now, *temptress*."

She rolls her eyes and finally I see that classic Alex grin. "Alright, *incubus*. Let's go."

WE HEAD out in my Range Rover, driving through the hills

of northwestern Illinois, driving on country roads toward nowhere in particular.

Alex doesn't say anything as I drive, the sun's golden light ebbing as it falls toward the horizon. It's a comfortable silence. We're used to hanging out in the room together and not having to keep talking to each other nonstop. But after a few minutes I feel the urge to break it.

"My life is anything but perfect," I finally say.

"What's up? If you feel like sharing."

"Well," I start, turning onto a road that angles directly into the sun. I put on my shades. "I suppose it started when I was in high school. That was the first time we found out my dad was cheating."

"Seriously?"

I nod.

"Damn." She blows out a loud breath, then turns to me. "I want you to know that I really do feel bad for assuming you had, like, the perfect upbringing."

"It's okay. Everyone does."

I find I'm driving on the same road I took to Bald Bluff where I snapped my photos the other day. It's the golden hour, and I figure it'll be gorgeous there now, so I continue down the two-lane country road that brings us there.

"No, it's not okay," Alex says, putting her hand on my shoulder and squeezing. "People shouldn't judge a book by its cover."

"But they always do. That's why we *have* covers," I point out. "And I'm a blue-eyed white boy from rural Illinois with a dorm building named after me. They don't know that the whole *reason* the dorm is named for my grandfather is because when he passed away, he and my grandmother left all their millions—*every penny*—to the University. They didn't leave us a dime."

"Holy shit. Really?!"

I nod. "Grandpa and Grandma Dalton loved Greene State. They met here. And when my father rebelled against him and slighted the family business, Gramps didn't take too well to it. I was young, but I still remember the air of tension at our family parties when my dad and Gramps would be together."

We pull up to the Mississippi River, and there's a breeze rolling toward us from the west as we watch the sunset.

Alex's face lights up when we arrive and gets out of the car. The whole place is empty. Not another car in sight, tonight.

"Oh my gosh!" She displays a wide grin. "It's beautiful! That picture you showed me doesn't even do it justice!"

She runs toward the cliff, and I get out of the car to chase after her. "Careful," I say. "Long way down. It's not a beach."

When I get to her, she's spinning around and leans her butt on the metal railing.

She's got jeans and a hoodie on, and her black hair blows around in the wind.

"Thanks for taking me here," she says. "I really miss the water."

A few more pirouettes and she looks out over the Mississippi. "You're right. So Beautiful."

We work our way down to the spot where I saw the couple lying the first time I came here and we lie down on a blanket I brought.

"Question," she says. "So how did you buy a Range Rover if you're not rich?"

I snort. "First of all, it's used. Second, I bought it with my own money."

"How did you make your own money?"

"I'm a knife salesman in the summer."

"You're joking." The look on her face is priceless.

"I'm not. Any shot at an NFL contract and a payday is a long ways away. College athletes don't make any money. So if you know anyone who needs some kitchen cutlery? I'm your man. The commissions really aren't bad, let me tell you."

We both sit propped up on our elbows. The breeze is tamer down here with the way the cliff blocks the wind, and we can watch the last hour or so of the sunset comfortably.

She turns with a furrowed brow toward me. "So what was going on with your mom today specifically? If you don't mind me asking."

I hesitate. But then I figure this isn't something I'd probably share with the guys. They don't need to know about my family drama. Plus, most people don't understand.

"My sister has serious body image issues...and depression. She had the worst sophomore year of high school a girl could have, right when I was about to head to the West Coast to play football at USC. But I turned the offer down, stayed in Davenport and went to a community college to make sure she got treatment. Because my mom and dad seemed content to just pretend everything was fine and dandy! Anyway, she was doing okay for a while until her boyfriend broke up with her a few days ago, and now she's had a relapse. Which might be triggered by my dad being shady and distant. I mean, he does live in Galesburg for the whole fall term. It's not a good situation, because then my mom will probably start self-medicating with pain pills...again."

"It's like a whole chain reaction," Alex comments.

"Yep, our family is a web. When I was in high school, I pretty much made it my job to be the glue and hold us all together. I feel really guilty about not being back home right now to help with this crisis."

She inches her elbows toward me, and I can feel body heat radiating from her. She looks so sexy, even with messy hair, wearing a hoodie.

Her soft hand runs through my hair. "Your parents can't expect you to parent."

"Maybe, but my sister...she needs someone."

"Are your parents helping her?"

"My mom is. At least she's in the hospital getting treatment. I just think I should be there. I'm going to leave tomorrow."

"Don't you have a football game tomorrow?"

I shrug. "I'll just skip it for now. And my dad isn't letting me start on the team, even though I'm way better than our senior starter. It's like he's fucking with me.

"I can't believe I haven't seen one of your games yet."

"If I'm ever starting, I'll let you know."

She nods, then sits up, and narrows her eyes at me. "So what about you and your trauma?"

"My trauma?"

"Yes. Your sister is depressed, your mom relies on pills sometimes...what's your trauma?"

"Besides Jessica?"

"Yes. And great job ignoring her, by the way. I haven't seen her around in a while."

"Me neither," I say.

"That's not your trauma, though. Being cheated on doesn't count. Or are you really Mr. Perfect, the glue guy who holds his family together?"

She pushes up the sleeve of my flannel shirt, takes hold of my forearm and rubs it.

"Hmm. I've never thought about it like that."

"Or were you just born this sexy beast with a golden tongue for going down on a girl?"

I squint. "Who told you about that?"

"Oh, word gets around. You'd be surprised."

I laugh. "Well, I appreciate you calling me a sexy beast. But no, I wasn't always like that."

"Do tell."

I guess this is confession time. What the hell. "Jessica told everyone about that during high school before she cheated on me. But honestly, if I was so golden-tongued, why did she cheat?"

"Some people just want more than their fair share," she says. "Jessica seems like one of those, to be honest. And judging from my interactions with her, I think you've dodged a bullet."

I smile. "Thanks."

She shrugs and then scoots in a little closer to me, lets go of my forearm and lays her head on my stomach. "Maybe you just weren't the one for her. And she had a tough time letting you down."

"I suppose."

We sit in silence for a while. I wrap my arm around her stomach. Warmth flows through my body, and I buzz with her touch. I don't know what we're doing—I don't know if we'll hook up. And I kind of like the ambiguity, actually. For right now, we're just a couple of friends chatting about deep thoughts.

And that's when I realize I've been the one doing all the chatting.

"You're a great listener," I say.

"Why, thank you."

"So what about you? What traumas have you been through?"

I feel her abdominal cavity clench.

"Quite a few."

"Care to share?"

"My father tried to kill my mother, then committed suicide. Then my mother died of cancer a year later."

My skin tingles, and a heavy feeling takes over my stomach. "Oh my gosh. I'm so sorry to hear that."

"Yeah. I was seven when my dad died, and eight when my mom died from cancer. My family is like yours—we like to keep our problems hidden until they explode."

I pull her in tighter to me. "So where did you go? What did you do after that?"

She nods. "Since both my parents were dead, I got to move in with my Aunt Mia in San Francisco at age eight. Life was okay for a while. She taught me a lot. She was the best mother—and father figure, come to think of it—that I ever had."

I could tell there was more to that, so I ask her, "Yeah? So what were some of the good times you had with her?"

Alex sits up with memories in her eyes, "She loved the libraries around there and she'd take me a lot. She was a big reader, something my parents were never into, so I learned a lot about things through books. We'd read the same book and have our own 'book review group', just the two of us, and discuss the aspects of the story. I think that's where my interest in psychology came into play. You know? I think I'm lucky, actually. Compared to some of the shit other people go through."

We sit up, and I wrap my arm around her.

The sun has set now, and we both look at the river as it flows along.

"I don't even know what to say. Alex, God, what you've been through —I can't imagine how that must feel."

"Honestly, it makes me happy for every day I'm alive," she says. "My mom was the inspiration for my first tattoo. The golden retriever was her spirit animal."

Without warning, she whips up her hoodie and shows me the tattoo of a happy dog on her skin just above her bra. "See? It's like she's always got my back."

She pulls up the back of her hoodie, but I don't forget the impression of her flesh and that beautiful coffee with cream color of her skin.

She tells me about her aunt, her therapy and how things worked out for the best for her. Her parents were toxic and it would have infected her had things not have happened the way they did. She was young enough to overcome it and learn from it.

"Wow," I say, holding her hand tighter. "You barely even show it. How do you do it?"

She shrugs. "I don't know. I just do. I think I'm lucky for my Aunt Mia and my friends."

I nod. "That reminds me of a story my Grandpa Dalton used to tell. Have you heard the story of the alcoholic father with two children?"

"Tell me."

"Two men are born to an alcoholic father. While they're children, he's really bad, always acting out, doesn't treat his wife right."

"Wow, okay."

"So the first son sees how bad his father has become because of the drinking. He works his ass off and vows never to drink. His path is difficult, but he eventually finds a light at the end of the tunnel, and from his hard work he starts his own business and makes something great of himself. Now, the second man sees his father and decides that's 'just the way he is too.' He drinks, gambles, and dies an early death."

"Wow. And?"

"So on both of the brother's deathbeds, they are asked, 'why did you turn out the way you are?' The successful businessman and the lazy alcoholic both have the exact same answer: 'My father was an alcoholic.'"

She pumps my hand. "I just got chills."

"You impress me, Alex," I say, and it's true.

We sit in silence for a few moments, until she giggles.

"Think we could go surfing on the Mississippi River?"

I laugh. "I don't think we'd want to try it. It's so muddy. Why, you want to go surfing?"

"I'm kidding of course. I guess I have a 'thing' about surfing. My dad used to always promise me he'd take me surfing. He never did. He had a lot of those empty promises."

"Damn. Sorry to hear that."

"Let's chat about something lighter," she says. "I'm feeling really heavy right now."

"Yeah, you're right."

"I mean it's good to cover these topics. Better to dig them up and expose them than to keep them buried. But wait, there's one more trauma I have to tell you about, I mean, since we've bared our souls tonight," she says with a grin.

"Oh, boy. What's that?" I brace myself, because honestly what else could this girl have gone through.

"Well, when I got to college, they put me in the boys' dorm," she says.

I chuckle and raise an eyebrow. "Oh? And that was traumatizing how?"

"Very bad. Luckily I met these great girlfriend and we all got matching Triangle tattoos."

"Sounds horrible."

"Well, it wouldn't have been so bad...if they didn't put me with the sexiest one of them all."

I lie back, and she climbs on top of me. My erection presses up into my jeans, barely held back.

"That sounds awful. You must have a ton of tension built up with this guy."

"I do." Her voice sounds extra sexy right now as she slowly moves her hips, straddling me.

I fist a clump of her hair in my hand and guide her body slowly down to my face for a kiss.

Through the hoodie I can feel the weight of her body on me and I love it. Her hands pressing lightly into my chest. Her lips are soft. When she opens her mouth, my tongue races in, and I twist it against her piercing.

"I love the way you taste," she whispers.

"Me, too. Want to get out of here and go back to the room? Promise I won't jump your bones, but I'm feeling the chill now that the sun's almost gone."

She giggles. "Yeah, agreed. What do you want to do in the room?"

"Oh, I don't know. I could think of a few things."

"So can I." She laughs, then lowers her voice. "A little light making out never hurt anyone, did it?"

"Not that I'm aware of," I joke.

We get in the car and head back, and I know she's right.

I won't let things get out of hand. I have her back now and I don't want to lose her.

As I drive back to campus, I call my dad. "I'm not going to the game tomorrow," I tell my dad over the phone.

"What?! Boy, you've got another thing coming if you think you can just cop out like that.

I raise my voice. "Felicity just texted me, and I can tell she's in a bad spot. Mom is on the brink of...who knows what. So yeah, I'm not going. Why should I? You're keeping me out of the lineup for being one fucking minute late, anyway."

I'm frustrated when I hang up. Alex puts her hand on my shoulder and massages it.

"You alright?"

I shake my head. "I'm going back to Davenport tonight. I'll drop you off at campus. I have a bad feeling."

"Really?" She asks.

I nod. "As much as I want to hang out with you...family has to come first."

"I get that," she says. "And I respect it."

Damn if I don't want to spend tonight with Alex, though.

But I've just got a funny feeling about something.

28

DJ

Sunday afternoon I head back to the Greene State campus.

My sister wasn't as bad as I thought. Neither was my mom. Better safe than sorry, though.

But I still get the feeling like there's something they're hiding from me, and it bothers me that I can't tell what or why.

A few of the guys call me and they're concerned, but I just don't feel like talking with them right now.

I want Alex.

As I'm pulling up to campus, I see her name buzzing on my phone.

"Hey," she says. "Everything alright?"

"Yeah, it's not as bad as I thought...I think."

"Okay. Well...can you do me a favor? I need to stop at the pharmacy for some snacks."

"A snack?"

"Yes. My pretzel supply is really low."

I shrug. "Okay."

I wait in the parking lot for ten minutes until she comes

down. I drive her over to the pharmacy, and there's a notable electricity in the air during the ride.

She grabs what she needs, and when we pull back into campus and I park, she catches me staring.

"What?" She asks, flipping her hair.

I can't resist.

I kiss her.

I intend to make it just a peck, but once our lips are together, I can't let go.

Neither can she.

Next thing I know, my hand is rubbing her thigh and Alex is petting my cock over the fabric of my jeans. It's dark and we have no shame. Even if it was still light out, I don't think we would. She leans onto me awkwardly from the passenger's seat, and we make out like it's quarter to twelve on prom night and we have a midnight curfew.

"Hold on," I manage to spit out. "Let's get to the room."

She nods, and we walk briskly across the street, into the Dalton building and head up the stairs. A few people try to say hello to us as we walk by and ask what we're doing, but neither me nor Alex see them. I'm holding her hand, leading her to the room, and it feels like we're in a fog.

We barely close the door behind us before I attack her. She eagerly accepts my assault as I press her up against the blinds, kissing her lips. I work my mouth down the side of her jawline to her ear and slide my tongue onto her neck. I feel her tremble and I stop.

"Hey," I say, massaging her cheek with the back of my hand. "You okay?"

She nods but doesn't say anything or make eye contact. I take a step back.

"Look, if you don't want to do this, we should stop right now." I rub my forehead and wipe the sweat.

Her dark eyes are radiant. "I want to do this. I want everything with you, DJ."

"I'm obsessed with your body. I'm obsessed with you. Do you realize how hard it is not to stare at you all day?"

She shakes her head. "Enlighten me."

"Don't mind if I do. First things first. There's your *voice*. The way you talk kills me."

"I think I have a monotonous voice."

"I think it's amazing."

"Go on then."

I run my hand over the tattoo of a triangle on her inner right wrist. "How did you decide on a triangle?"

She blushes. "It's a delta, symbolizing change."

"Then there's your smile. Your soft lips which are like landing pads for me." I kiss her sweetly and deeply for a minute, then pull off.

I go on. "Of course, your skin is amazing. So soft and beautiful." I run my fingers slowly down her cheek to her neck and clavicle, stopping just short of her breasts.

I can feel her heart racing, and her breath shortening. "Keep going," she whispers, a smile pulling at her mouth. "I like this game."

"And then there are your hips." Leading her over to my bed, I straddle her body with my legs, running my hands back and forth along the skin I find between the fabric of her hoodie and jeans.

"Kind of hard to play this game in this clothing. Let me help you out," she says, and points her arms straight up in the air. I help her pull her hoodie off, revealing the grey tank top she has on underneath.

She smiles and slips her hands under my flannel, running them over my abs. I can tell she likes those.

"Anything else you want to mention?" she asks.

"Yes, your eyes. I love how they're dark." I squint. "Would you call them black or brown?"

"They're black when I'm angry. Dark brown when I'm not."

"*That's* the mystery I've been trying to solve. Finally, it makes sense," I smirk.

"Anything else you're missing?"

"Voice, skin, hips, eyes," I say, counting on my finger. I tap my chin.

"What about these?" grabbing my forearms, she places my hands on her tits, and I get an instant jolt of energy straight to my loins.

"What? Your boobs? Hardly noticed 'em."

She chortles. "Okay. Now I *know* you're lying. They're impossible to hide."

"They *are* nice. What size are they?"

Her eyes widen. "You seriously haven't secretly checked my bra size while we've been living together?"

"I might stare at you, but I *do* try to give you your privacy. I'm damn impressed."

"Take your best guess," she says.

I close my eyes. "Maybe if I got a closer look I could make a more accurate assessment."

"By all means," she smiles, sticking her hands up in the air. I help her pull her top off. While I'm leaning in, she grabs my head, nibbles my ear and whispers, "Let me help you get this flannel off, too. You know, so we're even."

Alex's focused eyes, wearing just her bra and focused on unbuttoning my flannel turns me on so much.

"So is it okay if I stare at your tits now? Because I am," I announce. "Newsflash: they're amazing."

"Thank you," she smirks and she takes down the last button. "So are yours."

I grin, biting my lower lip. "My boobs are amazing?"

"Yeah, your boobs. They're really incredible. You do have a bigger chest than a lot of guys." She laughs. "Well, and these..." She rolls her hand slowly along the ridges of my ab muscles.

"You can do more than just touch them," I whisper in her ear.

Leaning down, she kisses my flat stomach just above my belly button.

I can't hold back any longer. I grab her hips and position her body so we're pressing together lengthwise on my twin bed. I cup her ass with one hand and her tit with the other. She grinds into me and moans deeply as our mouths find each other for another kiss.

She pulls back. "You still haven't made your guess on what size they are."

"My brain is scrambled right now. Let's just say they're really nice. Whatever they are, they're perfect."

"Damn, you're good!" She grins, smiling. "They're perfect! How did you guess?"

I reach my hand around her back and snap her bra off. "I don't know, but I think I deserve a reward for that."

"Which would be?"

"This."

I flip her onto her back and make out with her for several minutes.

At one point, she stops kissing me and opens her eyes.

"So I'm your reward?"

I nod. "Yes."

"I like that."

She tips her hips up and into me, sparks flying between our denim. I can't get enough of the feel of the hot flesh of her soft breasts as they press into my hard chest. I'm so turned on right now, I worry my cock may rip right through these jeans.

I cup her ass and then let my hand slide up to her tits, then lick down her neck until it's perfectly positioned to flick my tongue lightly on her nipple, then use extra tenderness when doing the same with her nipple ring. She arches her back and lets out a simpering moan, nails digging into the mattress as her body writhes underneath me.

"Oh God, DJ," she mutters. I enjoy every second of how she tastes, of how privileged I am to suck her beautiful tits. I love how her voice sounds when she moans softly, and I love how her hand feels, running through my hair.

Finally, my right hand steals its way down her stomach and lands between her legs, rubbing softly between them.

She is *hot* and she is *wet*.

Her hand slides down my abs, landing square on my cock.

"You're hard," she mewls, her mouth hanging open, eyes half-lidded.

"Wonder why that would be," I smirk.

"No idea." Her eyes flicker with some sort of amusement. "So what about you?"

"What do you mean, what about me?" I ask.

"Are you going to make me guess?"

I laugh. "You've seen me before."

"Yeah, but I didn't get a close look."

"Well, we can certainly fix that."

I stand up and pull off my jeans. She puts her legs up like she's a dead beetle, and I help her take her socks and jeans off so she's just lying on my bed in panties and nothing else.

Nothing else.

"Fuck, you're sexy," I manage to say, because I can barely *think* I'm so turned on right now.

"You, too," she says, and gives me the sexiest once over anyone's ever given me. "Those abs…" Her hand slides slowly down the ridges of my washboard stomach, until her fingers reach my boxers and she hesitates.

"May I?" she asks.

"Please," I grit out, my voice gravelly. "Do the honors."

She pulls my boxers down slowly, revealing my cock inch-by-inch until it springs free and slaps against my abs.

"Ohh! That's fun," she jokes, and then puts her hand on my base and gently pulls me toward her. I let out a bear-like groan. She licks her lips and focuses on my cock. "I don't have any guesses yet. Let's see, though." Her left hand lands on my cock and she turns over on her side a little, bringing her mouth closer.

"Wow. You're really hard. Definitely a two-hander…and my hands aren't small. Let's see what else I can fit on here."

Leaning in, she stretches her tongue out and just barely nicks my tip.

Even that tiny touch of her tongue launches a quiver of desire up my spine. Her eyes find mine, and I run a hand through her long black hair. The metallic feel of her tongue ring adds to the sensation as she takes an inch or two of me in her mouth, then pulls back, making a popping sound.

Her tongue runs back and forth on my cock, and then she fists the slickness of her spit and my precum up and down, sending bolts of pleasure tearing through my body.

"Two hands and a mouth. That's the official measurement."

She runs her hand back and forth on me a few times, then kisses the head of my cock.

"You've got a beautiful cock," she says, licking her lips. "I'm sure you know that, though."

I smile. "Rest assured, I've had my cock called many things but 'beautiful' is not one of them."

Wrapping a hand around my ass muscles, she pulls me forward, closer to the bed, and takes me into her mouth.

A loud groan escapes me, and I throw my head back in ecstasy. She expertly swirls her tongue and mouth in tandem with the hand she slides and twists up and down from the base of my cock and back. With how incredibly turned on I am, I'm leaking cum, and she doesn't seem to mind it. My throat bubbles up with a deep growl, and I bring my head back down and watch her. God, she looks sexy, so focused on my cock. Alex is a giver and I'm the beneficiary of her generosity. And expertise.

Fuck, she is good.

My heart speeds and I slide a hand onto her nipple with the piercing, which makes her tense and moan. I'm gentle. I switch my hand to her other breast, and I flick my thumb over it a little harder.

She flips her body into position and takes me as deep as she can, then taps her tongue on the underside of my cock. Feeling the metal of her piercing as she slowly draws her mouth back makes me shake with pleasure. Without thinking, I grip her breast just a little harder, and the vibrations of her humming vocal chords reverberate through her whole body, and I feel my orgasm hovering. And it's going to be an explosion.

"Stop," I mutter, but she smiles—*yes, as much as you can smile with a cock in your mouth*—and keeps going.

I fist her hair and yank her away from my dick. She lets out several deep, greedy breaths.

"Do you want a fucking volcano in your mouth?" I mutter. "Because that's what's about to happen."

She licks her lips and parts them. "I mean I've already swallowed plenty. You've got a leaky hose down there."

"If you think I'm going to come yet, well, you've got something else coming."

She sticks her legs straight in the air, and I accept her invitation to slide off her panties. I kneel next to her in bed for a moment, hands on my hips, and I take a few breaths just to admire her. Her long black hair sprawls out on the bed behind her. Dark eyes full of fury.

The feeling I got in my gut when I first saw her, that was *real*. She wanted me just as much as I wanted her.

"Stop staring at me like that. I'm getting afraid you might eat me."

I lick my lips. "And whatever would give you that idea?"

Her breaths are short. "Just be careful, okay. My piercing is sensitive. You don't have to do much."

My eyes widen. "You have a piercing *down there,* too?!"

She smirks. "I have many more secrets. You don't even know."

"Maybe I'll have to torture them out of you."

She snorts with laughter and I spread her legs slowly, and slide my hand across the flesh of her thigh until it lands right on her clit, and her stomach tenses.

"Be gentle until I'm warmed up," she adds.

I nod, and watch her body twist as I barely press into her clit with my middle finger.

"Oh, fuck *me*, DJ," she utters, and throws a hand over her mouth.

I grab her wrist with my free hand. "Just what are you doing?"

"Keeping quiet."

"Why?"

"Uh, I don't know."

With my hand still pressing into her clit, I hover my face close to her and kiss her on the cheek. "Please don't stifle your moans. That's how I know if I'm doing a good job."

She nods and I press a little harder. Her mouth jumps to my shoulder and she bites me.

She fucking *bites* me.

"Ow, fuck!"

"Oh shit, sorry! You okay?"

I raise an eyebrow. "A biter?"

"Yes," she admits. "Hot?"

"Hot. Now that I know, I'll be ready...but you better be ready, too."

She laughs. "I'm ready for whatever you have to give me."

She's as wet as a river now, and I press a little harder into her clit with one hand, while I kneel at her side on the bed and massage her neck with my thumb. I run my finger up and into her mouth, and she sucks it. Her hand reaches up and grabs the base of my cock.

"I just need..." she stumbles on her words, breaths escaping her. "...something to anchor me down so I don't fly away."

Well she's not wrong about that.

I finger her clit for a while longer, listening to her moans and answering the swivels of her hips with the perfect touch. I don't even know how long I do this for. A minute, ten, a half hour?

All I know is eventually, she's begging for more.

"Please go inside," she mewls. "Please."

"Well, when you ask so nicely," I grin. "How can I refuse?"

Kneeling to the side of her on the bed, I slide two fingers inside and curl them gently.

She lets out a yelp and grabs my arm and bites it. A gravelly groan emanates from the back of my throat.

"Sorry," she says when she lets her teeth off.

"Trying to mark your territory, are you?"

"Oh fuck, I'm going to come, DJ," she whimpers.

Leaning up, she lunges forward and plunges her mouth onto my cock as I wrap my fingers into her.

"Mmm," she moans and then lets her lips pull away from me so she can scream.

Her entire body shakes and she lifts up her hips and drags her nails down across my abs lightly, almost tickling me, and a few moments later she's breathing hard and looks exhausted.

"I just came," she mutters. "Your turn."

I shake my head. "No. I still haven't gotten to taste you. I've been dying to."

"Why don't you just fuck me?" she says, point blank.

"Are you on the pill?"

"No."

"Do you have condoms?"

She narrows her eyes. "You don't have condoms?"

I shrug. "I wasn't really planning on this tonight."

She sighs. "Well...what else can we do?"

I'm full of lust, and I can't *not* go the night without tasting Alex. So I do what any reasonable man would do. I kneel down on the rug, flip her body around so her legs are hanging off the bed to the side, wrap my hands around her legs, and gently lick her already soaking wet pussy.

I say *gently*, because as much as I want to devour her, a clit piercing is a new thing to me and I need to hold back and be careful with her.

Plus, the way her whole body is shaking, I think my gentle tonguing and sucking of her clit is doing just the trick.

She rocks her clit back and forth into me, and I wrap a hand around and bring two fingers into her.

"Coming again," she moans. *Already? Damn.* I love how easy this piercing makes it for her to come.

Or maybe I should give myself at least a little credit.

Climbing back into bed, I put her legs up against my shoulders and dive down into her again, but she grabs a tuft of my hair and pulls me up.

"No, no, no. I want to taste you again, D."

"Is that my new nickname?"

She giggles. "Don't get a big head or anything. I'm too lazy to say DJ all the time."

"I like it. And I've got an idea for us to both get our way."

"Oh? What's that?"

I scooch my body over so I'm on the bed, and we're head to toe. She's lying next to me.

"Sixty-nine," I say with a smirk.

"Oh. I've never done that."

"Hop on. Don't be shy."

She doesn't hesitate, and the next thing I know, my tongue is on her again and my cock is taken in by her magical mouth. I love the weight of her tits on my abs as she bobs up and down on me.

I wrap my arms around her waist, and as much as I want to see what she's doing that is making me feel so amazing, I love how I can make her wiggle in this position. Her body shudders again, and I wonder if she's coming. I damn well hope so.

I feel some combination of her hands, mouth, and tongue on me as she slides up and down, slick hands on my rock-hard erection. I gyrate up and down a little, rocking my hips into her.

Our bodies press together in an explosion of sixty-nine heat and sweat and sex.

For a moment, I pull her hands behind her back, forcing her to sit up and on my face. She's hesitant at first, but I think my enthusiasm overrides any shyness she might have, and she's twisting into me as she comes again.

I know because she tells me, even though her words are barely a whimper at this point.

She lifts her body up and off me, then kneels between my legs and pushes her hair behind her head.

"D, tell me how you want me to finish you," she says as she runs her hand up and down on my cock.

I bite my lip. "I'd be lying if I said I didn't want to fuck your tits."

"Well, I'm glad you're not lying." She looks down. "Fuck these things? And how would you do that?"

I narrow my eyes. "You've never done that?"

She shakes her head. "Never."

"So I get to take your boobs' V card?" I exclaim.

"Let's not make a big deal out of it."

She lies down on her back and I position my legs on either side, straddling her upper body. I slide my cock between her breasts, and just enjoy the beautiful view for a moment. When I lean back with one arm for balance, I find myself fondling her clit again—*instinct*—but she grabs my arm. "Nah-ah. This is about you, now. This is about D."

Grabbing my cock, she pulls me toward her face and leans forward at the same time, then takes me to the back of her throat, leaving me nice and slick.

She puts my cock between her tits and then presses them together.

"You like that?" she asks, and I nod vigorously.

"Very much," I grit out.

"Good. I like watching you do it."

Her eyes flicker with excitement and that turns me on even more. I press her boobs together myself and she grabs hold of my ass and slides her hands around my hips.

It's so damn hot and this is goddamn reckless abandon, and I feel like I can do anything sexually with this woman, like I'm free and she's my toy and I'm hers, too. I pump my cock between her tits again and she lets out a moan that puts me over the edge.

"Gonna come," I growl. "Where should I come."

"My tits, baby," she says throatily, and next thing I know I spurt ropes all over her breasts and neck. By some miracle, none gets on her face.

When it's all over, both of our hearts are racing.

She looks down at her chest, and then up at me.

"Wow."

"I would say sorry, but that would be a lie."

She touches a tiny bit of the liquid with her finger and taps her tongue. "You taste good, actually. I mean, I already tasted you before."

I laugh as I unstraddle her and go grab a towel. "I'll let you taste me as much as you want, babe. By the way, let me just say you kind of look hot as hell right now."

"Thanks."

I wipe her off, wipe myself off, and then lean down to kiss her. I envisioned a peck, but it ends up being a long, lingering kiss that promises more.

She takes my hand and I stand there for a minute, next to her.

"So...shower?" I ask.

"Definitely."

Luckily, Friday night means that our floormates are out drinking, so we have the floor bathroom all to ourselves.

Then Alex and I collapse under just my bedsheet, naked.

She presses her ass into me and my arm is all wrapped around me.

"Hey," she whispers as we fall asleep.

"Good night, DJ."

"Good night yourself."

"And you better get some condoms tomorrow."

"Roger that."

As we're drifting off, her phone buzzes.

"Need it?" I ask, reaching for it on her nightstand.

"No," she says, waving it off. "I don't care who it is."

I fall asleep against her, and I haven't slept so well since I got to school. Judging by her relaxed breathing, I don't think she has, either.

29

ALEX

The soothing sound of a rainstorm on our glass window wakes me up the next morning. The grey skies outside contrast deeply with the hot afterglow of sex and a copious amount of orgasms radiating from within me. I can still feel DJ's body pressing against mine as we did all those dirty things last night. They weren't things I would normally do, but with him I could do them. A faint smile comes across my face as I think about each moment with him.

I scoot backwards in DJ's bed, excited to press into him, but I end up backing my butt up into the wall before I realize he's not there.

I wonder if maybe he went to get condoms, and I wait around for a few minutes, stretching and gradually waking up.

He doesn't come back, though, and I notice his backpack and computer are gone from his desk. At the same time, there's no message from him on my phone.

I read for a little while, but after an hour, a sinking feeling rocks through my chest and I wonder where he could be, and why he would not text me after something like last night.

By ten a.m. he's still not around and I head to the library to study for the afternoon, read the books Professor Z gave me, and brainstorm possible research proposals. My mind is really flowing today, and I come up with several good ideas which I email to Professor Z.

By the late afternoon I'm ready to be done with work for the weekend. April has texted me that there's a low-key Sunday night party tonight and to bring something cute but formal so we can get ready and drink at her dorm.

I pack my backpack with my dress and shoes, as well as my makeup, and bring the bottle of whisky sitting on my desk.

As I walk over, the sinking feeling still sits inside me. What I had with DJ last night felt so *real.*

To get to the girls' dorm I have to pass the Lambda house, and when I do I see a few guys out on their porch, drinking outside, wearing raincoats.

DJ's right. They *are* the creepy frat.

I realize my hands are in tight fists, so I loosen them consciously. *Herman.* Ugh. It's not that he's a *bad* guy himself. But he is a psuedo-creep, at least. After the night I turned him down, he seemed to lose interest in texting me during the day, but sure enough he would text me from time to time, only between the hours of midnight and two to see if I wanted to come over and 'hang out.'

Even though I don't look at the Lambda house as I walk past, I get the feeling I'm being watched. I walk faster.

Is he doing the same thing Herman decided to do after I turned him down? Is he somehow...ghosting me?

I can't believe he would after the moments we shared yesterday. What I felt for DJ was way different than what I'd ever felt for a guy before. Not only did I have this visceral attraction to him, but once I learned what was behind his sea blue eyes, I wanted him *more.*

My heart races with anxiety. Maybe he drove back to Davenport to be with his sister and his mom. That's the only plausible excuse I can give him. But couldn't he give me a heads up?

A girl from one of my classes is heading inside the dorm area, and she opens the door for me so I head to Maya and April's room. April opens the door with a straightener in her hair. Maya is lying down on the bed, staring up at the ceiling.

"Hey," I smile, coming inside. "I brought whisky!"

"Good. That's good. We'll need that tonight," April said in a slightly shushed voice.

"What's the matter?" I ask. "Why are you talking like that?"

April takes a deep breath, and glances over at Maya. I've never seen her like this.

"Babe, do you want me to tell her?" April says.

Maya just nods with her arms folded, her expression glazed over. "You tell her."

My palms sweat, and I half-sit at the foot of Maya's bed.

"Maya's parents," April says, "are getting a divorce."

So that's why they're so gung ho about a Monday night party.

I glance at Maya, then look back at April. "You just found this out."

Maya clears her throat. "Just found out an hour ago." She sits up in bed. "They were the most in-love couple I ever knew. I learned everything I know about being sex positive... and for what?"

"Come here," I say, and slide over on her bed to hug her. "That sucks. It really does. I'm sorry."

We hug, and when she pulls back she looks at me like I'm an alien. "Are your parents married? Sorry, I just realized we've never talked about this and I have no idea how. I know you mentioned your aunt raised you."

I try to loosen up by rolling my shoulders a little. "We've talked about it...but I kind of glazed over the details."

I tell them the story. She puts her hand over her heart.

"Dear God! I mean, sorry. Wow. I just wasn't expecting that. You're so put together. I wouldn't expect it."

"I was eight when it happened. I guess that's lucky, in a way. You're eighteen, so this is going to affect you a lot differently. But the fact is, a lot of parents get divorces once their kids move away to college. It's a thing. And you're the youngest. Stop me if I'm overstepping. I'm doing a lot of research in this area. I've kind of lived through a lot of weird stuff." I unzip my bag and take out the bottle of whisky. "You know what's funny, though? I've stopped talking to most people about the full story around their death because they feel sorry for me. But the truth is, I've become so much stronger and independent because of those things. It's true what they say, what doesn't kill you makes you stronger."

Maya stands up and grabs a few shot glasses. "Am I an asshole if I say that hearing you say these horrible things you've experienced in your life makes me feel better already?"

"No, absolutely not. Happiness is relative."

My thoughts wander back to a book Professor Z gave me, *Man's Search for Meaning*. And how the narrator found happiness—some slice of it, at least—in the greatest humanitarian disaster of the twentieth century.

Maya pours us three shots of whisky. "To us," she says.

"To our friendship. I freaking love you both from the bottom of my heart."

We cheer and take the shots and it feels good.

"So, where were *you* last night?" April says when we finish. "You didn't respond to any of my snaps."

"Oh. Yeah. I was..."

I look down and clear my throat, deciding what to share with them. When I blush, Maya's eyes widen.

"So I kind of hooked up with DJ last night."

"No!" April yells.

"Oh my gosh! I knew your skin had sex afterglow! Tell. Us. Everything." She's like a hawk when it comes to reading people's sexual activity. I should have known there would be no escaping.

Maya nods, surprisingly unfazed. At least I got her mind off of her worries. "Tell me about it. Was he good, were you drunk, how big is his business, are the cunnilingus rumors true, etc.? You know. The important details."

"Well, he got some weird news from back home, so we went to the Mississippi River and hung out for a little while on Friday. He came back Sunday and we kissed...and I realized that DJ isn't as big of a spoiled asshole as I thought. He's actually a decent guy."

"Oh, come on, like you wouldn't want to screw an asshole," Maya says, then narrows her eyes at her own comment. "Huh. That sounds a little dirty when you say it out loud. Anyway, go on."

"So we got back home and we couldn't keep our hands off each other." I shudder with pleasure, thinking of how sexy DJ looked when I finally got his boxers off.

"What was *that*?" April asks.

"Um, you just like, *shook*."

I clear my throat. "Did not."

"Yes, you did," Maya seconds. "You literally just wiggled in your seat."

"Okay, fine. DJ is *very* hot. I was thinking of him just now. I was so turned on the whole time we were doing stuff and I came multiple times. That's never happened before. But the dam just burst and I couldn't hold it in anymore."

April parts her lips. "I wish someone would burst my dam."

Maya raises an eyebrow. "You're not going to get your dam burst when your boyfriend at home won't even *visit* you."

"He's been backed up, okay? He's working overtime lately. Anyway, sorry for interrupting. Go on. The more details, the better."

I smile, and decide I'll be channeling Maya for this explanation. If they want full details? Well I will give it to them. "Well, we didn't have any condoms. So we decided not to go all the way. His vibes were hot AF. Let me tell you about that dick though...it was like it had a magnet attached to my mouth. I couldn't help but always zone in on his pleasure as he was trying to please me so hard. And succeeding. Finally he caved and made us 69...fucking hot...where he arched my back and sucked my soul from my vagina."

April's jaw is practically on the floor. I get up and walk over to Maya's desk, where the whisky is and pour myself another drink.

Even Maya puts her hand over her heart, and I wonder if I've impressed even the queen of hookups. "How was *el grand finale*?" she asks.

I giggle. "Oh, he just titty fucked me and really seemed to enjoy it."

"That's totally hot," Maya says as she wiggles into her

jeans for the night, then glances at my chest. "I totally wish I had tits like yours, no lie."

Maya shrugs. "Same, although running track with those boobies would be a bitch."

"Jogging's not really my thing."

"Where did he...you know...by the way?" April asks.

"What are you talking about?"

"I think what my puritan friend here is trying to ask is, where did DJ's special sauce go?" Maya explains.

"Ewww! Gross!" April shrieks. "I'm never going to be able to eat at Taco Bell again."

"Honestly, I'd rather swallow than eat at Taco Bell," Maya says. "Unless I'm drunk."

"Wasn't the special sauce a McDonald's thing?" I chime in.

They laugh, and I sigh. Being friends with Maya means it's a requirement to tell all. Which, honestly, I wouldn't be ashamed of if DJ had freaking *talked* to me today.

Thunder strikes outside, adding a dramatic effect. "He came on my tits."

"Well done! Well done," Maya says, and pours a few more shots. "Welcome to the big girls' club, Al. I'm really proud of you."

"What are we cheersing to this time?"

"How about to Al's boobs?" April jokes.

"Done. May DJ forever be the beneficiary of your one beautiful, pierced nipple. And the other one, too. But right now we're cheersing to the pierced one."

We laugh and take the shot down. "I'm starting to feel it already. We should get some food."

"On it," April says. "I'll order us a couple of pizzas online."

"So when are you going to finish what you started?" Maya asks.

The unease returns, and I shift on the bed. "Well, he has not texted me all day today, and was mysteriously gone from the room when I woke up."

"What a dick!"

"Seems like they all are."

"Whatever. We're going to the cool frat tonight."

"There's a 'cool frat'?"

April and Maya nod together. "All the girls have been talking about it this week. Alpha Z guys are cool as shit."

"How do you know that?"

"Because Maya's in love with Grant and he's joining the Alpha Z's," April blurts out.

"Oh, please," Maya says. "I am *not* in love with Grant. He's not my type."

"Tall, shaggy-haired, handsome, and smart isn't your type?" I retort.

Maya shakes her head. "We're just friends."

"Just friends who hang out like every night!"

"We don't hang out every night."

"Sorry. Four nights a week."

"Have you two, you know, hooked up?"

Maya shakes her head. "God, no. I'm *telling* you two, it's not like that with Grant. We're just friends. Plus, I don't even know what he's up to right now. He hasn't texted me for a couple of days. We're chill like that."

"You need to give Alex the full story. You two *totally* had a Snap streak going for a week and then it broke yesterday, and you've been checking your phone every few minutes to see if he's snapped you."

"You know what? Enough about Grant. The point is, we're going to the Alpha Z house tonight and we're going to have a great time. It's a low-key party, nothing too out of control. Just a little basement beer pong happy hour thing. Just a few cool people and that's it."

I shrug. "A few cool people? Sounds good to me."

Maybe it will take my mind off of DJ for the night...*maybe.*

30

ALEX

We brave the pouring rain and make it to the Alpha Z house about a block away from campus. One of the fraternity brothers who knows Maya lets us inside, and to our surprise, the first floor is empty and totally quiet.

"So, uh, where's the party?" April asks.

"Downstairs," he says. "Leave your jackets over there." He points to a black leather couch in the front of the room, and we see a host of other jackets laying there.

As we head down the winding stairs to the basement, the music gets louder and an array of voices can be heard below.

Once at the bottom, we see a beer pong table in the middle, a bar countertop to the side of the room, and a mix of maybe thirty guys and girls standing around chatting.

Maya stops and puts her hand up. We both stop.

"What's up?" April asks.

Maya nods, and turns around to us. "This room has a good energy. Can you feel it?"

I shrug. "I think so."

April twists her face up. "How can you tell the energy of a room the minute you step inside? Isn't that a little ridiculous?"

Maya shakes her head vigorously. "Not at all. Our instincts process information one-hundred times faster than our brains. So you've got to go with your gut feeling."

"Come on, Al, back me up. There's no way Maya can be right about this. That's some new-agey-type stuff that my crazy Aunt Zelda talks about."

I look around, and people seem to be smiling, relaxed, and the girls have open body language.

"I have to hand it to Maya, I think there may be something to her crazy philosophy."

"Yes!" Maya says, pumping her arm.

Just then, a smiling guy in jeans, a white button-down and a blazer walks over to us.

"Hi. Welcome to the Alpha Z house. I'm Ian, the president of the house."

The guy is smiling so hard as he shakes our hands, I wonder if he has a problem. We tell him our names and he repeats them back to us.

"Maya, Alex, and Avril."

"It's actually April."

"April like the month. Got it. Well, thanks for coming over tonight, ladies."

"So, question," I say. "How are you having this party if you're on social probation?"

I tip my head in the direction of the thirty rack of Keystone Light on the bar top.

"Ah, we've got a smart one here," he says, tapping his head. "Well, the thing is, we're just breaking the rules tonight. If we get caught, we're fucked."

We all laugh. "No, really," I say.

"I'm dead serious," Ian says, stone-faced.

"Like they'll shut the party down?" April asks.

"No," he says, and I have no idea why he's still smiling. "Like they'll shut the fraternity down, most likely."

"So why are you having a party, again?"

He leads us over to the counter and grabs a can of beer for each of us and hands it out. It's cold.

He cracks a beer and we do the same. "We laid low for September. What are we going to do, *not* have a party all term? That's lame. Plus, who's going to tell? Almost all of the girls here are girlfriends of guys in the house. I know the name of every single person in here."

"Wait, so how did *we* get invited to this party?" I say, turning to Maya.

She shrugs, and looks Ian in the eye. "I hooked up with Turner."

Ian nods. "Did you?! I had no idea."

"You didn't? So why did you invite us?"

"Who invited you?" Ian says. "I know it wasn't Turner."

Maya blushes and presses her lips together. "Hmm, I kind of forget, honestly."

April crosses her arms. "Well, I didn't forget. It was Grant. Grant Taylor. Remember? He told you about this on Thursday."

"Okay, fine, he *may* have mentioned it to me."

"Definitely. It was Grant who said you three were legit. Anyway, have a good time, and let me know if Roger gives you any trouble." He looks down at the end of the bar and winks at a man with black hair and darker skin.

"Hey, fuck you, Scooter!" the guy says with an intense face. He instantly jumps off the bar stool and strides over to Ian with crazy eyes.

They bump chests and tip their chins back, staring each other down.

"What you gonna do about it? Huh? Punk," Ian says back to him. He's fuming.

"Guys, stand back," April says, putting her arms in front of me and Maya like a mother hen.

I look around and a few people glance at Ian and Roger, but no one seems to *care* that a major fight might break out between the president of the Alpha Z's and one of the brothers.

"I'm gonna fuck you up so bad, Scooter. You have no idea. Oh, man. I've just been waiting for this moment."

They keep chest bumping and staring at each other with these wide-open, crazy eyes like shit's about to go down.

"I'm going to crush you, then call your mom and let her know she can come pick you up because little Rogie couldn't take a little jokey-pooh."

"Oh, do *not* bring my mother into this. And don't use that voice, man. You know I can't stand that voice!"

"Guys!" April hands me her beer and squeezes in between the two of them. "Violence is not the answer! Please!"

Now a few people look over. But they don't seem freaked out at all. Instead, they're *laughing*.

April covers her head like she needs to shield herself from the blows.

My heart races, and Maya grips my shoulder hard. "Why does everyone else just think this is funny?"

Ian's fists are clenched. So are Roger's.

And then, just when I think they're about to start throwing fists, they burst out laughing.

"Oh, shit, man. That was good. Too good," Roger bellows in between laughs.

"Me? You should get a fucking Oscar! Did you see the looks on their faces!" Ian says, pointing to the three of us.

April grabs onto my arm, mortified. "Wait. That was...a joke?"

Ian and Roger slap hands and hug each other, still unable to stop laughing. "Works every time on the freshmen," Roger says. "I love you, man."

"Love you, too, son."

"Whoa. Son?" I cut in.

"Yeah," Roger says, putting his arm around Ian and taking a swig of beer. "Ian's my pledge dad. Helped me through some dark times last year."

Ian nods, that goofy smile still attached to his face. "So, welcome to the Alpha Z house, ladies. Now that you've officially been hazed, you're welcome here. Just remember the three rules. One: Let me know if you have a problem. Two: Drink but don't drink too much. And three: Have fun. Cool?"

"That was...hazing?"

"Yeah. We don't really believe in hazing, so that's about the extent to which we go."

"Wow. Cool," I say.

"So I'm getting a game of flip cup going," Roger says, unstacking some red Solo cups. "You guys want in?"

Maya puts her hand on my and April's shoulders and whispers in our ear. "Told you they were the cool frat."

I feel my phone buzz and I jump to get it.

My heart sinks when I see it's Herman, saying *'sup*.

I don't respond. Creeper.

Where are you, DJ?

31

ALEX

The night rolls on and the Alpha Z guys are absolutely hilarious. We have a blast playing flip cup all evening, and the vibe is a one-hundred-eighty-degree turn from the Lambda house.

Maya, April, and I take a break and huddle in the corner for a few minutes while we're waiting for our turn to play beer pong.

"Guys, is it weird I haven't been hit on *once* tonight?" Maya says. "And these are my sexy butt jeans."

"This is just a more casual atmosphere. Where's Grant anyway? If he invited you," I say.

"No idea. He hasn't texted me all day. Or snapped. What about DJ? Have you heard from him?"

I purse my lips together. "I hate to say it, but I almost *hope* his family emergency took a turn for the worse and he had to disappear. Because treating me like he did last night without a text the day after is *not* acceptable."

"Preach it! This is why I'm glad I'm not hooking up," April says. "I'd get too emotional."

"I thought you said you wished someone would burst your dam."

"Well, yeah. Under the confines of marriage, some day."

"Really? Don't tell me you're going to wait for marriage," I chime in. "Be real."

"Not marriage but…I don't know what I'm waiting for, necessarily."

"Is your family like really religious?" Maya asks.

She shakes her head. "Just regular Irish Catholic. Why do you ask?"

"Just curious."

At that moment, Ian waves us over to the beer pong table. April just wants to watch, so Maya and I will be playing against the guys who just won the last game.

We hear a ruckus of male voices coming down the stairs, and when they come through the basement doorframe, a big cheer erupts from all the brothers in the house.

It's DJ, Grant, his roommate Finn, and their other friends, Nelson and Chris. Clearly, they have friends here.

My muscles stiffen when my eyes lock on DJ's through the crowd. He smirks at me.

Smirks.

The bastard has the nerve to make that expression after we did what we did last night, and now I know he clearly did not have to go back home for a family emergency.

The start of the beer pong game is interrupted, which gives me and Maya the time to take some much-needed practice shots.

DJ grabs a beer and walks around the room, stopping and shaking hands with most of the guys. A few minutes later he finds me on my side of the beer pong table.

"Hey," he says.

"Hey," I say flatly, staring ahead and concentrating on my shot.

"Cool you came here," he says.

"Totally." I don't make eye contact.

One of the other guys, Hunter, comes over to us. "Hey, man, Woodlock and I just won like eleven games in a row. We're going to retire as the beer pong champions of the night. You wanna play against the ladies?"

"It'd be my pleasure." He turns and calls out. "Hey, Grant. Want to play against Maya and Alex?"

Grant's ears perk up from the conversation he's having.

"Fuck yes, I do."

The game starts, and Maya and I hit a couple of quick cups and take the lead.

"Damn," Grant says. "The girls can play ball."

"That's not all we can do," Maya winks as DJ shoots and nails a cup. I pull it away and drink it down.

"What's that supposed to mean?" I whisper.

"Nothing," she says. "It's all about the distractions in this game. Pull your shirt down, show some cleavage. Clearly, DJ has skills." Grant misses his shot and it's our turn.

"So, where, uh, were you guys all day?" I ask.

They look at each other and smile. "We tried to go camping," DJ says as I shoot and miss.

"Tried? What do you mean, tried?"

"Well, we went to Green Oaks campgrounds, we locked our phones in the trunk per our no-phones pact, we set up our tents, and then it started pouring rain."

Maya and I make eye contact at this information.

"It was raining when we woke up this morning," Maya points out.

"Yeah, but we thought we could out-run the rain. Turns out we were wrong about that. We got absolutely soaked and called off the trip a few hours ago, packed up our tents and came straight back here, basically," Grant shrugs. "Oh, well. We tried. We had been planning it for a couple of weeks."

"On a Monday?"

A pang of annoyance creeps up inside me.

Really? No phone pact? And DJ, you couldn't think to mention this to me?

We play until there is one cup left for each of us. Then Maya steps up and says, "It's been a nice game, boys," before she hits the last cup.

"Like you said, girl can ball." DJ shrugs as he drinks the last red Solo cup full of a third of beer.

Four other people want to play, so we graciously walk away from the table, even though since we won we have winners' rights to stay.

DJ grabs another beer, then comes and finds me in the corner. Maya and April disappear to the other side of the room.

"Hey, is everything okay?" DJ asks.

"I don't know…is it?" I bite back.

"I'm not sure. You've been looking at me with dead eyes all game. It's kind of scaring me. And I thought we really connected after last night."

"So did I! And then you ghosted me all day!"

"Ghost you? What are you talking about? I'm your roommate. How would I ghost you?"

I fold my arms, and lean in. "We're not doing that…*again*. We're done."

That gets his attention. "Alex, c'mon. You're not serious. We both know after last night what there is between us."

"So then why no goodbye this morning? Why no text all day?"

"I *did* kiss you goodbye. You must have been sleeping. I would have told you about the camping trip, but it totally slipped my mind after everything that happened last night."

He brings his head down. "Sorry I didn't text you. Service was bad where we were, but I should have. Did you not get my note?"

"What note?"

"The one I left on my pillow."

"Seriously? I didn't see it."

My hearts pounds furiously, and I try to remember through my buzz if I accidentally touched a piece of paper when I was getting out of the bed this morning.

"Well, I thought that would be nicer than a text." His hand lands on my hip and he leans in to be close to my ear, and whispers. "Alex. You really think I don't want a repeat—many repeats—of last night? And I'm not just talking about what we did in bed. I'm talking about the whole night. Well, Friday night. That romantic night looking over the river. I want to do that again."

His eyes fasten to mine as he awaits my response.

Just like that, all the walls I've built up today melt away. It's just not fair what those baby blues and deep voice are able to do to me.

But he wrote me a *note,* for goodness sake.

Our moment is interrupted when Ian comes by with his jolly demeanor. "Hey, you two. You okay, or need a refill? Another beer?" He slaps DJ on the back.

"Yeah, sure, I'd love one."

"I'm good," I say. "Thanks, though."

"No prob. Better get those pants cleaned up, man. That's a lot of dirt," he says, glancing at DJ's jeans which are a little muddy around the ankles. He winks, and as he walks away, I see him stop by and do his same double pointy beer fingers at April and Maya. He puts his hand on Maya's shoulder, and I wonder something out loud.

"Does Ian have a girlfriend?"

DJ looks at me and cracks up.

"What!? It's a legitimate question."

His face straightens. "You don't have very good gaydar, do you?"

"Um, I usually do. Wait, you're telling me..."

DJ nods, a slight grin comes over his face. "Ian's gay."

My eyes widen. Not because I haven't been around a gay person. I've lived in San Francisco for a decade, for goodness' sakes.

But a gay president of a fraternity? That goes against every single stereotype I've seen in the movies.

Ian comes back and hands DJ a beer, then looks at me. "This is a good guy, I tell ya," he says to me. "I don't care what his enemies say. He's a good guy. Thanks for coming by tonight."

"Our pleasure," DJ says. "Thanks for hosting."

Ian leans in, and motions with his hand for us to lean a little closer, like he's going to tell a secret.

"And remember, this party? *Never Happened.* The first rule of Alpha Z basement parties is..."

"You do not *talk* about basement parties."

"Good man," he says, then turns to me. "And you, too. You're welcome in the Alpha Z house now. Once our probation gets lifted in January, we can be more open about parties and what not. But for now, secret bdsm parties in the basement it is!"

We laugh, and he shakes our hands before he heads over to another crowd of people.

"He's very presidential, isn't he?" I say, and DJ laughs.

"Absolutely."

"These guys are so nice, though. Totally not what I thought a frat atmosphere would be like."

We wrap up the night and head back to the dorms. DJ and I are belligerently drunk, holding hands and skipping on the sidewalk to the dorms and singing random 90's songs that we both happen to know the lyrics to.

When we get back to the room we also realize we don't want the night to end.

We order some food to be delivered to the dorm, DJ cracks open a couple more beers (because we definitely need those), and we cuddle and chat. When he gets up to go to the bathroom, I can't resist checking my email to see if I've gotten a response from Professor Z today on the independent study proposals I sent him for winter term.

I don't even notice when DJ is back in the room until he speaks. "Why are you checking your email at this hour?"

"I, uh, have an independent study I'm kind of stressing over getting a topic for. And I really need to get into Professor Faulkner's upper-level psychology class next term."

He comes and stands behind me in my desk chair and rubs my shoulders while I space out looking at the screen. Because there was no response from Professor Z.

"I hear that's an amazing class. Everyone talks about it. What independent study topic did you propose?"

"Well, I've proposed to study the effects of guided meditation methods utilizing the Alfred Adler school of thought and visualization on trauma recovery."

"That is a mouthful. So no word from Z yet?"

"No, not yet. But I need to get into this class. It's three-hundred level but if I get in I'll be setting myself up for success. That feels amazing, by the way. Please don't stop."

"Can't stop. Won't stop. So you think you'll get into that class? When do you find out?"

He continues working his hands down my back in a non-sexual manner that releases tension I didn't think I had, "Next week is registration, after mid-terms. It's *everything*."

"You'll get in. I have a feeling."

"By the way, was your sister okay today? You didn't mention that. Have you heard from her or your parents?"

"Yes. I had a weird feeling so I called her this morning and talked to her, actually. I was about to abandon the camping trip to drive down and see her again, but she wouldn't have it. She said she's doing fine and that my mom was overreacting."

"You think that's true?"

"It's possible. My mom's a bit of a drama queen sometimes."

I spin around. "Hey. I've got an idea tonight."

"What's that?"

"Let's push the beds together so we actually have some space to cuddle. And...whatever else."

He smiles. "Oh? Were you wanting to do something besides cuddle tonight?"

"Yeah, I was thinking of some specific things that would be beneficial to us both."

He jumps up and snaps his fingers at me to move so he can push the beds together.

The funny thing is that we're so drunk we fall asleep in the middle of making out, all tangled up together.

And it's completely perfect.

32

ALEX

When I wake up the next morning, I'm still drunk. Well, maybe drunk is overstating it.

But I'm definitely buzzed.

And it's Tuesday, so there's that. Yay for college. And getting drunk on days that aren't Friday or Saturday.

I get up and go to the bathroom, then head back and get in bed. I'm just wearing my panties and bra, and I try to be the big spoon because DJ's back is turned from me.

I drag a finger down his oblique muscle, sliding it down until it lands on his hip. He stirs, sounding like a bear, and reaches a hand behind him and cups my ass and pulls my body into him.

I can't tell if he's awake and moving or just in that zombie state in between dreams. I nuzzle my nose into his back, enjoying the feel of his warm hand as he sleep-palms my ass. All I can think is what an unlikely duo of a couple we are. The allegedly spoiled, possibly soon-to-be frat boy, and the girl with the most tattoos on campus who swore she'd never be with someone like him.

But DJ's like a book with a cover that doesn't accurately

describe it. Or maybe he's like one of those books that you don't like for the first several chapters, but once you get into the middle of the story you're hooked.

I'm definitely hooked on him.

He swivels his hips against me. I pull him tighter, pressing my breasts into his back. He lets out a low, throaty moan, running his hand up and down my thigh.

Okay then, he's got to be awake. I wonder if he's just messing with me right now. Pretending to be half-asleep and turning up my temperature with his caresses.

Asleep or not, what he's doing is definitely working to make my heart race. My body heats, and my clit throbs.

I decide to go out on a limb and mess with him a little bit. I bring my hand around to his abs and slowly slide it down, past his belly button, then rub it on top of his boxers.

A shiver of surprise runs through me when I feel how hard he is. I can't resist slipping my hand beneath his waistband and grabbing the base of his ready and willing cock.

He inhales a deep breath and turns over onto his back, and grins at me.

"Well good morning."

"Good morning," I sing.

And just what do you think you're doing?" he asks.

"Being naughty," I smirk.

He laughs heartily, wraps his arm around my head and kisses me deeply.

"Oh, yeah? Just how naughty do you want to be this morning?"

"Up to you."

I let go of him and he tilts toward me on his side to face me, then reaches under the pillow and pulls out a crumpled piece of paper. He reads:

"Alex, I need you to know that I really like you. Taking

off today for a camping trip with the guys we've been planning for a while, but I'll be back probably tomorrow. Can we pick up where we left off last night?"

My heart warms. "I don't know how I missed it."

He brushes my hair behind my ear. "It's true you know. I like you a lot."

I wiggle my eyebrows. "Like a *lot* a lot?"

He nods. "Like *a lot a lot a lot.*"

"So do I."

We kiss again, and this time, we don't stop. Our hips gyrate against each other and we make out for a good long while like that. Our bodies heat and his cock rubs against me through the layers of fabric that separate us. My bra comes off. His boxers come off. And then there's just my soaked panties left.

"I need you," I finally say, desperately. "I want to feel you, DJ."

He nods. "I know."

Reaching below the bed, he grabs a condom and I slip off my panties.

"You want to start on top?" he asks, sliding the condom on.

I shake my head. "Let's just see where this goes," I say. "Go slow."

I'm so wet he slides in with ease. I grab the bars behind the bed to brace myself.

"Oh, God, yes, DJ," I mutter. My inner muscles tighten around him.

He blows out a loud breath. "Fuck, I wasn't expecting you to be this tight," he groans, then leans forward. His two muscled arms are on either side of my head.

He nibbles my ear before he whispers the next word. "*Temptress.*"

As he says it, he thrusts just a little deeper into me, and the touch of his cock rubbing against my clit sends a blast of pleasure through me. When I moan, he covers my mouth with his and eats it up.

"Fuck, that feels good," he mutters.

He feels so damn good inside of me, and his cock on my clit feels amazing as it rubs against me every time he thrusts in and out.

Gripping my chin with his thumb and forefinger, he forces me to look at his eyes, simmering with pleasure.

"Jesus, you really do have a perfect cock," I mutter.

"Why thank you. You're really complimentary during sex."

"I am when you're..."

I take shallow breaths, arching my hips up and into him. My stomach rolls with pleasure, and I feel the first orgasm building.

I run a hand through his thick hair, and his big hands run down my backside until they reach my ass. Every thrust of his sends another bolt of pleasure through me. He leans down into me, rubbing his cheek against mine. I grip his back with my nails, and dig into him, and he lets out a growl.

"Yes, Alex. More of that."

His low, throaty voice combined with his light scuff rubbing against my soft skin is the last straw.

My entire body pulsates with need for this man, and my first orgasm comes crashing through me. DJ swallows up my moan with a deep, passionate kiss.

I'm so pleasure-filled I feel high. He pulls out, then whispers in my ear, "Flip over."

I do as he says, getting on my hands and knees.

He pushes into me from behind, and my stomach knots

again as he fills me up. I look over at a mirror on the wall, and my God, we're a sight to see. And *feel*.

DJ holds onto my hips as he thrusts into me relentlessly. The cloud of pleasure takes us over, and any actual dialogue becomes difficult. I think I hear DJ say something about 'fantasy girl,' but I'm lost in my own world so I'm not sure.

I let out a yelp when he pulls a knot of my hair. I arch my back and lift my head so upward toward his. His fingers grip my neck and he kisses me.

"Alex, you look so sexy from behind. Do you know that?"

"Yes?"

"Say it again. Not like a question."

"Yes, I know."

"Good."

He pushes my head back down and I feel his hand slap my ass. I groan.

"Do you like that?"

"Yes."

"Damn. Fuck me, Alex. You're so damn sexy it's crazy."

My body throbs.

So sexy it's crazy? There's a compliment I won't soon forget.

Just when I think he might finish, DJ reaches down and touches my clit while he continues thrusting into me from behind. It doesn't take long for me to come again.

He presses my body down so my stomach is flat with the bed.

"Alex," he whispers in my ear. "You should know something.

"I like you a lot. A lot," he says in a low voice.

I muster a hazy grin, as my body shakes with pleasure again.

"If you like me so much then why don't you come?"

He growls again, and this time I know he's going to finish from the way his thrusts are completely overpowering and wild. He reaches around and grabs my tits.

Heat explodes between my legs one more time.

A few moments pass.

"I came," he says.

"I could tell," I smirk.

He pulls out, ties off the condom, and throws it away, then jumps back next to me in bed.

"Damn, Alex. I just feel so…I don't know what the word is."

I roll over so I'm on my back.

"Connected to you," I fill in his blank.

He kisses my stomach, then lips.

"Yes. But it's more than that. I really like you."

"I like you too."

This is going to be a fun term, I think, but I'm afraid to say it out loud.

Hell, a fun *year*.

DJ stares at my naked body, running a finger up and down my flesh.

"What are you thinking about?" I ask.

"That was incredibly hot. You're so fucking hot."

I giggle. "So are you."

A grin crosses his face.

"What are you thinking about?" I ask.

"Do you want to do that again?"

I nod. "Yes, please."

He slides his hand down my thigh and my cheeks redden all over again. "I have a feeling we're going to be doing a lot of this."

33

DJ

October rolls on, and it *is* a fun month. Alex and I find a sweet spot, and—turns out we have the ability to be very nice and generous with each other. Plus, she's super smart and a great study partner.

Instead of trying to figure out how we can avoid each other, we coordinate our schedules to make time for our extracurricular activities that we are enjoying.

You know, things like homework, movies.

And let's not lie: we're fucking like rabbits.

Time flies so fast I barely realize October is ending. Halloween week is legendary on college campuses everywhere for the parties, and Greene State is no different.

Even though the date of Halloween falls on a Sunday this year, all of the best parties are on Friday and Saturday.

Friday night, Alex and I get dressed up and head to our favorite restaurant in our costumes.

After she finishes putting her makeup on, she grabs her jacket.

"Let's go," she says, putting her hand on the doorknob.

I'm frozen staring at her, though. She twirls her head around. "What is it?"

"Just confirming something."

Alex furrows her brow. "Confirming what?"

"That you're the hottest Jasmine."

Her cheeks redden. "Yeah, okay. Let's go."

She goes to pull the door open and I shut it, then push her against the wall, pressing my hips into her.

"I don't think you understood me."

"I heard you."

"Well, you don't believe me."

"That I'm the hottest Jasmine ever?"

I push a lock of her hair back behind her ear and clench my jaw up and down. Her breathing gets louder as I press my body into her, feeling her warmth.

Holding onto her hips, I kiss her long, hard, and deep until she moans into my mouth. I can feel her body heating from my touch as I slide my hand under her jacket and onto her midriff. My cock stiffens against my ridiculous Aladdin pants. I love the way she melts into me.

"Well, hello there," she says, running a hand over the thin fabric around my crotch.

I smile and open the door. "Come on, we need to go now before I keep you here long past the costume parties. Ready to eat?"

She rolls her eyes. "You're such a tease."

I run my lips over her earlobes. "Was I teasing you this morning when I made you come five times?"

She bites her lower lip. "Seriously, stop. I thought you were hungry."

I wink. "Come on, temptress. Let's go."

. . .

It's a short walk to the restaurant, and not too crowded inside. We order our food and sit down to eat.

"So did you find out if you got into Faulkner's class yet?"

Alex shakes her head. "No, and I have a bad feeling about it."

"Have you thought about just going into his office and asking him?"

"Professor Z's office? Why would I? He already knows how badly I want to get in."

"No, not Professor Z. Ask Faulkner."

"It's not a bad idea." She sinks in her chair a little. "But I think the rosters get sent out next Monday. And it's Friday. Where would I even find him to ask him this weekend?" She reaches across the table and wraps her hand around my bicep. "Some things just aren't meant to be, Aladdin. Maybe if you were a genie you could help me."

The TV in the restaurant flashes on, and it's Greene State U's sports channel. They're summarizing the season, which has been a pretty mediocre one for our team. Farnsworth, our quarterback, has been throwing interceptions left and right and basically giving away games.

Alex watches the screen for a moment, then turns back to me. "So...why aren't you playing again?"

"Because my dad is a dick." I shrug and take a bite. I wonder how many college athletes have to deal with their dad being their coach.

"It's so weird. I thought you were this big football star. From the first moment I got on campus, everyone was talking about your talent. It's like he's trying to sabotage you or something."

My stomach grinds. I try to think the best of people—even my asshole father. In my mind I'd always thought he was just a hardass. But all of a sudden I'm wondering if he might be manipulating me to...

I put my food down, my appetite suddenly ruined.

"Holy shit," I exclaim.

I look over at Alex who is using a napkin to wipe her mouth.

"Everything okay?" she asks, furrowing her brow with concern.

I shake my head. "I think my dad might actually be trying to sabotage me and my future."

She recoils. "Why would he do that?"

"I don't know. He's always been pushing me in football since I was really young. So it's weird that he would do that and I'm probably just imagining it."

"I don't know anything about football past Greene State U gossip, but the consensus is that Farnsworth just sucks."

I take a sip of water and put up a finger. "Well, that is an interesting question. The original reason he benched me was because I was one minute late to a practice."

"Why were you late?"

"Remember the day you moved my shoes?"

Alex puts her hand over her mouth. "I'm so sorry!"

I wave her off. "It's got nothing to do with you."

"I remember that day. It was my fault."

"Maybe." I motion for her to give me her hand. "But is it your fault I couldn't stop staring at you?"

Her eyes widen and she grins. "I knew it! You *were* staring at me while I was sleeping."

I crack up. "Guilty as charged." I motion for her to give me her hand, and she does. I pull her body closer, gently, and lower my voice like I have a secret to tell her. "Have I told you yet today you're absolutely stunning?"

She smiles and shakes her head. "I forget if you have."

"Well, you are, Alex. Inside and out."

I kiss her and she's delicious.

She sighs and leans back.

"You look like something is on your mind," I say.

She nods. "DJ, what are we?"

"What do you mean?"

"I mean, are we together? Are we seeing other people? This fall has been amazing. I know it's been a short time but it—"

"Feels like it's been forever."

"Yes." She purses her lips together. "Where do we go from here?"

I'm silent. I take one last bite of food and give myself some time to think.

Her body stiffens. "You know what, it's fine. I shouldn't have brought it up. We're just having fun, right? I should be enjoying the ride."

"Alex, come here."

I motion for her to come on my side of the booth. She moves over to my side.

"You're right—we're young. I'm basically a sophomore, well, a freshman, academically. You're young, too. I don't think either of us can know what this is, or how far it'll go. We've just got to take it one day at a time. If I ever get the urge to be with another woman, I'm going to tell you. If you ever want to be with another guy, you tell me."

She nods. "But we've got almost four more years of college left."

"Alex," I growl, wrapping my arm around her. "I'm not your father. I'm not my father. To be honest, I'm still figuring out who I am. Will I play professionally some day? Maybe. But I'll tell you this. My grandpa and grandma were married sixty-two years and they met freshmen year of college.

Maybe we're too young for this to be...whatever it could be. But we're also too young to figure out what it *couldn't* be. Does that make sense?"

She nods. I go on. "You've been a positive influence on me since you appeared, crazy as this whole roommates' adventure has been."

"I have?"

I nod. "You're a great person with a kind heart," I say, then smirk. "Your lips aren't bad either."

She giggles, taking one of my hands and putting it on her breast. "What about these?"

"These are what I like to call the eighth wonder of the world."

Where we are in our booth in the back, no one can see us. I run my hands under her shirt, up her stomach, pausing before I reach her breasts.

Her voice is breathy. "Oh God, DJ. Stop...they'll see."

"What if I want them to see?"

I think she's about to protest again, so I kiss her to cover up her mouth.

"Mmm," she groans.

I kiss her neck, bring my hands up to fondle her breasts, then whisper in her ear, "I can't wait to suck on these beautiful nipples later."

"Seriously, stop, DJ. You're going to make me come right here. I don't think these people want to hear me scream."

I kiss her jaw line once more, then pull away, acting like none of that just happened.

"Alright, so are you ready to go for a walk around town?" Although I need to wait a few moments. These white Aladdin pants hide nothing.

Alex smiles and shakes her head. "You are the worst tease ever."

"And you love it."

WE AMBLE around town in our costumes on this beautiful fall night. The houses of Galesburg are remnants of a bygone era. Old colonial builds from the 1800s when the town was a major stop along the cross-country railroad, and booming like never before.

As we walk in silence, I suddenly realize something.

"We're passing the block where my dad rents a house during football season," I observe.

"Wow. This is a nice area."

"It's called professor row. The professors make a lot of money compared with the other people in town, so they're just about the only ones who can afford to live here."

"I wonder if Professor Faulkner and Professor Flores live around here."

I wink. "What about Professor Z?"

"Oh, yeah. So many girls have crushes on him."

"Do you?"

She shrugs. "I might, if I weren't so overwhelmed by this one guy I'm seeing. He keeps me pretty satisfied."

"Just *pretty* satisfied?" I say.

"Well, he's kind of a tease," she whispers in my ear.

"Maybe. But it seems like he always delivers."

We come closer to my dad's place, and I notice the lights are on.

"I wonder what he's up to tonight," I say.

"Have you not visited him here?"

"I did on orientation day. We all met here. Not since then."

"That's so sad you don't visit your dad."

I shrug. "I'm not super broken up about it."

"Maybe you should go say hi right now and ask for your starting spot tomorrow."

I purse my lips. "He'd probably tell me no, just on principle. Everything has to be his idea."

"It can't hurt, though," Alex says.

"Fine. I'll step in and ask. Do you mind waiting here? I'll try and be quick."

"No problem whatsoever. It's such a beautiful night, I don't mind."

She sits on the steps while I use the old-fashioned knocker to knock on the door. There is no answer, so I knock again, loudly. I end up having to call my dad's phone.

He doesn't pick up the call, but a minute later my dad answers the door, and he's weirdly sweaty, wearing shorts and a t-shirt.

"What are you doing here?" he asks coldly.

I push my way in. "Coach Sal, I need to talk about something."

"It's not a good time."

"It's the *only* time."

I brush past him and into the living room. Glancing around, I furrow my brow. I sniff, and a smell sends coils to my gut.

"Why does it smell like perfume in here?"

"Candles," he points to where he was having dinner.

I put my hands on my hips and stare at the two sets of wine glasses.

"Dad, were you having someone over here?"

"I had dinner with one of our coaching staff."

I squint at one of the wine glasses, and make my way over to it and pick it up.

"Oh? And does this member of the coaching staff wear lipstick?"

"Don't give me the third degree. What did you come over here for?"

My heart starts to race. I knew there was something that my sister and mom weren't telling me this month. Maybe they suspected what I'm seeing now, and just didn't want to break the news to me. Maybe they didn't have proof of his exploits, and just knew that he was acting shady.

I stare at the red lipstick up close and consider my father's poor excuse. I realize this is that moment when everything is about to change.

"It doesn't even matter much what I came over for anymore. Who is it? One of the professors? Someone from town?"

"Son," he growls, and pours himself a tall glass of pungent whisky. "You'll understand when you're older. This is just something a man does."

"Cheats on his wife? What about Felicity? Do you think about her and what she'll think of you?"

His face twitches, and for a moment he falters.

He swirls the ice cubes around in his whisky. "DJ. I'm forty-eight. I had you when I was twenty-eight. I've done my duty as a father. I'm done with that now."

I pull out my phone, pull up Felicity's number, and hover my hand over it. "Well, you want to break the news to them, or should I?"

"Calm the fuck down, DJ, or I'll calm you down."

I step up to him.

"Don't tell me to calm down."

Is this seriously happening? Is my own father insinuating a physical confrontation?

And even more so, is he saying that he would be able to take me?

"Old man," I say, looking him in the eye. "It'll take a lifetime to undo what you've done."

I clench my jaw and spin around, heading outside and into the brisk fall weather.

Alex stands up as soon as I come out.

"What did he say? Are you going to start tomorrow?"

I shake my head. "I didn't ask. I think I've got a bigger problem now."

"What problem?"

I take Alex's hand firmly in mine and we start walking down the sidewalk. We must look pretty ridiculous walking hand in hand "You don't want to know."

She reaches her hand under my jacket and squeezes my bicep, turning toward me as we walk with her pretty brown eyes. "Yes, babe. I do."

A soft grin comes over my face. "Did you just 'yes, babe' me?"

"Yes, I did. What's the matter?"

I stop at the end of the block. "My dad was in there with another woman. So I didn't exactly get a chance to ask him about the starting spot on the team."

The blood drains from her face. "You're serious?"

I nod. "Unfortunately."

"Who is she?"

"I don't know. She was probably hiding in a closet or something. But I saw all the proof I needed. He basically admitted it to me."

Alex thinks for a split second, then lurches forward to wrap me up in a tight hug.

"I'm sorry, DJ," she whispers. "How do you feel?"

"Honestly, I feel oddly calmer now than I did beforehand. I knew my mom and sister were hiding something they weren't telling me. Now I know what that is."

"There's nothing quite as bad as the tension of not knowing," she says, then pulls away.

I look down at her. "This is a crappy situation, sure, but it's not any rockier than things you've experienced."

"Every trauma is personal, though. No reason to compare them."

We walk back, and I do feel oddly calm, even though I wouldn't have minded landing a punch to my father's face.

We head back, and we seem to be avoiding all of the parties, the noise, and the shenanigans happening on campus tonight.

I don't want to be around anyone else tonight making silly conversation. I just want her.

And judging by her demeanor, she feels the same.

We spend the night solely focused on each other and bringing pleasure to our lives, pushing the pain aside and simply being in the moment. In the early hours of the morning I wait for my alarm to go off at seven a.m. for game day.

34

ALEX

I'm shaken up today, to say the least. DJ seems off in the morning, but I leave him with a very happy send-off that almost makes him late to practice again.

As I sit in bed in the morning, I stare out at campus and think about the story DJ told me about the two sons of an alcoholic. It was a simple story but it gave me chills.

An idea strikes me. *That's* an ideal research project: find the children of parents who have gone through something traumatic, and find out how they dealt with said trauma. I email the idea to Professor Z, and he gets back to me quickly with an encouraging reply that I'm on the right track.

I smile looking at DJ's things.

We've come a long way since the beginning of the term when he seemed like the type of guy I would prefer to stay far, far away from. All that thinking I had about my 'type' was misguided. I'd never dated or been with a guy like DJ, so how would I know he wasn't my 'type?'

I wonder why I tried so hard to put a label on him. Why do we always try to label people like we think they know them at a glance? People are so much more complex than we give them credit for.

Later in the day, April and Maya invite me to go to the football game with them.

We have a few drinks in their room and head down to The Bowl, where all of the students watch the games from the bleachers.

"You seem off today," April says. "Everything okay?"

I fill her in about how DJ still isn't playing, which makes me sad. I don't want to get into the details of what we ran into last night at DJ's dad's house in this rowdy environment so I just leave it be.

"Come on, DJ!" someone shouts from the crowd behind us. I turn and see a teenage girl, who clearly doesn't go here. She's got a sign that reads "GO, DJ."

I recognize the feminine handwriting. Where have I seen that before?

It dawns on me: the poster I saw when I was first filing into Dalton Dorms that said "We'll miss you, DJ!" When I look closer, I recognize the two faces.

DJ's mom and I make eye contact with his sister. "Hello, there!" I say. "I'm DJ's roommate, Alex."

A wide smile crosses her face. "Oh, my goodness. I'm Felicity! He's told me all about you!"

"He has?" I gulp.

She nods enthusiastically. "Thanks for putting up with him. I know he can be a lot sometimes, but he means well."

I laugh. "Thanks." I wonder to myself if he's filled in his sister and mom on our romance. Probably not.

Felicity smiles dimly, and Mrs. Dalton looks over at me with tired but hopeful eyes.

A tingle tumbles down my spine and I think about just how wrong I was about their family being 'perfect.'

I'm about to say something to Mrs. Dalton when there's a big cheer from the crowd, and I'm not sure what for. Suddenly, everyone in the crowd is on their feet.

"What just happened?" I ask, nudging Maya.

She wiggles her eyebrows. "What just happened is they put your boytoy into the game for the first time all season."

Felicity squeals behind me, and the entire crowd is roaring. We're playing our archrival today, Saint Simeon College, and our fans seem especially pumped up to beat them. Maybe it's Halloween, maybe it's the weather. I don't know for sure.

But when DJ comes in, the noise is so loud that conversation is now difficult.

On his very first play, he throws a touchdown pass to Luke Rutledge.

Talk of "where has this been all season" starts up from the crowd.

When Greene State gets the ball back, my skin tingles. DJ completes another pass down the field, and chants of 'D-J! D-J!' overtake over the crowd.

Down a few rows from me, I even see the cab driver who drove me here the very first day pumping his fist.

I never thought I'd date a man like DJ, much less fall head over heels for him like I have.

He throws another touchdown pass to Luke, and the crowd goes absolutely nuts.

Maya takes my wrist and whispers in my ear:

"How does it feel to be the one who's with the star?"

I grin. "Well I have to say he looks good in tight pants."

She wiggles her eyebrows and leans toward me to whisper. "You lucky girl. You get to hang onto that—"

Just then, there's another, much louder roar from the crowd. I look up and DJ has already thrown a long touchdown pass. He sprints to the end zone and high fives his buddy Luke, who caught the pass.

"Damn, he's good," April chimes in. "You two would have really athletic babies."

She covers her mouth. "Sorry," she adds. "Way too soon to start talking about that."

"It's okay, you're right. We would. I think it's okay to dream."

The game goes on and DJ absolutely dominates the Saint Simeon Team.

Maya nudges me again, and winks. "Hope you two have fun tonight."

I nudge her back, and point down to where we can see Grant standing with a few other guys. "We will. How about you and Grant? When are you finally going to stop playing this weird game you're playing?"

"I told you, we're just friends!"

"Yeah, friends..." April smirks. "Friends who stay up chatting until—"

"April, shush! And it's just chatting. Nothing more."

"You two are really cute roommates, you know that?"

The game ends in an easy victory. I see the taxi cab driver going nuts. DJ really did give the people here some happiness today.

As I'm heading out though, I see DJ's mom and sister who seem to be having an intense conversation.

A few moments later I get a text from DJ.

DJ: Hey, I'm having a family dinner with my mom and sister today after the game. Sort of a personal dinner. Meet up with you later?

Alex: Yes. Great game. Has anyone told you look incredibly handsome out there?

DJ: No, but tell me more! Talk to you later

As people are clearing the field, I notice that DJ's dad is lingering and looking at his clipboard.

"Wait here, I'll be right back," I tell Maya and April without waiting for their response.

Maybe it's the fact that I'm slightly buzzed, maybe it's seeing DJ's sister and mom in the flesh, but I'm feeling fired up right now.

I stop a few feet in front of Mr. Dalton. "Ahem."

"Can I help you?" He billows.

"Yes, you can. Thanks for finally playing DJ, first of all. Nice of you."

He does a double take in my direction. "Who are you?"

"Alex Reyes," I say with a smirk. "DJ's roommate."

Oh God, he's staring at my tits. I now regret wearing this low cut top on this brisk fall day. I zip up my jacket.

"Okay...great," he says sarcastically. "So that's it? You just wanted to say hello?"

"No, that's not it. I also wanted to ask you a question."

"Which is?"

"And this is just for my own selfish good, because I want to know how a man turns out like you."

He gives me a funny look, furrowing his brow. "I don't follow."

"How does a man end up like you? Is there something you had stuck up your rectum that turned you into an inflexible asshole?"

"I have no idea what you're talking about."

"Oh come on. I was with DJ last night. Don't play dumb.

I just want to know, for my own reference, what makes a guy like you—great family, beautiful daughter, son and wife, end up doing what you're doing?"

He crosses his arms. "You're way out of line here. Take a hike, Miss Reyes."

"I didn't think I'd get a real answer out of you. But that's fine. You know what they call someone who has to do what they do behind closed doors?"

"I don't have to stand for this." He grabs a headset from the bench, and starts to walk off.

"A coward," I say. "That's what!"

He snorts, turning around. "I would stay far away from DJ if I were you. Like father, like son. It's truer than we wish it were sometimes."

"I don't believe that," I say.

"Well, maybe you should."

35

DJ

"DJ, I have something I need to tell you."

I tense up. Mom seemed all restless and distant on the drive over to the restaurant so I'm definitely having a bad feeling about this.

"Your father and I are getting a divorce."

I pause with my spoon full of soup, halfway from my bowl to my hand. I put the spoon back in the bowl, and flash eye contact with my mother and sister.

"So this is why you've been being so shady lately?"

Felicity looks at my mother. They've always been a close pair, and I think it's good for both of them. They're not like a normal mother and daughter—most of the time they're like best friends.

My mother takes my hand. "Yes. I'm sorry, we didn't want to tell you until it was absolutely final."

I turn to Felicity. "When did you find out about this?"

"I've known since…for a few weeks."

I blow out an exasperated breath, my appetite dissipating. I look between the two of them.

I get why they didn't tell me, in a way. But I still feel for some reason like I'm outside the circle.

"So you've been keeping this from me?"

"DJ, I'm sorry I didn't tell you—" My mom says. "I wanted to do it in person. We were waiting for the right time. And part of me held out hope that things would turn around with your father. But they didn't. So here we are."

"I'll be right back," I say, standing up. "Gotta go grab some air."

Felicity tugs my forearm. "We didn't mean to keep this from you. We just..."

"I know. It's not like this is coming out of nowhere." I run a hand through my hair, then grab my jacket. "Just give me a moment, okay? I'll be right back."

I step outside and into the chilly fall air, an anxious feeling creeping up in my stomach. I feel around for my phone, and realize I left it in the restaurant. Oh well. What's the point?

I walk a block, slowly sauntering, and notice a group of girls outside a bar.

Hmmm... I know her.

"Alex," I call out. She's talking animatedly to Luke, the senior on the team, and I feel jealously start to bubble up inside me.

My heart sinks.

Alex doesn't notice me, and I take a chance to observe her without her knowing. We spend so much time together these days, and we're always so in sync.

But right now she's standing there with Luke and lighting up like a Christmas tree, and the feeling that's bothering me becomes clear: With everything that's gone down between my mom and dad, I'm worried about the 'forever-ness' of any relationship I start up right now. If it's going to go down in flames, why even start one up? It just seems...like a pointless effort, like swimming against the stream. And the way she's flirting with Luke right now gets my blood boiling. Like my mom and dad, maybe we're just not meant to be together.

I walk up behind her and tap her on the shoulder.

"Hi there," I say.

She turns around, and smiles broadly. "Deeeeej!" She wraps her arms around me and kisses me.

Luke winks. "I'll leave you two be."

"What are you doing?" I say, my heart pounding.

"I'm at the bar. Obviously."

"I know, but what are you *doing*?"

She squeezes her eyebrows together, then leans in and whispers. "Besides thinking about what we're going to do later? You looked amazing on the field today."

I swallow. "Yeah, so did Luke, didn't he?"

She shrugs, then bats her eyes at me, all flirty. "Yeah, I guess."

I squint. "No, you were. I just saw you two talking."

She furrows her brow. "You both looked amazing. Come here."

Alex wraps her arms around my neck, and I shake my head.

"I don't know if we should do this."

"Not here? You want to go back to the room? Well...I guess."

"No. I mean in general." I bring my eyes to Alex's. "What are we even doing?"

She peels her arms away. "Are you saying what I think you're saying?"

My eyes hood over. I notice Luke looking at us over his shoulder.

I don't want to be feeling what I am right now.

"What's the point, Alex?"

Her eyes hood over. "...The point?"

I nod. "I'm only going to end up hurting you in the long run. Sure, I like you a lot...today. But aren't we better off just calling it quits now instead of waiting until we're years down the road and we really hurt each other?"

Her expression is pained. "You want to break up?"

I nod grimly. I know I'm coming out of left field with this, and I see the confusion in her eyes. "I think we both know...it's better that way."

Alex's lip starts to quiver and a tear rolls down her cheek. "That's what you want?"

"It's not what I want...but it's what has to be."

She presses her lips together and takes a deep breath. "Excuse me."

She brushes past me and slices through the crowd of students on the sidewalk.

Luke watches her leave, then he turns to me with a concerned look on his face.

"Hey, Dalton, what the hell just happened?"

I don't turn around, I just keep walking away from the bar. Because fuck if I know what happened.

And in the direction of my dad's apartment.

A few minutes later I arrive in front of his place, and I just stand around on the sidewalk for a few minutes staring at the cracks with my hands in my pockets.

Today should be a giant day of celebration. We defeated our arch rival Saint Simeon College. I threw my first touchdown passes as a Greene State Flame. But overall, I'll always remember today just simply as the day my parents got divorced.

Maybe I'm being overly emo about the whole thing. As I

stare at my dad's door, I think about how many times when he told me growing up just to 'suck it up.' 'Be a man.' 'Don't be such a pussy.'

He wasn't always a bad dad, but every piece of advice that he gave me rings hollow.

I should just go back to the restaurant and be with Felicity and Mom. But I'm hurt at how they kept me out of the loop with their little mother-daughter secret thing going. Who do I tell my secrets to?

Alex.

I hear the front door to my dad's house swing open and I spin around, expecting to see him.

But what I see is ten times worse, and it makes my jaw drop.

"Jessica?" I'm nearly gasping for air. "What the fuck are you doing here?"

36

DJ

Her face turns bright red as she walks down the steps.

"Are you fucking serious? *You're* the one who's been sleeping with my dad?"

She won't look me in the eye. "DJ, I don't know what to tell you."

"Tell me that you haven't been *sleeping* with my dad!"

"Do you want me to tell you that? Or do you want the truth?"

I smack my face with my palm. "And I thought this day couldn't get any worse."

"DJ, I didn't think this would happen. I didn't do this to hurt you, if that's what you think. This just kind of happened."

I face Jessica and look her in the eye. "You're forgiven. My beef isn't with you. It's with my father."

"Really?"

I look her up-and-down. "Once, I cared for you. I don't know any more if what I felt was love. Once, I thought it might be. But yes, I'm forgiving you. I'm not going to hold on to hate in my heart for someone who now means absolutely nothing to me."

Her jaw drops, and she blinks a few times in surprise, but I'm not surprised that she has no response.

I step up and knock on the door.

My father answers, and when he sees me, the color drains out of his face.

"Expecting someone else?"

He sees Jessica behind me, and knows he's caught red-handed. "I just ended it with her, for what it's worth."

"Not a lot."

"Come in."

"No thanks, I'll stay out here now."

"You knocked on the door earlier. I assume you wanted to talk."

"I did. That was before I knew your mistress was my goddamn ex-girlfriend."

He looks down at his feet, then comes outside in his t-shirt, despite the fact that it's quite cold. Jessica reaches the end of the block and walks out of our sight.

"I made a mistake, DJ." He looks out into the distance, his eyes glazing over. "I shouldn't have done what I did. I was lonely last year living out here. I was drunk and I ran into Jessica at a bar—"

"I don't want a fucking replay of how it went down," I cut in. "It makes no difference."

He turns to me. "You know what made me end it?"

I shake my head.

He goes on. "That girl of yours. Alex. Came up to me after the game and told me just what she thought of me. I realized, I've become exactly what I promised myself I wouldn't become when I was her age. Your age. When I met your mother."

I swallow. "That's it?"

"Do you think you'll end up like me, DJ?"

I furrow my brow.

"Well that's what you told me yesterday, remember."

"Things change. I...I'm not even happy. For what it's worth I saw the look on Felicity's face..."

A tear rolls down the man's cheek. He's using that expression a lot. I've never seen him this broken up about anything. Not in my whole life.

I struggle with my gesture, because I'm damned pissed off, and put my hand on his shoulder. "I don't know what to tell you, Dad. Mom and Felicity told me about the divorce already."

He sits in the rocking chair on his porch. "I'm a fucking mess, DJ. I've lost touch with you. With all of them. I don't know what to do."

He turns to me with raised brows. Holy crap. Is my dad... asking me for advice?

"I have no idea what to tell you," I grit out.

"Just do yourself a favor. You've got a good one with that Alex. See how that plays out."

I bite my lower lip, and feel my heart sink even further.

It might be a little late for that, due to my own rashness.

As I'm walking out the door, I see an old man with white hair sitting on a rocking chair a few doors down from my dad's place on Professor Row.

"You're that quarterback, aren't you?" the old man says.

"That's me."

"You seem stressed."

"I am. I need some trauma management." I smile at the dude because, well, it's not his fault my life is shit.

"You need a girlfriend."

"I've already got one of those. Her name's Alex."

He laughs. "Alex? Sounds like a guy's name."

I keep going. "Okay, old man."

Crazy freakin' dude. There are some loonies out here.

Why did I even say that? Alex isn't my girlfriend. Well, not after our run in on the sidewalk, anyhow.

I HEAD BACK to dinner and finish up with Felicity and my mom. They want to know where I've been, and I tell them: I just needed to take a moment.

Although I'm still in something of a fog, we leave things on a somewhat good note, at least. I'm still upset with them for not telling me about this sooner. But then again I could have called them right up and told them about my dad when I knew he was cheating.

I say goodbye to them and they take off for Davenport.

On the way back, I stop at the bar to think things over. As I am buying a beer (thank you for not carding me) Luke taps me on the shoulder.

"Dude. What happened with you and Alex earlier?"

"Let me ask you something," I say. "Was she flirting with you?"

Luke shoots me a confused look. "What on earth are you talking about?"

My beer arrives, and I take a swig. "Yeah. She was so animated when I pulled up earlier today. What was the deal with your conversation?"

His jaw drops a little. "You thought she was flirting with *me*? Bro, all she was doing was raving non-stop about how great you were and how she couldn't wait for tonight."

My heart drops down to my feet. "What? *That's* what you were talking about?"

He nods. "She likes how you look in tight pants, bro. She

even mentioned how she doesn't get it. She went on that date with, ah, Grant, and he just didn't do it for her. She really likes you man. Alex was worried about you though, wouldn't say why. Said that's a secret between you two. God, she's a great girl isn't she?"

My entire chest cavity fills with butterflies. "Yes, she's great. The best type of girl."

"So what were you saying? Why'd you think she was flirting with me?"

I shake my head out. "My mom and dad told me about their divorce today. And I guess I've just been seeing infidelity everywhere."

"You thought *I* was moving in on your girl? Shit, man. I'd never do that. Not in a million years. Come on, man."

"I know you wouldn't. I just...Fuck, man. This divorce is really messing with my head."

Luke nods, and takes another big swig of his beer. "Play a game with me for a moment."

"A game?"

"Yes. Just play along." He wraps his arms around me and points out at the crowd. "Look around, and focus especially on the color red. Anywhere you see red, I want you to mentally note that. Okay? Take a minute."

I look around and note the color red. The booths in the bar, a neon sign on the wall, Many shirts and jackets. The red "C" in the numerous cubs hats.

"Done?" Luke asks.

"Yeah, got it. What is this doing?"

"Just play along like I said. Okay now close your eyes."

I do. "Now what?"

"Now tell me all the things you saw that were green."

"Green? You told me to look for red!"

"So? Are you saying you didn't see any green at all? Just

because I told you to look for another color you became blind to green?"

"I can't tell you a damn thing that was green. The door?"

"Open your eyes."

I do, and look around.

"The door is black," Luke points out.

"Okay, so I failed. What's the point?"

Luke spins around and looks me in the eye. "The point is, my man, if you look for something hard enough, you'll find it. You want to find someone being unfaithful tonight? I bet you'll find it if you choose to focus on that. Want to find people who are truly loving partners and would never consider infidelity for even a second? You'll find that too, if that's what you're looking for. But what you need to watch out for, is you can't look so hard for the color red that you start pretending orange is red. Alex likes you a lot, man. I can tell by the look in her eyes. If you're looking at her and seeing someone who could potentially be unfaithful, I think the problem is with you, not her."

I take a sip of my drink and try to process this information. Since I met him I noticed Luke has a wise way about him. I felt drawn to him for some unknown reason—like he had a message he needed to give me. Maybe this was it?

Even so, I'm defensive and skeptical with all this information being thrown at me so quickly.

"What are you, some kind of love expert? Have you ever been in love?"

He shakes his head. "Never. But I've also never had a girl rave about me like Alex talks about you. She passes the ten-minute rule with flying colors."

"What's the ten-minute rule?"

"If someone is into their partner, they'll bring them up within ten minutes of a conversation with someone who could be hitting on them. Forget ten minutes, she brought you up after like, ten seconds. She couldn't stop talking about how excited she was for you for getting in the game, and to see you tonight. She was worried about you, though. Wouldn't say why."

Hearing all that, I suddenly feel sick to my stomach. "She's a great girl who thinks the world of me. And I broke up with her."

"You what?!" Luke stammers.

"I broke up with her!" I repeat.

"Why'd you do that?!"

"I don't know." I think for a second. "You're right! I'm seeing the color red everywhere. I'm believing love can't last, because of seeing my parents' divorce. But that doesn't mean I should pre-emptively stop loving Alex."

"You're in love with her?"

"I think I am."

"Then what are you waiting for?" He leans in and slap me on the back. "She might take you back or she might not. But you'll never know if you don't ask. Go get her."

"How, though?"

Luke thinks for a moment. "What's something she loves?"

I think back to the conversation we had about her dad.

"Surfing!"

"Boom! Get her a surfboard!"

"Do they sell those here?"

"I don't know! We're pretty landlocked in Galesburg. But you never know what you'll find at Target!"

A TAXI CAB RIDE, fifty dollars, and one hour later, I'm getting out of the cab with a wake-board. Okay, not exactly a surfboard. It's a kid style complete with a Muppet design on it.

Surfboards aren't exactly for sale in the great plains.

But I have a feeling Alex will appreciate it based on what she said about her father.

It's the only hope I have.

I run up the stairs of Dalton with the board in my hand, which gets me quite a few stares and inquiries from other students about why I bought such a thing.

All I can think about is Alex.

Since day one, I've had a crush on her. Something drew me to her that I couldn't quite understand, and I knew I needed to make her mine. I *did* make her mine. I found out that in addition to being smoking hot and the ability to be a devil in bed with me, she's also incredibly smart, understanding, and maybe most importantly, *she's on my side.*

I open the door to my room.

She's not there.

I wait.

She doesn't come.

So I wait longer.

And I'm there waiting.

I text her.

No response.

Eventually, I fall asleep in a hopeless heap.

37

ALEX

"I'm an idiot. How did I—in a million years—think hooking up with my roommate was a good idea?" I say to April and Maya at our traditional Sunday brunch in the cafeteria.

I sit at brunch with my face in my palms.

"Cheer up, Al. It could be worse," Maya says.

"How? Tell me, how could it be worse? He's literally my roommate for the rest of the *year*. I've got to sleep in the same room as him, unless I stay over at your place every night."

"You can if you want," April offers.

"I know. And you guys are the best for that. But I just can't see how this is going to be an enjoyable year anymore."

April and Maya get up for some chocolate milk, and I look out the window at the fall landscape.

When I arrived, everything was so green and hopeful. Now I feel like the rest of this year is just going to be annoying. I tense up. Why would DJ so suddenly want to have nothing to do with me? He said it was not to hurt me? Now that he got in the game and he's the big star, maybe girls are after him. My stomach drops. Maybe Jessica finally got to him. Ugh.

My phone buzzes, with a notification and I pull it up. What I see sends my pulse racing, in a good way.

From: Professor Faulkner

Subject: Class

Alex,

My first name is Adam. Did you know you like people better when the first letter of their name is the same as yours?

I got the message from Professor Z about trying to get into class. He says you're brilliant and have experience with trauma management.

We need bright, young, passionate people coming into the field.

That's my way of saying you're in.

Professor Faulkner

P.S. Don't mistake the kindness of this email for how you will do in class. I'll probably have to be tougher on you than the rest since I made an exception to get you in.

My heart flies.

I want to squeal. I want to run and tell...who?

I text Aunt Mia and let her know.

But I really want to share this moment with DJ. Life is hollow without friends to share these kinds of moments with.

I look up with a sigh and see April and Maya caught up chatting with someone near the chocolate milk machine. I gaze out the window again, then I hear a body sit down across from me. I turn, expecting to see April, but to my surprise it's Luke Rutledge.

"Uh, hello."

"Hey," he says. "Have you seen DJ?"

I shake my head. "I haven't gone back to my room since

yesterday. I slept with the girls last night. Why? Everything okay?"

"Oh, uh, no reason, it's just…I'll let him tell you when he sees you."

"If he sees me."

"What do you mean by that?"

"I mean, he really hurt me. I wore my heart on my sleeve and he knocked me down out of freaking nowhere."

"He had a rough day yesterday," Luke says. "Just…I'm not going to tell you what to do."

Maya and April arrive and Luke stands up so April can have her seat back.

"Ladies," he says, greeting them. "How's your morning going?"

They make small talk for a few moments, but his eyes are on mine, laced with innuendo, and it makes me wonder what he meant with that comment about DJ.

Luke's a mysterious guy. I can't make up my mind if he's a lady killer or just a good, solid guy. I guess maybe life's not always simple, and people can't be put in boxes. Maybe he's both.

When Luke leaves, I grin and tell them about the class.

"That's so amazing!" April squeals.

"Eh, I knew you'd get in," Maya winks. "Piece of cake."

We do a chocolate milk cheers, and I'm happy for a moment. Still, the thought of DJ enters my mind. I wish we weren't…broken up. Wow. Broken up? It's like we stopped what we had before we even truly got started.

After brunch, I head back upstairs. As I turn into the hallway and walk toward the door, I have an eerie de ja vu feeling about the very first time I walked in, and saw DJ inside the room doing pushups, and a smile comes to my face that I quickly brush off.

Whatever the reason is, he doesn't want to be with you, Alex. Too much of a star, not your type, it doesn't matter.

Rage spills through my veins. He *played* me. Toyed with me, led me on, and dumped me. I ought to give him a piece of my mind.

I open the door, ready to tell him what I really think, and what I see makes me freeze.

He's got a mini-wakeboard, and he's standing in the middle of the room pretending like he's surfing.

"Uh, hello?"

His eyes widen when he sees me, and he puts his arms down.

"Oh. Hi there."

"What on earth are you doing?"

"I'm surfing. Duh."

"Why are you surfing?"

He steps off the board. "Alex...can we talk for a minute?"

"Yeah. We had better talk." I step inside and close the door behind me. "I know I tried before, but I'm seriously not going to live here winter term. I can't be your roommate, DJ."

He nods. "I understand. First, I want to tell you something about yesterday."

I put my jacket down, then put my hands on my hips, frustrated. "What do you want to say?"

He pauses for a beat, and blinks a few times.

"What?!" I bite out.

"You just look incredibly hot right now. I don't know what it is."

"Oh no, you're not charming your way out of this one. Not after what you said."

"Sorry. I meant to just tell you...my parents are getting a divorce. It's official. I know we kinda knew after we went by my dad's house and saw what was going on the other night, but hearing it from my mom and sister really made it set in."

He walks over to the window and sits. He's shirtless, just like the very first time we met.

My chest tightens. "I'm sorry. That sucks."

He turns, and his eyes are glossed over. "Want to know the kicker?"

"What?"

"It was with Jessica."

I gasp. "You're fucking serious."

He nods. "My dad was sleeping with my ex-girlfriend. Now that is some telenovela type drama right there."

"You're telling me." I walk over to him, but don't touch him. I just feel like I should be near him.

"And you want to know the second, worse kicker?"

"What?"

He turns toward me and locks his gaze on me.

"There's this amazing girl I started dating. She's beautiful, smart, everything I could ever wish for. And I ruined things with her because I started seeing red."

"You…started seeing red? I don't follow."

He nods, then reaches out and touches my side, ever so slightly. I don't fight his touch. It feels good right now, as a matter of fact.

"Yesterday when I saw you talking to Luke, I started imagining this reality where you wanted to be with other guys during college. Because, I figured, if my parents wanted to be with other people—or at least, my dad—then doesn't that mean everyone is going to sleep around? I mean we're in fucking *college*."

His Adam's apple bobs in his throat. I don't interrupt him.

"But then I realized, so what? If one, two, three years

from now we realize we're not meant to be together, so be it. But right here, and right now? Goddammit Alex, I can't help it."

My voice quivers. "Can't help what?"

"Can't help falling in love with you."

My body melts into his, a flash of warmth undoing me. I press my forehead to his, but don't say anything.

"I've never said that to anyone," he adds. "Maybe I'm too young. Maybe I don't know what it means. But I know, Alex, I want to fight for you and me. I love the way you taste. I love the way you feel next to me when I wake up. I could just keep listing the things I love about you. But I'd rather just tell you I love you. You don't have to love me back, I don't care. It's—"

I land my lips on his, pushing my chest forward and into him.

He stands up, a low rumble almost like a growl coming from his mouth.

"Do you know why I got you that surfboard, Alex?"

I nod. "I think so."

"I want to be there for you. In all the ways a man can be there for a woman. I want to start living—and loving you—right now. I'm not asking you to be with me forever. But I'm asking you to forgive me for yesterday."

"DJ!" I say, holding his jaw with my thumb and forefinger. "You're forgiven."

When I tell him that, I feel a wave of tension release from my body.

"Fuck, Alex. Fuck," he growls.

His hand slides slowly up my backside, riding over the yoga pants I wore to brunch.

I can feel his erection pressing into my thigh.

"Holy Geez, that's hard," I say.

"Yes. So hard for you, Alex." He runs his hand along my jawline, caressing it. "You make me so hard."

I giggle.

"What?" he asks.

"So is this our first time having make-up sex?"

He nods. "I guess it is."

I grab his hand as it rolls up the skin of my stomach. "Wait," I say. "I have to tell you something first."

His expression widens. "Oh my God are you pregnant?"

I roll my eyes. "No, Silly. I got into Faulkner's class."

"Fuck yes! I know how important that was to you." His eyes radiate that deep blue color, seeming to sparkle. "My girl, in addition to being an absolute vixen, is a genius. Damn, you're amazing. Have I ever told you that?"

"Not enough," I smile. "And I have something else to tell you, too."

"Oh?" He raises an eyebrow.

I take hold of his wrist, and guide it toward my waistband. He slips it down my stomach and in between my legs.

"Feel how wet I am," I whisper.

His eyes go wide with pleasure.

"Holy hell."

"And that's for you, DJ. Just for you. No one else makes me wet like that."

He smirks, and flicks his hand on my slick nub. "Oh yeah? Do you love how wet I make you?"

"I do. And I love you."

He slides my pants down. I tug his shorts, and they slide easily off his hips, revealing everything.

"Mmm," I moan, as he spins me around and into the window.

"I love you too, Temptress," he says smoothly, as he

kisses my neck. He swiftly grabs a condom, puts it on, and gently presses inside me.

"Stop being all sentimental and fuck me," I mewl, then lean in.

"Yes. You're wet. You want to get fucked right now, don't you?"

"You're so smart." I snort. "A regular Sherlock Holmes."

"Oh, my. You are..." he raises an eyebrow. "Are you telling me you want to get into some role-playing stuff? I can roll with this."

"Yes. But right now...I just want you inside me."

Need flairs inside me, my body burning up with desire. The heat grows between my legs until it's unbearable.

Luckily, he thrusts all the way inside me just at that moment, and I feel relief.

"Yes, DJ," I whimper. "God, I want to feel this forever."

He knots my hair and pulls my head back toward him. He stares at my eyes for a few moments while pumping in and out of me. "I don't know if I can be inside you forever," he growls, then kisses my throat. "But I can love you forever."

EPILOGUE - DJ

Monterey, California

THE SUMMER AFTER.

WE HEAD in from the waves after about an hour of surfing together.

"You're a natural," I tell Alex.

She shrugs. "Maybe it's all the dreaming about surfing I did when I was a little kid."

"Yeah, true. And I didn't do myself any favors growing up in the Midwest."

She laughs, and we walk through the sand over to where Aunt Mia is playing fetch with her dog Sandy.

"How's the water, you two?" She asks before she chucks the tennis ball into the water again, so Sandy can go grab it.

"Temperature is perfect, in the wetsuits!" I say.

Sandy brings the tennis ball back. Damn, that dog is one hell of a retriever.

"Wanna try?" Aunt Mia asks me. "Really launch it as far as you can. Don't worry, she's a terrific swimmer."

I launch the ball and watch Sandy go running after it.

"Hey I'm going to go grab the beers from the car," Alex says as she finishes getting out of her black wetsuit we used for surfing. "Anyone else need anything?"

"Just those beers," I wink, starting to take off my own wetsuit. "Oh, and Alex, one more thing."

"What?" She whips her head around.

I wink. "You're the best. Have I told you that today?"

She rolls her eyes and grins at our little inside joke.

I can't help but stare at her as she walks away. Damn she looks sexy in the red one-piece swimsuit she has on. Funny how one pieces have come back into style. With her curves she fills it out so well, it's all I can do not to follow her back to her car and have a quick make out session with her. Not in front of Aunt Mia, though.

Sandy gets back and drops the tennis ball in front of me in the sand, and I launch it again. Damn, that dog just seems to have endless energy.

"So, Mr. Dalton. We're finally getting some alone time."

Aunt Mia's expression is completely serious and unsmiling.

I glance over my shoulder at Alex, who is walking all the way back to where the car was parked. "I guess so," I say, turning back to Aunt Mia.

Her eyes sparkle. "I'm not going to beat around the bush. Alex is a gem, and I'm the only family she has at this point. If you're her boyfriend, you could be her family some day."

I steady her gaze. "You're worried about my intentions with her?"

"Should I be?"

I watch Alex as she comes back. "Aunt Mia, I don't know when most people figure out they're truly in love. I know we're young, but I'd do anything for her. I'd..." I'm about to say, kill for her, but that feels like overkill, no pun intended. "I love her," I say simply.

Aunt Mia's prodding expression converts into a smile. "Good. Because you seem to make her happy. And that's what's important to me."

As she finishes the statement, Sandy gets back with the ball again, and Alex approaches from behind.

"What are you guys talking about?" She asks, pulling a beer out of the cooler for each of us.

"Oh nothing, honey," I say, giving her a kiss while running my hand along her thigh.

We crack the beers and cheers.

"I really like California," I say. "Maybe we should move here some day."

I mean it.

I've had California dreams since I was a kid, if I'm being honest.

And with Alex, I feel like anything is possible.

THE END

Thank you for reading! Book 2 of the series is coming in April!

Want more enemies-to-lovers? Start reading The Lying Game Duet right now!

Preview:

I don't think I've ever felt such an intense focus on her. "Where's your boyfriend?" I growl.

She swallows, and her voice shakes. "I-I'm not sure."

I give her an up-and-down. "Come with me."

A look of fear spreads across her face. "No."

I take her arm, and whisper in her ear, my voice gravelly. "That wasn't a fucking question."

YOU'LL KEEP READING FOR FREE IN KINDLE UNLIMITED

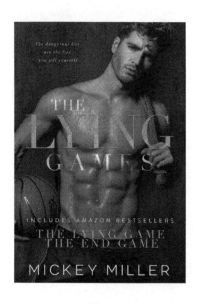

THE LYING GAME - CHAPTER 1
CARTER

It's natural to think hate and love are opposites.

They're not.

Actually, indifference is the opposite of love, not hate.

And indifference is precisely what I'm feeling right now as I stare at the tall blonde I met last night, who is still in my apartment. She's been lingering this morning, sticking around and watching TV in my penthouse.

The time has come for me to kick her out.

"I have practice soon, so it's time for you to go," I say, nicely but without room for discussion.

She blinks a few times, and leans over on the kitchen island, letting out a slow breath. Trying to be cute. "I can just hang out here while you're gone. And be waiting for you when you come back." She lifts her eyebrows and tilts her head as she tries to tempt me.

Clenching my jaw, I stare her down.

Last night, we were enjoying ourselves.

But this afternoon, I don't feel a shred of desire for her.

All I feel is the distinct sensation of wanting this awkwardness to be over, and for her to leave.

Am I an asshole?

Yes. And I'm fine with that.

I was very upfront last night with Natasha about my 'no strings attached' policy when it comes to pleasure.

I don't do relationships. They're not for me. Maybe I'm paranoid, but when you're worth millions of dollars you never know how a woman might deceive you. Maybe she'll play the part of a perfect girlfriend up front, then after a year you'll find out she has a giant secret she's been keeping from you, lying to your face every day.

And yes, that's happened to me.

Natasha stares at me, squinting and giving me this 'Blue Steel' type of look where she wants to seem like she's not trying too hard, but I see right through it.

My eyes drift over to my bookshelf. I notice my copy of *The Great Gatsby* put on top of the shelf. Natasha must have been reading it.

My muscles quiver, seeing the tattered copy of the book that I read junior year of high school. My then girlfriend Lacy and I would read the passages to each other after school. I was so into her, I thought I wanted to spend the rest of my life with her. She asked me why I didn't press for sex, like the other guys were all doing with their girlfriends. I had this zen calmness back then. I just knew we'd be together forever, so what was the hurry?

It's funny the things you think you 'know' when you're seventeen.

I 'knew' I'd be with Lacy.

I 'knew' I was a relationship guy. Not a fuckboy.

Then Lacy broke my heart with a lie.

Little did I know back then, I would become the king of

one night stands. And I thank Lacy for breaking my heart to show me that.

Like James Gatz himself, if I reached for a relationship, I'd only be a boat beat back against the current, in search of a green light that doesn't exist.

Shaking my gaze off from the book, I refocus on Natasha, my smirk returning.

I love my life these days.

I'm twenty-seven years old, just signed my first multimillion dollar contract with the Chicago Wolverines.

I enjoy my lack of responsibility when I'm doing anything besides playing professional basketball.

Noticing me drifting off, Natasha steps around my marble kitchen island and runs her hand along my shoulder.

"You look pensive. Everything alright?"

I swallow, suddenly thinking that maybe my slapstick version of Natasha isn't appropriate. At least she reads. Maybe I've underestimated her, maybe she is relationship material.

"I can be waiting for you . . . when you get back," she adds, her voice full of sultry suggestion. She runs her tongue over her upper lip.

I tense when her finger grazes me. "Look, Natasha. I think you're great. Last night—and this morning—was a lot of fun. But you don't want me, believe me. I have a lot of issues."

She furrows her brow, and a curious smile spreads across her face. "I like issues."

I run my thumb and forefinger across my forehead.

"You've never seen issues like mine, believe me."

"Doesn't seem to affect your, ahem, abilities." She lets her eyes drift below my belt.

I let out a slow exhale. This is probably most guys' dream come true. A hot blonde begging to be nothing but a friend with benefits.

Taking a moment to assess, I search inside myself for feelings. After all, she's smart. Attractive.

But I feel absolutely nothing for her.

Just then, my phone buzzes with a text. Picking it up, I play like someone's calling me.

"Hey Chandler, what's up?" I say to no one on the line.

"Oh we have a team dinner after practice tonight . . . oh totally forgot about that . . ."

She sighs, and I smile as I nod into my phone like Chandler is continuing to talk to me.

It's not that I mind being more forceful with her and simply telling her we are done. It's more that I enjoy the thrill of the lie.

Just then, my phone rings. For real. While I'm holding it.

Natasha shoots me a funny look.

"Were you just . . . faking a conversation?"

"Call coming on the other line," I say, waving her off. "Hi Mom."

Rolling her eyes, Natasha walks away.

"How's the best son in the world?" my mom drawls sweetly.

"Hey, Mama. What's up?"

"Well, the reason I called is, you obviously know Mrs. Benson."

My heart does a tumble at the name 'Benson.' I hold the phone away from my face, clutching it hard.

"No, Mom, I completely forgot that you two went to wine night together every Saturday in high school after my games. Why do you ask about her?"

"Well Carter, I have a favor to ask. Lacy is moving to Chicago for a modern dance tryout."

My heart skips a beat. I can already feel my blood pressure rising.

"Lacy's going to be in Chicago?"

"You didn't know? I figured she might have called you or you would have seen her Facebook updates."

My jaw tightens, and I try not to bite down too hard on my lip. My mom has no idea Lacy and I aren't exactly on speaking terms, and haven't been for years. "She must have forgotten to let me know," I say through clenched teeth.

"So, do you think she could crash at your place while she's there? Tryouts are an unpaid thing. Mrs. Benson is worried about Lacy having to pay rent. We were casually chatting at dinner last night, and I mentioned your new place and how you have that extra room. Apparently Lacy's living arrangements fell through at the last second. And Lacy is too shy to ask for favors, you know how she is. So that's why I'm calling."

I move my mouth to start talking, but nothing comes out.

It's just past the first of June. It's the tail end of spring, and we're headed into summer in Chicago, after putting up with one hell of a winter. This is the first summer I'll be living all by myself, in a place that I officially own.

I've already declared the theme of this summer to be freedom.

The freedom I've earned with a lifetime of dedication to my sport, which culminated just a few weeks ago when I signed a monster contract.

Freedom doesn't mean spending a summer with my ex-girlfriend.

My mom can sense my silent resistance.

"And you two always get along so well, anyway. It's only eight weeks and then she'll be out of your hair."

I grind my teeth.

Only eight weeks.

She's got me between a rock and a hard place.

Lacy Benson always knew how to fuck with me.

Still does, after all these years.

As big of an asshole as I am, I can't say 'no' to my own mother.

"Just eight weeks?" I bite out.

"Just eight weeks, and she'll be out of your hair. I talked with Mrs. Benson. She says her audition is at the end of July."

My cat Smokey brushes my leg.

She licks her paw.

I can feel the tension on the other side of the line.

"Of course she can stay with me, Mom," I finally bite out.

"I thought you'd be fine with it. I mean, you two get along so well."

"Of course we do."

"She'll be arriving on the train tonight around seven-thirty. I'm sure she'll be tired. She left yesterday morning."

"That's great. Just great. I can't wait to see her," I lie.

My mom and I say some more pleasantries, then we hang up.

"Smokey," I growl. "Come here. I'm done playing games."

I stare her down.

Finally, she rolls her neck and jumps into my arms. Maybe she senses the anger emanating from me just thinking about Lacy's name.

Well, if Lacy's going to be here, at the very least maybe I

can finally get some revenge and even the score for what she did to me.

Natasha walks back into the room in heels. She shakes her head, and puts her hands on her hip.

"How was your chat with 'your mom'?" she says, making air quotes.

I smirk.

"You're an asshole," she says, shaking her head.

I nod. "I know."

"I can handle asshole. But I can't handle a blatant liar. I'm leaving."

As the door slams, I feel nothing in my heart.

Not desire. Not hate or ill will. Just indifference.

The way my heart feels about Lacy Benson, however, is another matter entirely.

I'm not indifferent to her. I hate Lacy with every bone in my body for how she lied to me.

YOU'LL READ *THE LYING GAME* FOR FREE IN KINDLE UNLIMITED

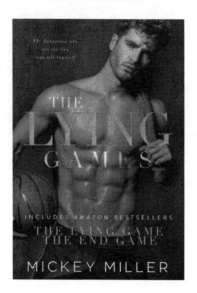

SPECIAL NOTE FROM MICKEY MILLER

Hello Wonderful Reader!

Hell yes! I hope you've enjoy reading this enemies-to-lovers-ish, roommates story that takes place at the "Harvard of the Midwest," Greene State University.

The name of this series of Standalones is *Forever You*. I think it's a fitting name for a group of friends who find their true loves in college.

One ask I have as you're reading: Send me your favorite lines/parts that strike a chord with you! These can be screenshots, copy paste or whatever works! (Send to mickeymillerwrites@gmail.com)

You are free to share lines as well as pictures of you reading, etc. on Facebook, Instagram, wherever. Not sure how other authors work but I am very pro-sharing. I love when you share my work.

A little about the book: This book has been in the works since last April. It was a little more involved since I'm planning out the characters for the future books, but need to keep them consistent. At least a few of the cast characters from this book will get their own novel, so you can feel free to make guesses about that ;)

I dipped into my own college experiences for this one, but I also wanted to make sure it was generally accessible and fun read for my readers who prefer contemporary.

As always, email me at mickeymillerwrites@gmail.com with any questions or concerns.

Thank you for letting you whisk you away into an alternate world for a little while!

XO,

Mickey Miller

P.S. I've written 20 books and you'll read most of them in Kindle Unlimited for free!

ABOUT MICKEY MILLER

Hello there! I'm Mickey Miller and I write light, hot, fast-paced romance that will make you smile and probably blush.

I've written seven top 100 Amazon Bestsellers, including my Amazon Top 25 Hit The Substitute, now available in audio featuring narrator Sebastian York.

The easiest and best way to stay in touch with me is to sign up for my email list (you'll get a free book when you sign up!):

https://dl.bookfunnel.com/mgr4nddhh2

Other social media:

Instagram: @mickeymillerauthor.

I have a wonderful Facebook Group here:

https://www.facebook.com/groups/MickeysMisfits/

Reach out and let me know what you think about my books! I love hearing from readers.

Lots of Love,

Mickey Miller

ALSO BY MICKEY MILLER

The Brewer Brothers Series:

THE LAKE HOUSE: Brewer Brothers Book 1

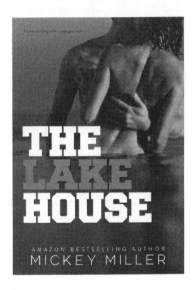

A summer fling with a younger man? Yes, please.

The love story of the youngest Brewer brother, Maddox.

"The **perfect escape read** that ticked all the boxes!! **Off the charts hotness,** a fun and addictive story that I inhaled before I even knew it."

-Book Haven Book Blog

THE HOLD OUT: An Enemies to Lovers Romance

Brewer Brothers Book 2

Impatient. Demanding. Sexy. *Bossy*.

I hate my new boss.

He's Everett Brewer: Football's smoking hot, superstar running back.

They say he's a monster, but I don't believe it.

Somebody pinch me. Because I can't believe I'm the girl having a forbidden romance with her hot-as-hades, football superstar of a boss.

And pinch me again. Because he might actually be falling in love with me.

<u>**THE SUBSTITUTE - New Standalone Contemporary Romance:**</u>

When the NFL goes on strike, Super Bowl champion Peyton O'Rourke ends up back in his hometown as a substitute teacher and high school football coach.

The one thing he didn't count on?

His best friend's ex being newly single.

Ballers (mostly) Sport Romance Series:

It was supposed to be just sex. But it became so much more.
(Chandler + Amy's Book!)

I've always been the good girl. Until one night in Tijuana. When a gorgeous stranger struck up a conversation with me. He was so damn cocky, I decided to play a trick on him. So I made up a fake name. It was innocent, even if he was sinfully sexy.

The Blackwell After Dark "Kinkiest Small Town in America" Series:

I'm studying to be a sex therapist, and I haven't even had sex yet. Which is why I decide that Professor Hanks is going to be the one to take my virginity.

How to find a wedding date at the last second: 1) Overheat your car on your cross country road trip 2) Make sure it's storming 3) Have a one night stand with the sexiest mechanic you've ever seen

Sebastian Blackwell isn't only the sexiest man I've ever met. He's also my boss.

My best friend's sister. A tiny white lie to get a loan. A fake fiance?

Standalones:

No sex for ten dates, which sounds easy. Despite the biceps bulging through his shirt. Despite the tattoos I desperately want to lick-- I mean, know more about. Despite the hunger in his eyes when he looks at me.

You'll get a free book here if you sign up for my mailing list:

https://dl.bookfunnel.com/mgr4nddhh2

To read a special sneak preview about Chandler, Carter's (secret) brother and how he fell in love with Amy, keep reading:

Made in the USA
Columbia, SC
04 April 2020